Tears
OF A
Class Clown

Sara Faith Alterman

AVON
TRADE

An Imprint of HarperCollinsPublishers

HarperCollins books may be purchased for educational, business, or sales promotional use. For information please write: Special Markets Department, HarperCollins Publishers Inc., 10 East 53rd Street, New York, NY 10022.

FIRST EDITION

Interior text designed by Elizabeth M. Glover

Library of Congress Cataloging-in-Publication Data

Alterman, Sara Faith.
    Tears of a class clown / by Sara Faith Alterman.—1st ed.
        p. cm.
    ISBN-13: 978-0-06-075592-8
    ISBN-10: 0-06-075592-X
    1. Class reunions—Fiction. 2. Waitresses—Fiction. 3. Comedians—Fiction.   I. Title.

PS3601.L825T43 2006
813'.6—dc22   2006006913

06 07 08 09 10 JTC/RRD 10 9 8 7 6 5 4 3 2 1

For KJR

Special thanks to Stacey Glick,
a tremendous agent and friend.

Infinite thanks to the luminous Lucia Macro,
and to Pam Spengler-Jaffee,
Kacey Barron, and Esi Sogah.

Thank you Mom, Pops, Dan, Mark Odlum, Michele Meek,
Georgia Riepe, Gabriel Unger, Becky Girolamo,
Will Luera, Elyse Becker, and the cast and crew of ImprovBoston.

Prologue

The moon was titian and juicy that first time.

It was my sixteenth summer and a sticky August midnight, the kind of weather lazy mosquitoes hold their breath for; air thick enough to float on if you have tiny wings. Swimming weather.

Walden Woods is exactly the way it was made to sound by the celebrities who walked to raise funds for it in the early nineties. Thickly untamed brush, a carpet of toffee-colored pine needles, a pond that simmers with algae on one end, harbors wading children in the other. A tiny beach marries the edge of the water to the cluster of forest nearest the notorious cabin. The trees play host to a slew of skulking creatures; raccoons, deer, a turkey or two. On especially muggy nights the air would be laden with the stink of spooked skunk mingled with wafts of motor oil from nearby Route 2.

That night the beach was littered with remnants of fussy summer vacations. A few abandoned sunscreen bottles, plastic shovels standing at attention from tiny hills of sand, a lonely looking beach chair, overturned by the wind or an angry child. During hot summer days, locals packed this beach, a gathering place for gleeful kids and their woebe-

gone full-time mothers who just wanted to finish their latest paperbacks and crisp their skin.

The sun drained the mystery from this place, but at night
the beach seemed to thirst for secret trysts, skin on skin
slapping together to the beat of cricket sambas.

It didn't smell like romance, though. Musty, like eau de
Thoreau's feet.

Under citrus moonbeams, his skin buzzed with fire. I
watched as he stripped off his black cut-off shorts and
dingy heavy metal T-shirt, down to a checkered pair of boxers and the tooth of a whale that he wore on a cord around
his neck.

The boxers fell to his ankles.

I hadn't seen him naked before, or any boy, for that
matter. I made a big deal of covering my eyes with my
hands, like the sight of his unabashed flesh would blind
me or send me directly to the perdition that my mother
feared above all other penalty. I splayed my fingers,
though, curious.

He caught me peeking and broke into a wicked grin,
backing slowly toward the water, toe to heel with unchar-
acteristic grace, never taking his eyes from mine.

With the finesse of a stingray he was gone, slicing through
the surface with Samurai ease. I held my breath along with
him until he finally emerged, fifty yards closer to the moon.

The instant I stepped into the water, my foot sunk through
a layer of sludge on the basin floor. I didn't want to think
about what I was stepping in; instead, I gritted my teeth
and tried to ignore the endless, sloppy pond pudding that
squished between my toes. My breath caught in my throat
as I fought the shock of the cold water and the fear of stepping in mystery.

I took my sweet time, abandoning any hopes of aquatic

elegance, instead panting and snorting like a bulldog in hot pursuit of a floating tennis ball.

From the middle of the pond the moon looked ever bigger, pregnant with light. I let my legs float up from under me and reclined, my ears flooded with muted underwater percussion. My hair was long back then, halfway down my back and tangled with the colors of autumn. Some of it stuck to my face while I listened to my Darth Vader breathing and pretended to be a mermaid.

He moved cautiously through the water, closing a bit of the gap between us while he stared—intent, intense. When I felt a hand brush my naked back I didn't flinch, relaxing into his touch as he guided me closer.

We stayed like that forever, plaiting our legs in pinwheels while we fluttered, right arms clutching fistfuls of flesh while our left ones flapped beneath the surface. Walden couldn't overwhelm the scent of his neck, pepper vanilla corduroy and freshly cut ryegrass.

I breathed him in while he put his lips to my ear and whispered for what seemed like hours, words I had heard a million times before, but never strung together quite like that, never directed at me. It tapered to a close at those tiny, giant words, that dot dot dot that begs to be echoed.

The moon hid behind a cloud, newly modest, as I buried my face in his smell once more, knowing that I loved him, too.

We shared a grin.

And sinned.

One

*H*e was squinty, the man flapping his yapper, with a Dippity Do and nostrils that twitched in time with his desperate lips.

"Hey, hey, how about some of *my* spicy tuna roll, huh, baby?"

Oh come on.

"So I says, 'Easy lady, that's my elbow!' Ba-da-BOOM!"

It had been going on like this all night; pathetic lines tossed out halfheartedly, like Frisbees on the beach in August.

"Sure, honey, feel free to use my dipstick to check your levels!"

Someone should slug this yahoo. Anyone? Anyone? Help a lady out.

All men, too. Honest to God. I'm not too surprised; it isn't often that we get chicks with balls enough to brave this crowd.

It's a tricky business, stand-up comedy.

I wished more of these morons figured that out before they got their paws on a microphone.

The moron du jour, sporting khaki pants, was nearly bursting out of a coral-colored shirt printed with birds of paradise—typical comic wear. His shoulders were broader than a Buick, and his strongman handlebar mustache glistened with sweat.

I've worked at Bellyaches Comedy Den for years now, and believe me I've heard it all. Mother jokes, sister jokes, jaded jilted-lover jokes, chick jokes, dick jokes, smart jokes, fart jokes, fat jokes. Boozers, losers, politics, pimps and hookers, bitches, tricks. Nobody's safe, no ethnicity ignored: honky, cracker, nigga, kike, wops and dagos, fags and dykes, jappy guidos, spics and chinks, the motherfucking kitchen sink.

My boss, Hal, actually wanted to use that rant as the club's motto, but City Council got a little nervous. I think some selectman had a problem with "cracker."

Bellyaches is small and dank, choreographed around a precarious platform that barely passes for a stage. Mismatched chairs accessorize two dozen tiny cocktail tables, which are packed together awkwardly to fill most of a shallow audience pit. The bar runs along the back of the room. I've spent the better part of my adult life stuffed back there like a helpless pimiento, yanking sticky taps and rolling my eyes at the sad excuse for entertainment. Make no mistake about my use of "better part." I'm talking majority. Believe me, I don't count my beer-bitch duties among the finest moments of my twenties.

The place defines "dive," but it's actually fairly popular; gross is apparently the new chic with Boston-area hipsters. It's gone far beyond thrift-store threads and pizza grease bedhead: I sell enough Pabst Blue Ribbon in a week to build a Tijuanan shanty village with the aluminum from the discarded cans. All that cheap beer is a beacon for amateur comics. Honestly, they flock like raccoons to shiny objects, likely comforting themselves as they leave with the notion that if their jokes bombed, the audience must have been, too.

You'd never catch me onstage in a million years.

Most of my friends are aspiring stand-up comedians, and I've seen more than enough rejection to stave off any limelight cravings. Time and time again I've watched grown men sniffle about jokes that failed or bits that bombed, while nursing Cuervos and dejected faces speckled with coin-shaped bruises. I don't need a crowd to make me feel bad about myself; superhuman celebrities and trendy department stores do a fine enough job of that, thank you very much. Watch any Lindsay Lohan movie and then shuffle into Express to try and stuff your ass into a pair of stretchy, sparkly pants. You'll leave the mall with a cinnamon roll and a pudge complex every single time.

So, I try to keep myself safe from heckling. It's much safer behind the bar, anyway, unless some wino gets fresh about my rack.

Though I man the booze, I wouldn't call myself a "bartender" per se. I wish. Bellyaches only serves wine and beer, so all I do is pull and uncork. (That's what *she* said. Badum . . . bum. Ha.) *Cocktail* it's not. Hal has owned this place for twenty years, bought it when he was fresh off the boat from East London. He's a pervy sort of Cockney, with lumps of doughy limbs and gravel in his throat. Saved his quid for nearly a decade so he could move across the pond and live out his dream of owning a moldy comedy dive. Not much stand-up in the UK, apparently. I guess they don't laugh too much over there. Ashamed to show their teeth, I'd imagine.

In his spare time, Hal fancies himself an amateur photographer, capturing weddings, christenings, bar mitzvahs, headshots, the occasional catalog campaign. His favorite shoots are portfolio jobs for aspiring models. He likes to dress the oblivious gigglers in thongs and drape them over machinery for "artistic effect." If you ask me, it's for his spank bank. For extra cash I help him out sometimes, loading his cameras, holding the light meter, and sponging the sweat from the back of his pasty neck. I keep that last part a secret.

Bellyaches was a butcher shop before Hal got his mitts on it; there are still bloodstains visible in the cracks in the cheap tile floor. There's a rumor that before *that* it was a Mob den, Tommy guns and all, but Hal waves that off.

Whatever its former purpose, the club still sports questionable ambiance. The walls are dingy, half the lights are blown out. Hal's even had the same Bud Light neon crackling behind the bar since 1985. Abe likes to remind me of that; he's an ageless Irish perch who started coming here five nights a week the very first night Hal was open for business. Retired from the force for twelve years, Abe stays home with his wife on Saturday nights, not out of dedication to his family, but rather to Jesus. Doesn't want to be hung over on Sunday morning; afraid he'll sleep through church and get tossed in the back of a one-way wagon to the fiery cell below. He's holding out for the big doughnut shop in the sky. And boy, does he love me.

"Hey Carrot Top, lemme get an O'Doul's!"

Carrot Top. *Everyone*'s a comic, eh? And they all think it's fresh material.

"Hittin' the sauce pretty hard tonight, tough stuff! O'Doul's? Jesus, we'll be wringing you out in the mop bucket, Abe. Better gimme your keys."

There are some things I love about my job. It's the only place I've ever worked where the staff is *required* to mouth off openly to the customers. In fact, keeping your disdain under wraps is grounds for termination.

Besides Abe, I have a slew of regulars, all blue collar, all of undistinguishable age. Every cheapskate one of them nurses single beers for hours, rationing them well beyond room temperature, and then leaves me a dollar after laying his most personal problems on me for hours at a time. Like Bill, the postman with four ex-wives and nine illegitimate children, or Jerry, the tough-talking municipal librarian who can rant unapologetically for hours about his slew of mysterious digestive disorders. What can you do? They all tell me I'm pretty. Hey, it's the only shred of romantic attention I'm getting lately. Hal thinks it's cute.

"Better not let your boyfriends see, love," he'll tease if a guy my age tries to flirt with me. "They'll run that fresh young whippersnapper clear outta town, Carrot Top!"

In case you were wondering, the carpet matches the curtains, thank you very much. My mother's half Irish, so the five kiddies came out with our heads on fire. Green eyes, too, the whole leprechaun lot of us. I lucked out and dodged the freckles, though. Got a big honkin' Jewish nose instead. (Thanks, Dad.)

"Hey, Red, when's your next night off?"

"Jerry, you ask me that every Friday, and every Friday I give you the same answer. There exists only one thing in this godforsaken city that I can't get off, and that's a night shift."

"Aaaah, Nina, you're breaking my heart."

"Impossible, Jerry, you don't have one. Here's your beer, smart-ass."

Speaking of asses, the guy onstage just didn't know when to quit. He was still trying to amble through his act, despite the disgruntled hisses and heckles spewing forth from the crowd. He finally got the hint when his fourteenth Eskimo joke was met with unapologetic boos and an explosion of bar debris. Someone actually threw a head of lettuce, and all of a sudden, vegetables were flying from every which way.

Huh. Who brought an eggplant in here?

The dude was still picking cocktail onions out of his toupee when the emcee hopped onstage to introduce the next act.

"And now, ladies and . . . wait, are there even any ladies in here? No? Well, there's Nina, our lovely bartender . . . wave hello to Nina, guys! But trust me, she's no lady, so she doesn't count. Well then, gentlemen, please give a warm welcome to our next comic. He's a Bellyaches favorite, and trust me, this one's actually funny. Give it up for Ben . . . Henry!!"

Oh thank you.

Ben Henry is the house comic at Bellyaches, meaning he appears every week because the club needs to guarantee at least one stretch of laughs for the people who fork over a cover. Ben is witty enough to pull off clever jokes, but not so uppity and satirical that his humor is lost on a blue-collar audience. He's got this sardonic kind of ease about him, like maybe he could be your best friend as long as you never turned your back on him.

I should know. He's been *my* best friend for years.

We've both been working at this place since we finished college (er . . . dropped out of college). Let's see, I'm twenty-seven, so it's been about . . . five years. He got hired as the busboy, and I started behind this very bar. I was barely old enough to drink, but the boss man is a horny man, and he thought a perky, flirty redhead would be just the thing to boost bar sales. He got the redhead part. I'm too abrasive to be perky and too awkward to flirt. Oh well. So it goes.

Hal figured out pretty quickly that Ben was funnier than the acts onstage. He noticed that the audiences had been laughing harder than usual, so he assumed the comics were hitting more marks—until he sat in the back of the club to watch one night and noticed that, as Ben made his way around collecting glasses, the people within earshot would erupt into giggles. Turns out the comics *were* bombing, and Ben was muttering sidesplitting comebacks to any table that would listen.

At first, Hal was pissed.

"I don't pay ye to be funny!" he'd screamed after the set was over, poor Ben separating silverware in a bin filled with muck. "I pay ye to be bloody tidy! To clean! *Not* be *funny!*"

"Well," Ben had shot back, "you pay those guys onstage a hell of a lot more than you pay me, and *they're* not being funny! The audience could at least get their money's worth!"

Touché!

Hal had stroked his chins with beefy fingers for a few long minutes, ultimately deciding to let Ben have at it with the audience for three minutes on a slow night, like a Tuesday.

A week later, Ben was headlining *every* show, *every* night we were open. It's been years, and he still has new material *every* week.

And I'm still the bar bitch.

Truth be told, the thought of being onstage is up there with getting my lungs pulled out through my nose on a list of things that I avoid like the plague, so I don't really mind staying out of the spotlight.

Besides, I give Ben most of his material, anyway. Offstage, he's kind of . . . shrill. And . . . whiny.

OK. He's worse than a woebegone Bridge-and-Tunnel

thirty-something window-shopping with her man at Tiffany and Co.

I'll admit I had a little crush on Ben when we first met. (He *is* pretty cute when he's not sniveling.) It was mutual, so we flirted in a totally seventh-grade manner, complete with hair pulling and note passing, until he had the guts to ask me out.

Disaster.

I remember thinking that things were going pretty well. I rarely get asked on dates, so when I do, I go all out. I even curled my damn eyelashes.

Ben took me to this place that serves hush puppies and Pabst Blue Ribbon in glass jelly jars. Perfect fodder for sarcasm, which is my specialty. Man, was I on top of my game that night. Usually when I'm nervous I have a hard time being funny, but *to this day* that date was one of the most successful I've had in terms of personal comedic best.

Unfortunately (and perhaps, especially), stand-up comics are no exception to the rules of gender-specific social code. It's a sad truth; men just don't like Funny Girls.

Let me explain.

I suffer from Funny Girl Syndrome, the female version of the more commonly recognizable affliction Nice Guy Syndrome. Men cursed with this miserable social malady are usually genuine and warm, polite and kind, inexorably chivalrous and hopelessly romantic. And they can never, ever, ever land a girlfriend. As any Nice Guy will tell you, women want to date assholes. I guess there's just something magnetic and mysterious about a dude who boots you out of bed before sunrise and never follows up with a phone call. (It's true; we *pine* for these idiots.) The most romantically successful guys I know are self-centered, beer-

guzzling blockheads who somehow manage to lead a pa-
rade of blonde goddesses around town like sexual Pied
Pipers. And the Nice Guys . . . well, they make great friends,
of course, but they're too eager, too attainable. Women want
a challenge. Apparently, men feel the same way.

Enter . . . the Funny Girl.

Sure, we're witty, quick on the draw, we love to rip people apart and we drink a lot of beer. But that doesn't make
us viable girlfriends; it makes us great drinking buddies.
And as any Nice Guy can tell you, once you're a friend, lust
comes to an end. It's a universal rule, like that liquor-
before-beer thing.

As far as I can tell, most men want a woman who has a
lot of hair, a lot of teeth, a whole lot of cleavage and a lot of
personality *that she keeps to herself*. It's a macho thing.

Many a male friend has denied my theory, but I have yet
to overhear a one of them whispering excitedly about that
blonde's voluptuous brain.

Since Ben's entire identity is constructed around being the
funniest guy in the room, it didn't exactly work out between
us. No loss, I guess. Besides, when we followed through
with the obligatory good-night departure, I discovered that
kissing Ben is a lot like getting CPR from a jellyfish.

I eventually got him to admit that he couldn't deal with
a woman who's funnier than he is, which was no surprise,
but then Ben hit me with the unexpected. He said that my
quick wit was intimidating, that most men didn't want to
feel like they couldn't keep up with their girlfriends. After
all, men were supposed to be the funny ones, the charming,
witty alphas. They don't like to be one-upped by their lady
friends, according to Ben. My sense of humor, he informed
me, would scare men away.

As it turned out, Ben wasn't so scared of my wit that he didn't have the nerve to steal my one-liners and put them in his act. Sure enough, the night after that disastrous date, I was minding my own business at the bar when I heard a few jokes that sounded awfully familiar. The weasel was repeating quips I'd made on our date, and getting a hell of a laugh.

At first I was mad, but when I heard how hard the audience laughed at bits that I had come up with, I started to get a kick out of it. It reminded me of high school. Ah, the days of yore. I used to crack up my classes with my outbursts and inappropriate comments. I'd forgotten how good it felt to be driven by an audience.

Still, watching the comic up after Ben that night get pelted with cocktail garnish reinforced my terror of public rejection. Rather then let him take all the glory for free, I convinced Ben to let me secretly write his jokes for a third of his paycheck.

Convinced is the wrong word. Threatened. I threatened the thief with two clenched fists and the promise of a balls-free bachelorhood. He complied. After all, friendship is all about compromise.

It's a system that works. Ben gets laughs and a stroke of the ego, I get the self-indulgent satisfaction of hearing my words tickle a crowd, and a hell of a laurel to hold over my best friend's head. That may sound exceedingly masochistic, but it's really just friendly competition. I swear. Keeps it fun. We bounced right back after that terrible date, and now we remind ourselves of a crotchety old married couple. We bicker, we nag, we pretend not to like each other. But, when I need him, he's there unconditionally, and I try to do the same. Beyond that, we spend a lot of time together and we don't have sex. Just like a pair of grandparents. Who have all their teeth.

Tonight was going especially well for Ben, since I'd had a bad week and was able to channel my frustrations into killer bits.

"So I've been trying to be extra nice to my sister's kid this week, because she's stuck in bed with the chicken pox," Ben was kvetching to an eager audience, "so I went to the video store to rent one of those Harry Potter movies. You know, keep her busy. So we sit down to watch it, and there's this scene where the boy wizard wonder fends off all these grim reaper guys by making some kind of shield come out of his wand. Hey, don't look at me like that, I didn't make this shit up. So the shield thing forms the shape of an animal, which apparently changes depending on who conjures it. It's called a 'patronus.' So Harry Potter's patronus is this giant stag; it all charges out of his wand looking like a reindeer late for Christmas. And my niece is totally into it, she's loving it. So being the caring, dutifully involved uncle that I am, I turned to her and I said, 'So, Caitlin, what kind of animal would *your* patronus be?' And she gives me this really weird look, like I've just sprouted fingers out of my head or something, and she says 'Uncle Ben, girls don't have a patronus.' Can you believe that?"

The audience erupted into laughter. Excellent.

The story wasn't true, of course. I'd quipped that thing about girls and patronuses last week after I'd curled up for an entire weekend reacquainting myself with the world's favorite magical teenager. Yeah, I like Harry Potter. (Go ahead, rib me about it. I will cut you.)

Ben finished his act with a bang, tearing off a few one-liners and closing with a gorgeous joke about crawfish.

As usual, I had an IPA waiting for him on the bar when he hops offstage.

"Good crowd tonight!" he said between gulps.

"Good thing, too, or you would have bombed, Henry. They were being nice to you."

"You seem to forget, Kurtz, that when you insult my act, you're insulting your very own jokes."

"The jokes were gold! It's the timing, Henry. The timing."

Not true, actually. Ben has terrific timing, and his stage presence is so likable that while watching him I can forget his manic depression, chronic phlegm-hocking, and the fifty bucks he still owes me from two weeks ago. The casual ease, hint of self-deprecation, and crooked puppy grin all add up to big laughs.

"Alas, Miss Kurtz, I'll just have to take notes from your comedic brilliance the next time you go up onstage. Oh that's right. Chickenshit."

"Shaddup and drink, you."

I like Ben the best when he's fresh off a gig. He's in his best place then, still coasting the adrenaline rush all performers get from winning a crowd. I enjoy these precious few minutes of happy banter with my best friend before he drifts back into Same Old Ben. Miserable. Crotchety. Eeyore with a chip on his shoulder.

When he starts to stare into the final dregs of his beer I know it's time to back off. It's been the same damned routine for the past five years, six nights a week except Christmas and Easter. When Ben has two swallows left, it's time to wipe down the bar. It's worked out to a fine science. Pathetic.

"You going out tonight?" he asked, as I swept crumpled beverage napkins into the trash.

"What day is it? Thursday? Friday? I don't even know

anymore. It's all the same fucking day. Friday. Yeah, I should go out."

"What did you make tonight?"

"I don't know, I haven't counted the drawer yet."

Ben kept staring into his drink as I tallied the cash register, scrutinizing every coin, shuffling every bill into bundles of twenty, snapping them together with rubber bands. I start each night with two hundred bucks in change. I'm supposed to take that out, print out a sales report from the register, figure out how much we pulled in for booze sales, take *that* out, and then the remaining money is what I made in tips.

In theory.

I always manage to feel shortchanged somehow. I don't know if it's because I feel like I should be making more money for having to deal with the same chuckleheads every night, or if it's because my counting skills are lacking and I end up giving Hal too much money at the end of the night.

"Shit. Only eighty-three."

"That's not bad."

"For a Friday? That's fucking dismal. Jesus, we should start offering tax write-offs to the regulars. Maybe they'd throw down a tip every once in a while."

"Why don't you look for another job?"

"And leave all this, Henry? You've gotta be crazy. Besides, where else could I get paid to stare at you all night?"

I batted my eyelashes mockingly while Ben swilled the last of his beer and slid me the pint glass.

"Well," he said, wiping his hands on the thighs of his jeans as he rose from the bar stool, "I'm going to grab a bite. Come if you want to."

"To where? Not Rosie's."

"What's wrong with Rosie's?"

Rosie's Diner has fed Ben twelve meals a week since he moved to Boston. It's the kind of place that would inspire nostalgia if disgust didn't plant itself in the way. Not a goddamned thing, the actual Rosie boasts proudly, has changed in that place since the day it opened in 1952. She ain't kidding. This includes the salt and pepper shakers, the fryer oil, and the V-necked T-shirt permanently stained with the armpit grease of Rosie's husband, Angelo. According to Ben, Angelo makes the best grilled cheese in Boston, which I'm inclined to believe. Not because I have any more faith in Angelo's culinary skills than I do in his personal hygiene, but because Ben is a certified grilled-cheese expert. It's all the man will eat.

No exaggeration.

When Ben was a kid, he got picked on. A lot. Don't feel too bad; it's like a prerequisite for comics to have had an underdog childhood so they have something to be neurotic about. Anyway, he was always getting wedgied and having boogers flicked on him in class and stuff, so every single day he would come home crying, and his mother would make him a grilled cheese sandwich to calm him down. It was the thing he looked forward to the most each day, because he knew, Little Ben Henry, that at the end of an intolerable schoolyard torture session, he would be treated to gooey, melty orange love embraced by two welcoming slices of toasty white bread.

As a result, he became psychologically conditioned to associate happiness with a grilled cheese. When his mother died while Ben was away at college, it sealed the deal. Now he eats grilled cheese every day in her loving memory. And soon he'll be able to join her; his cholesterol just peaked off the charts.

"Ben, shouldn't you eat something else once in a while? Like a vegetable?"

"No vegetables."

"What about a grilled cheese and *tomato*?"

"No vegetables."

"Tomato's a fruit."

"No fruit."

I sighed.

"Well, I'm broke, so, pass."

"You sure?"

"Yep."

"OK." He shrugged. "I'll call Cuse. He should be done with his midnight gig by now."

Our friend Bill Becker, better known as "Cuse," fancies himself a comic but is really the walking, talking definition of fledgling. At best his routine is mildly funny but never escalates beyond forehead-smackingly stale. Even a deaf mute could mouth along to the punch lines of Cuse's "best" jokes; they're that predictable. Besides being hopelessly awkward and sweaty beyond the boundaries of reasonable biology, the poor kid is about as attractive as a ham steak the morning after your twenty-first birthday. Not just over-weight, Cuse is literally round—perfectly spherical thanks to a pie-baking mama and an affinity for Three Stooges marathons.

He's a fellow redhead, but instead of the rich, auburn hue that I was, thankfully, blessed with, Cuse is cursed with tangerine tufts and freckle-flecked flesh. He earned his nickname one painfully clumsy midnight gig at Faneuil Hall, a few years ago during March Madness. Poor Cuse had the misfortune of performing for a group of Boston College frat boys who had just spent the evening watching

Syracuse University wipe the floor with a forgettable collegiate opponent.

"Dude!" one of them cried at the first sight of jolly Bill Becker. "It's the Syracuse Orangeman! OrangeMAN!"

"OrangeMAN!" the crowd of monkeys gleefully replied. "OrangeMAAAAN!"

Poor Cuse. Cursed with the physique of a basketball mascot. And not even a cute or respectable mascot. A nickname like "Wolf" or "Chief" probably wouldn't be that bad. But to physically resemble a basketball? Ouch. Accurate, but ouch.

Still, our sympathy was no obstacle. Cuse he became. Cuse he shall remain.

God bless him, though. He still gets up onstage as often as he can. He even counts his roundness as audience drawing power, and I'll be damned if club owners don't agree. Those guys don't care if the comics are actually funny, as long as they bring customers through the door. And let's face it; who's going to pass up the opportunity to watch a walking, talking basketball?

"The last thing Cuse needs is Rosie stuffing him with fried food."

"That's not untrue," Ben said, "but I can't stand going into Rosie's by myself. Whenever I do, she's on my ass about fixing me up with her daughter."

"Rosie has a daughter?"

"Yeah, the one who runs the register."

"That's a girl?"

"Nina, that's just mean."

"No, seriously, that's a girl? That thing has a mustache!"

"Well, she's Eastern European. What do you expect?"

"I expected Eastern Europe to have access to at least a primitive method of hair removal."

"Well, not everyone can be as naturally adorable and hairless as you." Ben reached across the bar and tweaked my nose, grabbed his coat from a bar stool and tossed a hand in the air toward Hal, who nodded in return.

"I'm taking off, Kurtz."

"Later. Say hello to Rosie for me."

"I'll eat a grilled cheese for you, too."

"Ick, no thanks. Have you seen the way Angelo sweats? It drips all over the grill. You eat that. You eat his sweat."

"Mmmmmmmm!"

"That's so gross, Ben."

"It's delicious!"

"Deliciously sweaty."

"Mmmmmmmm!"

"No wonder you can't get a date, sweat mouth."

"Hey!" He flicked a stray bar peanut in my direction, missing completely and instead landing it in a bin of cleaning fluid.

Ben has a love life that's nearly as pathetic as mine, and boy, does he love to bitch about it. I learned long ago to never ask questions about any girls that he may be interested in, lest I be sucked into a three-hour stint as a sounding board for sad-sack musings. Every so often, though, I slip.

"She's so cute, Nina. What am I supposed to do?"

Shit. Here we go. *Come on, Ben, it's one in the morning.*

For weeks now, he's been moping about some chick that he keeps seeing around town. First it was on the subway, then a few chance glances at a Harvard Square coffee shop, *then* he caught her eye across the crowd while squeezing cantaloupe at a Sunday farmers' market in Arlington.

"I don't know, Ben."

"She's got the prettiest, bounciest hair."

"I know, Ben."

"I'm just not sure what to say to her."

"I *don't know*, Ben."

"What would you do if some guy came up to you in a coffee shop? Would you think he was a dork?"

"Yes."

"*Nina!*"

"What? You asked!"

"So I shouldn't say hi to her?"

"Ben, you know as well as I do that men don't come up to me in coffee shops, so maybe I'm the wrong person to be asking about this. I never even make it past the first date! Why don't you ask Cuse when you see him? He's got more experience than I do."

"He's got more experience failing completely, maybe. You might not get a second date, but that kid can't even get a first. He gets turned down more than . . . more than . . . um . . ."

"More than the stereo volume at a preteen sleepover? More than the sheets at an airport Sheraton? More than—"

"Yes, yes, more than all of those things. Stop rubbing it in."

"Rubbing what in?"

"That you're snappier than I am."

"Snappier, but not luckier in love. That's my point."

"Well, maybe if you weren't so *snappy*, more guys would take you out a second time."

No, he didn't.

I bristled, turning my back on Ben and my attention to the oversized jar of maraschino cherries, which was in desperate need of a wiping before I returned it to its stock space in the tiny refrigerator under the bar. Wipe wipe wipe. Wipe. Wipe.

After a minute or two of superficial scrubbing, I shot a glare at my offending best friend. He was looking down at his feet while kicking at the bar, clearly embarrassed by his schmucky outburst.

"Well . . . I'm gonna head to Rosie's. Are you sure you don't want to come?"

"Nope. I wouldn't want to embarrass you with my offensive sass."

"Nina, that's not what I meant."

"No, no, it's cool. I'm a redhead. I'm supposed to be feisty and outspoken. Don't you watch TV?"

He smiled, a half smile, shoving his hands in the pockets of his faded black jeans.

"See you tomorrow, Kurtz. Maybe you want to grab a drink after your shift? I'll buy."

"We'll see."

"Okay . . . 'night."

Last one left—as I always am—scraping the last layer of beer scum from the battle-scarred bar, listening while Hal whistled "Tiny Dancer" as he put up the chairs.

"Do all right tonight, Nina?" he called from across the club after Ben had shut the front door behind him softly.

"Eighty."

"Not bad for a Friday."

"Not enough."

My meaty boss placed the last chair upside down on a rickety table and waddled to the bar, still whistling.

"Chin up, love. I've got a shoot on Sunday if yer interested, portfolio stuff. Pay ye a hundred bucks to listen to me gripe about how ye get yer sodding fingerprints all over me lenses. Deal?"

Hal's not so bad sometimes, for a portly wanker.

"Deal. Here's the drawer. I'm cashed out."

"All right, Red. Get yer arse home safely."

" 'Night, Hal."

I was almost out the door when it came, just as it always did after a Friday shift.

"How long ye been working for me, love?"

"Five years, Hal."

"Five years. Flies by, doesn't it?"

"Hal, like clockwork you call out that question to me every Friday as I'm on my way out the door, you know that? You're turning into a goldfish."

"A what?"

"A goldfish, Hal. They have really short memories. That's why they're happy to swim around the same damned tank for their entire lives."

"Bloody hell. Turning into a goldfish. That's funny, love. But it's you that's been swimming around the same tank for five years, isn't it?"

"Don't remind me."

"Well, don't quit before tomorrow. I need yer charm and quick hands."

"Funny, I don't hear that enough."

"Get off it, Red! We'll find ye a lad."

"I'm not worried."

"What about that first git we had up there tonight?"

"Chris Campbell?"

"Yeah!"

"The one in the 'Jesus is my Love Slave' T-shirt?"

Yeah!

"No."

"No?"

"Good night, Hal."

"Aw, can't I have a bit of fun?"

"Good night, Hal."

"Good night, me girl. See you tomorrow."

And the next day. And the next.

Blech.

Two

"Mrrrrrreeeeeeooooooowwwww!"

Oh God, it's so fucking early.

I'll tell you one thing about living with a roommate; it sure can be fodder for material.

"Mrrrrreeeeeeooooowwww!" She's singing in the shower . . . with her cat.

Take mine, for example. I'd been living with Jaime for about ten months now; found her by putting up a few fliers around my favorite neighborhood hangouts. I figured anyone who knows about the Brat-Scat underground jazz club and German sausage bar couldn't be all bad.

And she's not. Not . . . bad. Just . . . different.

Jaime was one of the few people to answer my ad, and I sort of liked her right away. By "sort of," I mean, you know, she seemed like a girl I could get along with—maybe not develop a platonic life-partnership with or anything, but I definitely didn't see myself tearing my hair out and devising crafty ways to get out of my lease. She's pretty shy and quiet, has shoulder-length brown hair, mousy clothes, sensible shoes. And she works as a teller at some nondescript bank branch, so the steady job was a plus, especially since my previous roommate had been a "phone actress." I still can't hear a Nokia ring tone without cringing a little.

Our apartment is in Somerville, the poor man's Boston, the top half of a small duplex that boasts avocado kitchen décor and tired gray carpeting. Since neither of us is what you would call a "career woman," Jaime and I have furnished the living room with an assortment of flea-market finds that makes the apartment look like . . . a flea market.

The couch is red plaid with wooden arms, scratched to smithereens by Jaime's cat and looking like it belongs in the bedroom of a horny fraternity scoundrel. It's my favorite perch in the afternoons; I usually eat a few bowls of crunchy chocolate cereal and watch *Law and Order* reruns until my ass is numb. I have a lot of naughty dreams about Jack McCoy. Which is shameful and weird.

We have a tiny kitchen that's accidentally retro chic, what with its before-mentioned green appliances and black-and-white linoleum. Down the hall are two bedrooms; mine has sunshine walls and a complimentary orange velvet comforter, and is littered with knickknacks, like porcelain art deco teapots and novelty ashtrays from my annual road trip to the Jersey Shore. Jaime's room, on the other hand, looks the way you'd expect a bank teller's bedroom to look; white walls, navy blue comforter, tidy oak desk laden with office gadgets. Basic. Boring.

Life gets a little hectic for me sometimes, so I thought having a bland roommate might keep me from adopting maniacal coping skills, like eating my own hair.

And it might have, were Jaime not a closet fruitcake masquerading as a deceptively harmless All-Bran four-eyes.

I started to get a little suspicious the first time I caught her talking to herself in the bathroom mirror. Not an entirely unusual act, sure, but as I listened more carefully (yeah, yeah, I'm going to hell) I realized that Jaime was role-playing a bank stickup. She would gesture to her reflection, motioning with her hands in a calming manner while apparently trying to appease an imaginary bank robber. It was kind of fascinating, actually. She looked like she'd keep it under control pretty well if some maniac ever shoved her a hastily scribbled note and a paper bag. You know what they say about practice.

The next quirk to be unearthed was a bit more alarming; the woman who swears by khaki daywear and comfortable loafers apparently plays lead guitar in a cross-dressing David Bowie cover band. Yow-sah. I discovered that one when Ben dragged me to watch his "key-tar"-toting dweeby roommate open an amateur night at some indie rock club. Imagine my shock when the woman that I watch nibble dry Shredded Wheat each Sunday afternoon in front of *Meet the Press* stormed out onstage in seven-inch purple stilettos and began to grind her Gibson.

Yep yep. So, while I don't have the balls to forge a five-minute stand-up routine, Miss Priss rocks the damned mic for an hour and a half, Mondays and Saturdays, at Club Sassycat.

Pretty fucking humiliating. Ben didn't let me live that one down for a few weeks.

But wait, there's more!

There's . . . Kitty.

Jaime's cat is a seventeen-pound creature of questionable character. Black as a walnut tree and equally shady, Kitty clearly has a hold on Jaime that's tighter than a nervous virgin. From day one the cat has owned this fucking apartment, skulking around the living room and throwing me predatory glances wrought with feline angst. I'm not making this up! That cat is *evil*, besides being totally spoiled.

First of all, he won't answer to his real name (though I wouldn't either, if my mother had named me Peaches), only "Kitty," and he seems to relish the fact that Jaime experiences extraordinary separation anxiety. It's so bad that she takes the cat into the shower with her. That's right, *into the shower*, where they proceed to serenade each other blissfully with total disregard for my sleep habits. I generally awaken each morning to primal screaming, usually regurgitated in the form of some Alan Parsons Project tune.

I actually think that the cat is out to get me. When Jaime's around he's perfectly placid, but as soon as she's out the door, Kitty changes, letting loose a fiendish and undeniably evil alter ego. After a prolonged stare-down, the cat will circle me, painstakingly slow, a snarl simmering in the back of his throat.

He's a bad kitty.

Kitty also seems to be completely unaware that he is supposed to be an inferior subhuman organism. Probably doesn't help that Jaime feeds him his meals from a spoon. Kitty's relative size is of no consequence to him; he parades around the apartment like Napoleon on the battlefield, just waiting for me to turn my back so he can attack and conquer. I've actually caught him stalking me around the apartment, hissing and spitting until I'm so intimidated that I retreat to my bedroom. The little fucker has figured out that he freaks me out, so he uses his evil feline voodoo to secure the run of the place.

I've always been more of a dog person myself, but I haven't actually had a pet since age thirteen, when I had to give away my Pomeranian, Nelly. She was the cutest, fluffiest little stinker. In the summer it would get too hot, so we'd shave everything but her head, leaving her looking like a teacup lioness. She ate like a snail and produced tiny little bee-bee turds, which ultimately contributed to her being given away.

In seventh grade, my best friend was Ali Bowen, who happened to live down the street from Ms. Norma Neuhauser. Ms. Neuhauser, spinster extraordinaire, was our sixth-grade earth science teacher and a real, live lesbian. Now, at the time I didn't really know what that meant, but I *did* understand that to be called a lezzie on the playground was akin to being caught eating your own boogers.

Determined to "get" Ms. Neuhauser, we experimented with various gross-out schemes until we discovered that Nelly's poops fit perfectly underneath the handle of a car door. Enough said.

To this day, I still wonder how she knew I was involved.

So, I had to give the pooch away as punishment for my "crappy" prank. But that was how I first learned that it was cool to be funny. I may have lost a dog, but I earned a coveted social status, a label that, apparently, will follow me to the grave: Class Clown.

Nothing could have prepared me for this destiny.

I was raised not too far from where I live now, in a nondescript suburb called Ashford. Mom cranked out five kids, and I was the only girl, sandwiched between two older-and-wisers and a set of chubby, impish twins.

All redheads. All in serious need of therapy.

I guess it wasn't too bad, just . . . a little warped. Fodder for sitcom, actually. Brilliant formula.

My mother, Margaret Ann O'Connor, was a perfectly pious, contentedly bland Catholic goodie from the Connecticut suburbs. She had perfect teeth, perfect grades, and a perfect track record with the Big Guy in the Sky. Not surprisingly, these assets landed her a scholarship to the University of Massachusetts.

They also landed her a hippie.

Gideon Kurtz was one of those dudes who sweats patchouli. In the nineteen sixties, he was double-majoring in political science and applicable bong mechanics on the very same campus as my prudent mother. Needless to say, they didn't run in the same circle. Hell, my dad couldn't even walk in a straight line most of the time, if you catch my drift. Somehow, however, fate took over . . .

Actually, student protesters took over, to be more precise. Took over the dean of students office for a week and a half.

Dad can't remember exactly what he and his comrades were protesting; just that he and a bunch of other flower children chained themselves to whatever furniture they could get near, and sang folk music for spiritual sustenance.

When my father awoke on Monday morning (day three of Operation Do Something Politically Radical and Snag Some of the Glory from Kent State), he heard someone humming softly. Strange song, though—not Bob Dylan or Joan Baez. It sounded more like . . . a hymn. He rolled over and noticed that the desk he was chained to was inhabited by an adorable woman, wearing a demure navy blue dress and a crucifix the size of Texas.

Ah, young love. Ignited by work-study.

They got married right after college, despite Mom's fervent religious values and Dad's lack thereof. Right away, they started playing the ole Vatican Roulette, and *voila*! Five kids in ten years. Four boys and me; Jeremy is the oldest, followed by Paul, me and the twins, Adam and Cory.

It was a childhood filled with bellowing testosterone, and I thought I had it pretty rough.

Turns out being in the company of estrogen is no better. It's louder. Weirder.

I went from living with a cross-bearing church groupie

and an organic atheist to an ornery kitty and a nerdy plain Jane who performs well under pressure and harbors a wanton, gritty yearning to rock.

"*If I could turn back time . . .*"

"Mrrrrreeeeooooooowwwww!"

Enough.

Six o'clock, Saturday morning. Miss Priss was smack in the middle of daily shower number one. One of *three*. First thing in the morning, right after work, and just before she went to bed. It's a mystery. How dirty can you get counting money all day?

I couldn't sleep after I got home from Bellyaches last night. I hadn't hit the pillow until nearly 5 A.M.

Now, call me crazy, but in my opinion an hour of snooze isn't even enough beauty sleep to keep a Stepford wife looking good.

I threw back the covers and stomped down the hall, successfully ignoring the temptation to pick up the autographed baseball bat leaning against my desk. At least three days a week I must remind myself that smashing Jaime's face in isn't worth the desecration of David Ortiz's sacred name.

"Jaime!" I bellowed, banging on the bathroom door. "*JAIME!!*"

The rock-a-thon stopped.

"Yes?"

"Jaime. I *just* went to bed. Could you keep the karaoke down this morning?"

"Oh sure. Sorry Nina. I'm done anyway, just need to rinse Kitty off. Oooh, bad Kitty! Don't scratch Mama!"

"Mrrrrreeeooooowwwww!"

"Awww, you cranky munchkin! Little grump tator!!"

Jaime went to college in the South, where she picked up

all sorts of endearing little colloquialisms like "grump tator." My personal favorite is "A-do what now?" Translation: "What?" Interesting culture down South. Can't get their mouths around "you all," but add on three extra syllables when they need you to repeat something.

"By the way, Nina," Jaime called as I lumbered back toward my delicious-looking bed, "you got some mail yesterday. I put it on the—"

Wha . . . hey . . . CRASH!

Ow.

I guess she was going to finish her sentence with "floor outside your bedroom," since that's what I slipped on.

"Thanks," I called weakly, rubbing the elbow I smacked on the way down.

The offending pile of mail didn't look too spectacular. A blue envelope of undoubtedly useless coupons, my cell phone bill, a bank statement. I miss being a kid sometimes, where every piece of mail was a check from your grandmother or a colorful party invitation shoved into a huge, tacky envelope.

Hold on. A huge, tacky envelope. Here's one at the bottom of the pile.

My full name trailed across the front of the cream-colored rectangle in loopy calligraphy. MS. ANTONINA ELIZA-BETH KURTZ, the script yawned, 259 DIRENZO AVENUE, SOMERVILLE, MA.

Great. Probably another stupid wedding.

The year I turned twenty-four, the magnetic fields in my cheap iron mailbox suddenly shifted, mutating the post slot into a virtual beacon for endless wedding invitations and birth announcements.

I don't know what it is about our twenties that's making everyone so antsy.

If you're going to spend the rest of your life with someone, what's the damned hurry? I never understood those girls who've faithfully renewed their subscriptions to *Brides* magazine every August since their eighteenth birthdays. You know the type: They orchestrated childhood wedding role-plays with reluctant boy cousins, doodled big poofy gowns in math class, selected complementary seasonal fruits to accompany their color-coordinated centerpieces. I mean, sure I'd like to have a fancy party of some kind. Wear a pretty white dress and dance with all of my friends and family. Sip on kiwi champagne cocktails under a cream-colored linen tent that's set up under the silvery twinkles of a blue moon, swaying with my groom to the sweet hypnotic torch of Julie London (tracks one, seven and nine on her greatest hits album), dancing off Argentinean tapas and mocha espresso wedding cake. Not that I've given it any thought.

But, alas, no matrimonial empanadas for me anytime soon. I'd have to get beyond a first date for that, right? Instead I keep getting suckered into pews at Presbyterian churches, following up sweltering June ceremonies with picking at banquet hall beef or fish or chicken, watching aqua-clad bridesmaids throw back Amaretto Sours and scream along to "We Are Family." Ben usually accompanies me as my pity date, but he refuses to dance.

I wonder who it is this time.

Antonina Elizabeth Kurtz.

Not many people know my full name, so it seems likely that it's family, or maybe some colleague of my parents. Who could it be, who could it be?

My Uncle Danny's kids were out, since they were all still in middle school. Uncle Jay's got a daughter my age, but she got married last year; enormous Catholic to-do at the

Arlington Street church in downtown Boston. The reception was in the Boston Public Garden. Disaster. Homeless people left and right, trying to hone in on the buffet spread. Who knew the homeless dug pâté?

Let's see . . . on Dad's side there was Aunt Barbara, who's a recluse, and Uncle Samuel, who has five kids, only three of whom I'd met. Dad hadn't talked to Samuel in fifteen years—some spat over a time-share. So, if one of his brood was getting married, I doubted I'd be invited.

That left Auntie Patty, Dad's baby sister who lives on a cliff in Los Angeles, overlooking Catalina. She did Dad one better and moved to Haight-Ashbury when she was sixteen—never looked back. She was married three times before settling down with her current husband, Norman, a stockbroker who thinks it's cute that Patty won't shave her pits. I think this one will stick; it was Patty's first marriage that wasn't induced by hallucinogens. They didn't have kids, but it wouldn't have surprised me if they were having some wacky beachside ceremony to renew their vows in front of friends and family. They got hitched in Vegas, and although Patty still raves about the post-ceremony pig roast with Fat Elvis, I think Norm secretly wanted to seal the deal in a tux.

I could hear Jaime finally wrapping up her shower, and the last thing I wanted was to listen to her coo about registries and tiny bags of sugar-coated almonds. Jaime loves weddings; she gets inappropriately excited whenever I get an infamous calligraphy invitation, and hangs all over me until I tear it open and tell her what the bride's parents' names are, what kind of sauce will be served over the chicken, if I can bring a guest, etc.

All I wanted was to crawl back into bed and mummify myself in pilly T-shirt sheets until the *pffft* of school-bus brakes woke me up around afternoon snack time. But curiosity was enough to keep me awake for another three minutes while I tore into the envelope, tried to figure out if I knew the bride or the groom and whether or not I'm related to them and had a brief pity party for my sad single self.

This invitation was heavier than usual, and a little larger. Must be some hipster creation designed to one-up celebrity avant-garde invitations. Amazing how competitive people get over wedding accessories. I overheard some lady bawling last week while I was at Mike's Pastry in the North End, apparently because the caterers had failed to track down the exact hybrid of exotic saffron necessary to duplicate the appetizer bisque consumed at J-Lo's last wedding.

This was interesting. Just one square of paper instead of the usual multitude of announcements and RSVP cards. And some kind of booklet . . . what, we're printing wedding rosters now? A bridal playbill? Come on.

"You are cordially invited . . ."

Wait. What *is* this?

"Nina? Come on, Kitty. Nina? Oh, there you are. How come you're on the floor? I couldn't help but see the envelope at the bottom of that pile. Did you get another wedding invitation? What's the soup going to be?"

"It's not a wedding," I swallowed, and read it again.

"You are cordially invited . . ."

Oh no.

It can't be ten years already.

Three

"Oh my goodness, Nina, this is so exciting! I wonder if there's enough time to get your prom dress dry-cleaned?"

"I didn't go to prom, Mother."

"You didn't?"

"Nope."

"Huh. I thought you did. What's that green gown hanging up in your old closet, then?"

"That's the horrible dress you bought thinking you could *convince* me to go to prom."

"Really? Well, nobody will remember that you weren't there. Maybe we could get *that* cleaned and you could just pretend you wore it to prom."

"Why the hell would I want to do that?"

"That used to be the thing to do! All of my girlfriends and I wore our prom dresses to *our* high-school reunion. Can you believe they still fit? It was such a scream! Hmm. Is there a tailor near your apartment, honey?"

Wow, seven whole minutes into the meal this time. It was a new record.

Like an idiot, I always retreat to my parents' house in the

suburbs when I'm feeling upset, assuming that they'll coddle me, advise me, soothe me. How easily I forget.

It feels like I've spent a million Saturdays in my parents' sunny kitchen. To make up for Christmas and Easter, Dad was allowed to claim weekend breakfasts as the way to infuse his children with the religious customs of his own childhood.

Every Saturday morning, Dad would get up at five thirty, throw a ratty purple windbreaker over gray flannel handsewn pajamas, and race his emerald VW Rabbit to Sol Schwartz's Kosher Deli. The sweet incense of Sol's challah could tempt the Jew out of the most Roman of Catholics, and his meat-and-potato-filled pastries warmed the deepest chasms of my belly. Sol didn't open his doors until 6 A.M. sharp, so Dad would usually have to wait a few minutes, pressing his nose to the glass double doors, hopping back and forth on his slipper-clad feet like a child held back from his birthday presents.

"Always the first one there!" he would boast when he returned to the house, clutching a greasy paper sack. "Rain or shine or locust shower! Fresh knish! Dig in, knids!"

And we did. Mom would nurse her coffee and delicate English muffin and watch, horrified, as the six other members of her family tore into those pastries like famished lions relishing their victory over the first gazelle of spring.

Unfortunately, enjoying the hearty glory of a Saturday-morning knish meant enduring rapid-fire questioning from Dad, who regarded the Sabbath not as a day of rest, but rather a thinly veiled inquisition about our personal lives. He'd get us all to the table with the irresistible aroma of indulgence, and then BAM! We'd open our mouths so wide for the pastries that words couldn't help but fly out.

As we got older, Dad relinquished the interrogation duties to my mother. She takes them very seriously, as she is
extremely nosy.

I had arrived in Ashford this afternoon in time for lunch,
too late for a knish but not for the grilling.

When I called my mother that morning—sniveling about
that cursed piece of mail, that calligraphied card inviting
me to showcase to my entire graduating class that I'm single, childless, and working for minimum wage—I should
have immediately read her lunch invitation as a front for
the glorious opportunity to make me feel three inches tall.

"Are you afraid the gown won't fit? I'm sure you just
need to have a few seams let out. More gravy, honey?"

They're tricky, these "nurturing" sessions. I'm always
welcomed with a ten-minute hug from Mom followed by a
high five and a sympathetic chuckle from Dad; then I'm
presented with a plateful of my favorite foods, a glass of
wine, some kind of cookie or pie and a box of tissues. I
really would have no cause for complaint if these gestures
weren't accompanied by intense scrutiny, hyper-analysis,
and gentle suggestions that perhaps if I started working out
and paying attention to my diet, things would fall into
place. Basically, I get stuffed like a Thanksgiving turkey and
then picked apart like its cold, dead carcass.

"Do *you* think I should have more gravy, Ma?"

"Don't answer that, Margaret Ann," Dad chimed in over
his crossword puzzle. "Nina, I need a five-letter word for
'cow.' "

Well timed.

"*Vacca*," I grumbled, stabbing a forkful of roast beef with
a vengeance.

"*Vacca*? What is that, Spanish?"

"It's Latin, Dad."

"Aaah. Good work, Jellybean. *Vacca*. Crafty bastards at *The Globe*."

"Anyway," I shoved the *vacca* into my mouth, "I don't think—"

"Antonina Kurtz, chew that before you speak, thank you very much. Would you talk with your mouth full in front of the Queen?"

"We don't have a queen, Ma. Democracy, remember?"

"Well, I'm just saying. Don't you think your husband will appreciate looking across the table and seeing that he's dining with a lady?"

"What *husband*, Mom?"

"Someday he'll come along, Nina, right when you least expect it."

"I'm not really that concerned."

"How's my Ben doing, anyway?"

"Ben's fine."

"I love that young man. Smart as a whip."

"I know, Ma."

"He really is my favorite."

"I *know*, Ma."

"I don't see why you couldn't have made it work with him, honey."

"Because the thought of sleeping with Ben makes me want to hire a community college undergrad to carve into my flesh with a toothpick and nourish a crop of carnivorous gypsy moths by allowing them to feed on my reproductive organs."

"Oh *honestly*, Nina! I am trying to eat!"

"Well, so am I. Stop talking about Ben. It's ruining my appetite."

"I'm just trying to help you figure out your love life, dear. Believe me, I understand; romance can seem like such a mystery. Sometimes you need a third party to point out what's floating right in front of your nose!"

"Ma, you're starting to talk just like the mothers in those girlie novels you're always reading. I am not Bridget Jones, OK?"

"Leave the kid alone," Dad said absentmindedly. "What's a three-letter word for 'Possesses annoying horse sense'?"

"Mom," I grumbled.

"No, there's no 'm.' Oh, it's 'nag.' "

Same thing.

"Well, I think reunions are exciting." Mom smiled, leaning over to wipe a speck of gravy from my chin with her sleeve. "Did you bring the invitation with you?"

"It's in my bag. In the foyer."

"Want to grab it for me, pumpkin? I'll freshen up your chardonnay."

Sweet talker.

I grabbed my green canvas Army bag from the front hall and returned to the kitchen table. It took me a minute to fish through the stash of candy wrappers, half-melted lip glosses, loose change and gas receipts, but I finally found the invitation and handed it to my mother.

"Oh how nice," she cooed. "Let me just . . . hmm. Gideon, have you seen my reading glasses? Gideon, honey? GIDEON? Deaf as a doornail." She nudged my foot with hers, clucking a tongue in my father's direction. "It's from smoking all that dope when we were kids."

"Marijuana does *not* make you go deaf," my father said, still completely immersed in his crossword. "What's a seven-letter word for 'Blind Motherfucker'?"

My mother gasped. "Jesus and Mary, Gideon! That is *not* amusing! Read us the real clue."

"I kid you not, Margaret Ann. They must have a ballsy new intern."

"Try 'Oedipus,' " I said.

Dad filled in the letters and shook his head in amazement. "The Jellybean does it again. 'Blind Motherfucker.' I suspect there will be an entire section dedicated to apologies in tomorrow's edition."

"You should have used that brain to finish college," Mom sang as she pushed her chair back from the table, checking the counters in vain for her drugstore reading glasses. I keep trying to convince her to go to an eye doctor and get real glasses, but she insists that she'll just lose them anyway, so better to spend fifteen dollars on a pair from Walgreens.

"And give up my glamorous rock 'n' roll lifestyle?" Rather than use my steak knife to slit the wrists that pulsed with the blood of a loser, I concentrated *really* intensely on trimming the fat off my piece of roast beef.

Marriage is only a distant second to my mother's greatest wish for me. She was the first woman in her family to go to college, and it kills her that I let academia kick my underachieving ass outta town with two and a half semesters to go.

Mom would never come right out and say that she's disappointed in me; it's more her style to drop hints in a singsong voice and then hand me a cookie or a glass of wine. Personally, I'd have preferred to have a one-time, knockdown, drag-out, kicking, screaming, clawing, primal fistfight over my academic mutiny rather than spending what I suspect will be the rest of my life listening to my mother make implications about what a screwup I am. In truth, I dropped out because school felt like an obligation, like just something to pass the time until I had to make an actual decision about my future. Ironically, walking away from college was just about the only definitive decision I've made with my life so far.

Dad finally looked up from his crossword and stuck his tongue out at my mother, shooting me a sly wink. "Leave her alone, M.A. You want our little girl to work for The Man? Swathe herself in a three-button monkey suit and spend her life staring at three plastic, movable walls? You've done us right, Jellybean. Damn The Man."

Well put, by a man who gets to go to work in his pajamas. Dad's been a disc jockey for thirty years, and he prides himself on never once in his entire career having worn pants to the office.

My mother just chuckled.

"What?" Dad asked. "What's funny?"

"Gideon, sweetie, your sense of irony has deteriorated along with your hearing. Now where in the good name of Jesus are my reading glasses?"

"Wait, wait." Dad was really paying attention now. "What the hell does that mean, 'your sense of irony'? Nina, can you make any sense of your mother?"

"Not a clue, but that's part of her charm."

"Oh, listen to you two! Nina, I cannot find my reading glasses to save my life. You're going to have to read this to me."

"Not before we discuss my sense of irony," Dad said.

"Yeah, this should be good," I agreed.

"Oh, Gideon," Mom sighed. "Haven't we been over this? This 'working for The Man' complex? I mean, honey, where do *you* work?"

"I don't see where you're going with this."

"It's a simple question, Gideon."

"You *know* where I work, M.A."

"OK, so I'll answer myself; you are the most popular, charming, and, dare I say, handsome, DJ in New England classic rock, past, present or future."

"Devastatingly."

"Devastatingly handsome."

"So, I bring good old-fashioned tunes to the masses, soothe a weary soul or two. Last I checked, Bob Dylan and Joni Mitchell didn't cater to The Man."

"Honey, you work in commercial media. Clear Channel. Ring a bell? Aha! Here are my glasses! I knew I wasn't going out of my mind." Mom had discovered what Dad and I had been holding out on; that her reading glasses were, in fact, perched atop her head. Giggle. "Now, hand me that invitation, please. I'm dying to see it."

Dad stuck his nose back in the paper, grumbling to himself as he always does when the wife one-ups him. It's his own fault; he never gives her enough credit. She may be a nag and a Jesus freak, but my mama's one smart lady.

I handed her the heavy envelope.

"You are cordially invited," she read, "to an evening of old friends and new adventures!"

That line, when I read it the first time, nearly made me gag.

" 'Ashford High School is pleased to welcome you to join your classmates as you celebrate the tenth anniversary of your graduation.' Gosh, Nina, I can't believe it's been that long! 'Saturday, the ninth of November. Boston Harbor cruise, departing from the Long Wharf at seven P.M. Cocktails at seven-fifteen, followed by dinner, dancing and memories.' Isn't that lovely? 'RSVP by October twentieth, blah blah blah, please feel free to bring significant others, party shoes required.' Oh Nina! This will be so good for you! You'll get to see all of your old pals!"

"Malaria couldn't keep me away."

"And look at this!" Mom continued, ignoring my bitterness. "They put a booklet in here with all of your updated information! 'Where Are They Now?' Oh isn't this cute! Honey, look. Did you see this?"

"No."

"You mean you didn't even look at it?"

"Why bother? I can guess. All of the cheerleaders have kids, only a few of them lost the baby weight, all of the jocks are fat, bald, gay or a combination of the above, the nerds have taken over the world and that one chick who picked her nose all the time had a boob job and a full makeover on one of those reality shows, and now she's one of Hef's girlfriends."

"Uh-huh. Anything else, Miss Know-it-all?"

"And somebody's a trannie."

"Nina!"

"You asked."

"Why are you having such a bad attitude about this? I thought you'd be excited; you loved high school!"

It's true; I *did* love high school, which is unusual for a cynic, especially a redheaded one.

I was one of those social insects who flit about from clique to clique, totally unaware that the long-reigning hierarchy of high school mandates that one must pigeonhole oneself amongst a group of one's peers. Said group is required, by unspoken law, to dress the same, act the same, speak the same, like the same music, loathe the same people, date only within a particular realm, and practice the same activities. These rules are applicable to all teenage castes identified by Rosalind Wiseman, and employ an interchangeable set of variables, such as Abercrombie and Fitch, The Gap, Your Father's Old Flannel Shirts, Nine Inch

Nails, Pearl Jam, Dave Matthews Band, cheerleaders, jocks, goths, band nerds, drama snobs, lacrosse, the student paper, the golf team, French club, chess club, key club, etc. Each characteristic is a key component in the equation for thoughtless categorization.

I managed to somehow transcend all that. I had the power, baby. The power of comedy.

With four messy little boys to compete with as a kid, I had to fight like the French Resistance to get anyone to pay attention. You'd think it would be the opposite; my being the little lady, Daddy's girl, the apple of everyone's eye, gleaming red and shiny and perfect amidst an orchard of mischief. But the boys took up so much of my parents' energy that I was forced to compete if I wanted any of the glory. It didn't take long to figure out that tantrums were ineffective, that whining was repellant and that running away from home only got me in trouble. So, I learned from a very young age to make Mom and Dad laugh. If my mother was tearing her hair out trying to control the twins in a supermarket, I could diffuse the situation by doing a monkey dance in the cereal aisle. If Paul and Jeremy were brawling to the death over the newest G.I. Joe accessory, and Dad was visibly fighting the urge to hit either the kids or the bottle, I would put a colander on my head and reenact the latest episode of $M*A*S*H$. My rendition of Hawkeye killed every time.

So it began, my role as the wise-talking firecracker, and it spilled over into the schoolyard the very day I started kindergarten.

Right off the bat I had a million friends; I mean, who doesn't like to laugh? The giggles of my classmates only egged me on, and I grew to feel the most comfortable when I had the attention of everyone in the room. Of course I got into trouble all the time; it seems the grown-ups at school weren't as amused by my antics as my parents and their friends.

"Act like a young lady!" teachers would admonish me after school. "Leave the monkey business to the boys!" And, when I got older, "Your attitude is very . . . *abrasive*, Ms. Kurtz. Perhaps it's time to give the stand-up routine a rest and try to be more *ladylike*. College admissions committees will agree."

Back then I didn't give a damn what college admissions committees, teachers, boys or anyone else thought. Hmm.

"Look at this!" My mother's command reeled me in from my nostalgic drift. "Michelle Grove had a nose job! Remember the honker on her, Nina? Oh my God, all the mothers used to worry about that girl's self-esteem."

She was leafing through the memory booklet, scanning each page and unleashing periodic squeals of distaste and delight.

"You're going to get a kick out of this one. Remember little Tommy Branblatt?"

"The captain of the Math League."

"He's a professional wrestler."

"Get out!" I grabbed the booklet from her and took a look for myself. "Oh my God, that's Tommy the Tank Engine!"

"You've heard of him?"

"Ben's, like, obsessed with him. He's some up-and-coming WWF dude. You've seen him before, Mom; he does those new commercials for Turkey Jerky. Son of a bitch, that's Tommy Branblatt?"

Seeing that piqued my curiosity, so I couldn't help but flip through the pages.

The booklet was flimsily bound, in our school colors, of course, and the copy was bursting with exclamation points, like a literary pep rally. It was laid out like a yearbook, only instead of pimply faced teenagers, it featured my classmates as they look today, those of us who had bothered to send in pictures anyway, and blurbs about what everyone had done with their lives over the past ten years.

"Married. Married. Married. Divorced, that's not surprising. Married. Married to *each other*? No way! Married. Still single. Married. Still single. Married. Married. Married."

See what I meant about the memo?

"Ross Miller is a *doctor*? He used to set girls' hair on fire! Sandy Hinley is a nutritionist. Ha! That girl started the eating disorder *trend* in our school. Holy shit, Mikey Ives got *hot*!"

"Let's see yours, Nina." Mom grabbed the booklet from me greedily. "What picture did you send in? Not that one from the boat trip last summer, I hope. I wish you hadn't put that on your Christmas cards, dear."

"What? Seaweed pubes are funny!"

"I still don't know how you managed to slip all that down your bathing suit without anyone noticing."

"Paul saw. He kept you distracted until Uncle Jay took the picture."

"I should have known your brother would have something to do with it."

It's true; my brother Paul is kind of my partner in crime. Not that I hate the other ones or anything, but we always understood each other, I guess, Paul and I. Jeremy was always too caught up in being the "responsible big brother," and the twins spent most of their time in their own little world.

Anyway, Paul and I are still pretty close; he's the only brother still living in Massachusetts. I don't get to see him as often as I'd like; he's getting a PhD from MIT because he's a G.E.E.K. The twins are at college in Connecticut, and Jeremy lives with his wife, Kelly, in San Diego. They have two kids and a slew of grown-up responsibilities that give me a headache.

"Nina!"

"What?"

"You're not in here!"

Shit. I knew she'd have something to say about that.

"Sure I am, Ma. There's my name right there. See? Antonina Kurtz."

"But there's no picture above it. It's just a blank square with a question mark! Didn't you send in a picture?"

"I thought the seaweed pubes embarrassed you."

"Nina Kurtz, you didn't even give them any information about yourself! It just says 'not available' under where your picture is supposed to be!"

"Oh well."

"A gray question mark. My daughter is pictured as a gray question mark."

"It's not a big deal."

"Are you joking? It's every mother's nightmare to see her child depicted as a gray question mark! What happened, Nina? Didn't the reunion committee send you the forms to fill out?"

"I guess."

"What do you mean, 'I guess'? Either they did or they didn't!"

In truth, I *did* get a thick envelope a few months ago, from Tom Vanderhoof, president of my senior class, and Amy Heyman, class secretary, but, honestly, I thought it was another wedding invitation. So I left it on the kitchen table and forgot about it until Jaime got curious one night.

"Aren't you going to open this, Nina?" she had breathed, visibly itching to tear into the sucker and devour every savory detail about dinner choices and wedding gift registration.

"Do *you* want to open it, Jaime?"

"Oh no, no, no, it's your letter," she said, "but I just thought, well, it's been sitting here for so long, and what if you have to RSVP by a certain date?"

"Open it, Jaime."

"No, I . . . OK!"

Like a ten-armed kid at Christmas, she tore into that sucker and sifted through its contents. "Oh." She sniffed, disappointed. "It's just forms."

"Forms?"

"Yeah, like, from your high school or something."

"What do they say?"

"Um . . . it's asking you to send in a recent picture and fill out a questionnaire. For some kind of memory booklet."

"Ugh. Throw that shit out."

"Really?"

"Yeah. They're just trying to scam money out of alumni again. I get a crafty fund-raising mailing once a year or so. Pathetic."

My bad.

So now I'm a gray question mark. Well, what can you do? My head is filled with gray question marks most of the time anyway.

"Everyone else in your class sent something in." My mother shook her head and sighed, no doubt mortified by her school-spiritless offspring. "They're going to think you're a spoilsport."

"Better a spoilsport than a loser."

That got Dad's attention.

"Why would anyone think you're a loser, Jellybean?"

"You tell me, Pops. You and Mom seem to have a pretty strong opinion on the subject of my lifetime successes."

"Now hold on a minute." Mom set down her glass of wine and stuck her hand out urban teenager style before my Dad had a chance to open his mouth. "Your father and I certainly do *not* think you're a loser."

"Sure you don't."

"We just want you to be successful and happy, and to have the tools to do so. If you can honestly tell me that you're one hundred percent satisfied working in that roach motel, well then, honey, I'll never breathe another word about college. Or cosmetology school."

"It's a comedy club, Ma, and when did you ever say anything about cosmetology school?"

"Well, I was going to bring it up to you tonight, Nina. One of the ladies in my Pilates class has a daughter who's going to Best Tressed Beauty School and she just loves it! I brought you a brochure."

"You take Pilates classes?"

"Sure, honey. When you get to be my age, even your flab gets flabby. But don't change the subject."

"Fine. Well, I'm *not* one hundred percent happy, but—"

"Oooh, look, your class superlatives!" Mom squealed, before I had a chance to finish.

OK, I guess my heartfelt declaration *can* take a backseat to decade-old popularity contests.

"Biggest Flirt: Angie Sullivan. Whatever happened to her? Let's see . . . here she is. Stay-at-home mom, four kids. Hmm. Most Athletic: Devin Moore . . . uh-huh . . . Oooh, he's the manager of a minor league baseball team! Not bad! Most Musical: Courtney Kurtland. Where's Courtney's page . . . mmm-hmm, first chair French horn in the Washington Philharmonic. My goodness, these things were so accurate! Most Likely to Succeed: William Brent. CEO of a pharmaceutical company. Uncanny. Class Clown . . . Nina Kurtz."

She paused for a few seconds, while I stared at my mashed potatoes.

They really are complex—mashed potatoes.

So . . . white.

And . . . potatoey.

"You never told us you were voted Class Clown," Mom squawked strangely, sounding fierce and bloodthirsty, like the bastard love child of a Broadway stage mother and a Senegalese lion.

"So? That was high school."

"But people must have really liked you, honey!"

"Again, that was high school."

"Why are you still working behind the bar at that booze hovel? You should be up onstage, if you're so good at making people laugh. I never gave it too much thought, but that could be the answer, honey! No, listen, you could really make a career out of that!"

"Mom, would you stop?" I exploded.

"Stop what?"

"I am twenty-seven years old! I am not going to sit here poking at my dinner while you try to relive the glory days of my pathetic high-school popularity, force-feed me a career in hairdressing and criticize what I'm doing with my life! If you had let me *finish* a minute ago, I was going to say that I'm *not* one hundred percent happy, but I can't figure out what to do about it. I came over here because I thought you'd make me feel *better*, but you're just making it worse."

"I'm not trying to force-feed you a career in hairdressing! I just said that I thought you should do stand-up comedy!"

"Sure, Mom, because it's that fucking easy. Why don't I just 'do' neurosurgery?"

"I think I'll take the dog for a walk." Dad had been surveying our exchange with the nervousness of a tennis coach at his protégé's first Wimbledon.

"The dog died three years ago, dear."

"I'll find one." He scooted back from the table and bolted from the kitchen, grabbing a down vest from the hook by the spice rack and stuffing his arms through it.

Mom shook her head as she watched him go. "He never was good with confrontation. You should have seen him the first time he met my parents. It was the second night of Hanukkah, and Gramma was trying to force-feed him baked ham. The third time the platter was passed to him, he faked a coughing fit and hacked himself all the way out to the car. I thought Grampy was going to run after him with the carving knife."

"Anyway"—she turned back to me—"what made you Miss Crankypants all of a sudden?"

"I just *told* you."

"Are you nervous about your reunion? You know, the Atkins Diet works wonders in only a matter of weeks. And you have more than a month!"

She has this talent, my mother, this astronomical knack for pretending not to know what's going on while simultaneously honing in on exactly what I'm depressed about, then completely superseding the issue and making me feel like a big fat turd. I suspect that it's not just *my* mother.

"Terrific, Mom, I'll be sure to pick up three pounds of Canadian bacon and a vat of Crisco on my way home."

"Get some eggs, too, honey. Can't get too much protein on this thing. I think I have an Atkins cookbook around here somewhere. Hang on, and I'll get it for you."

She left me, defeated, at the kitchen table, staring at those rows of happy faces who all turned out either exactly how they were supposed to, or had done themselves one better and become doctors and professional wrestlers and jerky pushers.

Shit.

My alma mater, Ashford High School, was a psychedelic mess. Founded as a single-story schoolhouse in the early nineteen thirties, the building was since fortified by dozens of additions, wings and single rooms slapped on precariously like the celebratory high fives shared among jocks on the football field. The school was chaos personified; a layout that couldn't be more confusing if the students were forced to walk to class backward and blindfolded. Soon-to-be freshmen would spend entire summers sweating over maps and blueprints, desperate to brave their first day of high school armed with infallible knowledge of the hallways that slithered amid classrooms and lockers, the gym, the cafeteria. Tiny Magellans, praying that the corridors would eventually meet up with one another in a perfect circle.

In the nineteen seventies, the board hired a wave of young teachers—an entire scholastic generation of former hippies eager to reform the state of public education. Leader of the free-lovin' pack was Teddy Sheckman ("Sheck," as he preferred to be called by his students), a charismatic, gently powerful history teacher whose wacky approach to the state curriculum pissed off the school board but invigorated the students. He believed that the best way to educate the young masses was to allow them to "relive the moment." His students often found themselves sporting tricornered hats while foraging for roots and mushrooms in the woods behind school (in order to more closely identify with the minutemen of the Revolutionary War), or cowering under their desks, arms thrown protectively over their heads, trembling under the threat of a Russian missile attack.

In the mid nineteen eighties, Sheck decided that the school needed to be unified—not the student body, or the faculty, mind you, but the school itself. He felt that the building must suffer from some sort of identity crisis, since it had haphazard appendages jutting out all over the place, but no real structure, no heart. So, he organized a day of "artistic hooky" and armed the entire student body with roller brushes, paint and turpentine—a Benjamin Moore militia instructed to pull the school together with a spectrum of creative colors.

The murals were still there when I got to high school in 1992—swirly, girly confections of oranges, yellows, blues. Every square inch of wall space was crammed with colors that melded into one another like molten candy. My locker was smack in the middle of "Sunshine Square," so dubbed by the gaggle of senior girls who painted the junction in painfully vivid hues of gold, lemon and tangerine. An eyesore in the afternoon, "Sunshine Square" was nearly unbearable at seven thirty in the morning, the colors glaring more brightly than the aura of a deity. It was excruciating to look at; the only preventive remedy was a healthy dose of caffeine before hopping the school bus, or—most of us imagined—the Bloody Marys that teachers swilled from their Garfield coffee mugs.

The brightly colored décor set a hilarious backdrop in the early nineties, when every student that roamed the halls was fashionably depressed. Flannel was our uniform, Cobain was our master, and nobody washed their hair more than once a week.

The closest thing I had to a best friend in those days was Lizzie Lee, captain of the debate team and a string-bean strawberry blonde. Lizzie was a geek, and kind of in awe of me, only because I wasn't afraid to speak my mind.

We would meet at her locker every morning before class; she brought hot chocolate, I the nip of peppermint schnapps I stole from my brother Jeremy's desk drawer. He was already off at college by my freshman year and had likely forgotten about his stash of contraband.

Freshman year, I got a little lost in the crowd, but it didn't take long for me to feel comfortable enough with my surroundings to start commanding attention.

The trouble with high school is that it's so damned *boring*. All those stupid classes with stupid people, learning shit you'll never use again with people you'll never see again. I'm not a dumb girl; I'd like to think the opposite. But I never did well in school, because I just didn't have the patience for bullshit. Thanks to my anti-establishment father, I knew that the "facts" I had to memorize for classes like social studies weren't the whole truth ("History was written by the winners!" was one of Dad's favorite lines), that the formulas used in math and science were practically obsolete if you weren't anticipating a career in engineering. So, really, high school was good for picking up social skills and VD, but not much else. (Oh come on, I didn't mean *me*. I wasn't a cheerleader.)

What I *did* enjoy was making people laugh.

I definitely carried my goofball reputation from the sandbox to the schoolyard, which didn't help my grades but ensured a solid scholastic career of unwavering popularity.

Platonic popularity.

Even as a high schooler with raging hormones and that general teenaged cluelessness regarding most social matters, I knew from the moment my breasts erupted that being the go-to girl for zingers and one-liners would get me nowhere in the romance department. Being the eternal buddy was never so difficult as when Lizzie and the other girls we hung with started shopping for lacy bras and tissues to stuff them with. Oh, I was right along with them, giggling and modeling and forking over my babysitting money to the disapproving elderly lingerie saleswomen at Filene's department store. But while Lizzie and company were speculating about the prospects of second base on their upcoming Saturday nights, I hung back, feeling awkward and unattractive. Because while the other girls were getting pursued and propositioned in the high-school hallways, I was getting high fives and recap requests, begged by boys, not to date them but to entertain them.

When I developed my first big crush I finally had a reason to cruise the mall for Wonderbras and scented body lotion. Sam Craig was a skateboarder with floppy hair, and I did everything in my power to telepathically entice him to ask me to be his date for the Fall Fling, the biggest dance in the first half of the year and a guaranteed make-out fest. My hopes were crushed when I overheard Sam and his buddies in the cafeteria, talking about the girls in our class. When my name came up they all piped up and agreed that I was totally cool but I totally didn't count as a girl, and that none of them could ever put a move on me because it would totally be like kissing their sister.

That was bad for the self-esteem.

Not quite as bad, however, as a hyper-hounding mother with a fad-diet nutrition mission.

"Found the cookbook, honey. I shouldn't have made two different kinds of pie, but I guess we can call this your last hurrah and you can get started in the morning. More wine?"

"No."

"It's OK; chardonnay is pretty low in residual sugar."

"I'm fine, Ma. I'll drink more later."

Later, when I'm sitting alone on my Salvation Army couch, eating prewrapped slices of American cheese and weeping poetically.

"November ninth. Ooh, Daddy and I will have to take you shopping! What are you doing tomorrow?"

"I don't want you to take me shopping, Ma. And anyway, I can't do anything tomorrow. I'm helping Hal."

"With what? Inventory?"

"No, one of those photo shoots that he does. Remember? He's an amateur photographer."

"And he hired you to help? That's so thoughtful of him. He's a great boss. Too bad he's running a rat shanty. I bet he'd let you try out a night onstage, if you asked him."

"You amaze me, Mom."

"Why, honey?"

"The way you shift gears. During the course of the forty-five minutes that I've been sitting at this table, you've clucked your tongue at me because I didn't finish school, then suggested I become a hairdresser, and now you're harping on me to be a comic. Stand-up comedy is the furthest you can possibly get from job stability. Really, it's even less financially rewarding than being a freelance abstract artist, or working at a factory in a third-world country threading dental floss through the little metal holder in the container. Did you know that's a job? Somebody's job. Somebody actually gets paid to do that. They probably get paid more than stand-up comedians. And they don't have anyone throwing cocktail olives at them if they thread incorrectly."

My mother took a healthy gulp of her wine, running a hand through her crisp Clairol pageboy so that it stood on end in the front, like summer ryegrass. "You have this great big idea that your father and I are disappointed in you. And maybe that's a little bit true—let me finish! But it's more that I'm disappointed *for* you. We want you to take your life in a direction. *Any* direction. Pick something. If you decide you want to be a comic or a mechanical engineer or a ballerina, we support you completely, as long as you have a goal and you're pursuing it as fiercely as you can. And frankly, honey, I don't get the impression that you're doing that right now.

"I think you should be inspired by your classmates, dear, instead of discouraged," she continued. "Some of these people have had mountains to climb over the course of their short lives, and most of them have really made something of themselves! I mean, Dan Bray? Wasn't he the little retarded boy? Look; he's an attorney now."

"Dan Bray? Dan Bray wasn't retarded, Mom, he was just cross-eyed!"

"Oh. Anyway, an attorney. He's doing pretty well for himself, considering that I imagine pretty much everyone he's ever met has mistaken him for being retarded."

"Anyone else in there that you'd like me to carve out as my professional role model, or can I finish my pie and head home?"

"You know who I forgot to look up?"

"Meredith Rice, the field hockey MVP with chronic eczema? Maybe she's a dermatologist now and I can use her triumph as inspiration to become a go-getter."

"I forgot all about her. No, I think you know who I'm

talking about. I can't believe we haven't done it already. Aren't you dying to know?"

"Dying to know what the hell you're talking about? Yes, Ma, I am."

"So, then let's see!" Mom snatched the booklet up again and began flipping with a purpose, the tip of her tongue peeking through her pursed lips as she concentrated on her search.

"Here! Here he is. I'm surprised it's not dog-eared."

"Who?"

"Jacob!"

"Who?"

"Jacob Ryan. Your first boyfriend, honey! Wow, he looks terrific!"

Dammit.

"I saw the way you two looked at each other the time eleven or twelve years ago when we ran into him at the Mobil station in town center. And, come on, do you really think your father and I were that clueless about where you were taking the minivan every Friday night? Honey, we're not idiots; it always came back with footprints all over the back windows!"

"Ewwww!"

"What do you mean, 'Ew,' Nina? You were the one jigging the horizontal Highland fling in front of the Lord-knows-who at the drive-in!"

"I was not!"

"Oh, come on. I'm not judging, honey. Your father and I used to have sex, too."

This was getting way too weird.

"I'm going home, Ma. You cooked me a terrific meal, and I'd like to keep it in my stomach until it's good and ready to move on."

"Well, give me a minute to pack up the leftovers."

The drive back home to Somerville was a mess, a nostalgic blur that made my intestines cartwheel and my toes curl. Not because of the feasting, though, or the chardonnay or the nagging or even the idea of my parents fogging up the minivan.

It was Jacob Ryan.

Four

"Look at this guy! Does this picture scream 'trapped in a failed marriage' or what? Or this one! Holy shit, this girl was head cheerleader? She looks like she ate half the squad!"

"Carla Sandino?"

"Yeah, how'd you know that? You aren't even looking."

Ben was right where he always is at seven o'clock: slumped on one of my bar stools at the club, killing time before his first set. I'd forgotten to take the reunion booklet out of my bag after the day's stressful lunch at Mom's, so when he started whining about being bored I tossed it on the bar to shut him up.

It was true about Carla and I can't say I was upset about it. I'd never had a personal problem with her in high school, but she was one of those mean-spirited pretty girls who think that anybody who didn't wear a size four was a hideous blob and therefore subject to ridicule. Silly Carla. Clearly she skipped mythology class the day we studied hubris.

"Yeah, I always thought she was a fat person waiting to happen."

"Wow. And look, she's married to the president of the chess club!"

"Really? Let me see that."

I grabbed the booklet from Ben's clammy hands. Sure enough, there she was, Fatty Sandino, now Fatty Sandino-Little (ironically), married to Tom Little, arguably the nerdiest boy in our class and now, no question, the richest. The rest of us should have paid more attention in our mandatory computer science classes.

"He always did have the biggest crush on her."

"Talk about crush. I wonder how they do it?"

"Do what?"

"Do *it*. Look at him, Nina, the guy can't weigh in at more than one fifteen. She can't be on top or it's all over!"

"I suspect it's all over anyway, Ben. Would you still do your wife if she had that many chins?"

"If I really loved her."

"Really?"

He thought about it for a second.

"No. Not really."

"I didn't think so, you shallow bastard."

"Me? You're the one who brought it up!"

"I simply posed a question; I never told you how I would answer."

"So you'd still do your husband if he weighed four hundred pounds?"

"Sure. If I were drunk."

"See? You're worse than I am, Kurtz."

"Never claimed otherwise."

To my right I heard the scrape of a bar stool against the tile and looked up to see Abe sliding into a seat.

"Abe. Running a little late tonight, huh? Wife give you a tough time about coming to see your girlfriend?"

"Hey there, Carrot Top, how are ya? Listen to that, would you, Ben? She finally admits she's my lady friend."

"I was talking about this girlfriend," I chuckled, throwing down a cocktail napkin and placing a pint of local beer in front of him. "Tall, pale, and full-bodied."

"Listen to you." Abe chuckled. "I tell ya, Red, you're a live one. Pity the man who tries to tie you down."

"Not a word!" I pointed at Ben with a menacing look before he could spout off any jokes about bondage. "I'm not in the mood for your lip tonight, mister."

"Aww baby, I thought you said you liked my lips," Ben teased, flicking the booklet at me like a Frisbee.

"I like them best when they're *closed*, bitch."

"Whoa! Somebody's a sourpuss tonight." Abe laughed out loud, holding his belly. "You gonna take that from Carrot Top, Benny boy?"

"Eh. Nina's just a little cranky because she's feeling old."

"Old? Get off it, young lady. Why in the hell would you be feeling anything but young and sprightly? You should be out breaking hearts, not breaking your back to pour beer for old farts like me."

"She got invited to her ten-year reunion," Ben sang in the obnoxious little voice he reserves for when I'm already set to kill him and he wants to push me over the edge.

"Ten years after what? College?"

"High school."

"That's all? That's why the long face?"

"Pretty much."

"Bah!" Abe waved his hand dismissively and took a long swig of his Tall Tale Pale Ale. "That makes you all of twenty-seven? Twenty-eight?"

"Why do you look so surprised, Abe? Do I look older? It's the stress from this place. Gives me wrinkles."

"You don't look a day over twenty, Carrot Top. In fact,

some of these guys and I had a bet going as to whether you're even old enough to be pullin' those taps."

"That's kind of creepy, Abe."

"So it's been ten years! What's the trouble?"

Ah, the most loaded of questions. Gosh, the bar looks dirty. This spot right here needs a good scrubbing. La la la . . .

"See that, Benny? The wheels are turnin'. She can't think of a reason to be all bent out of shape."

"No, I have plenty of reasons."

"Name one."

"Here we go," Ben muttered under his breath, finishing off the backwash in his pint glass and stretching over the bar to pour himself another.

"Oh, like I've never listened to *your* bitching?" I growled. "You have more problems than an algebra textbook!"

Abe laughed. "There's the spirit, Red. One of these days we're gonna get you up on that stage yourself, give Mr. Henry here a run for his money!"

"Oh no!" Ben looked up from his pour. "That's never going to happen."

"And why, exactly, is that never going to happen?" Abe asked.

"Yeah, Ben"—I shooed him away from the tap—"I'd like to hear what you have to say about that."

"Well first of all," Ben began, selecting a maraschino cherry from the bar tray and popping it in his mouth (I don't know why we keep the damned things, since we only serve beer and wine. Cocktail onions, too. Makes no sense). "Nina has terrible stage fright. Can't talk in front of more than six people or she starts shaking like a leaf."

"That true, Red?"

"He's got a point," I grumbled.

"Second of all," Ben continued with a smirk on his face, "Nina is fully aware that she'll never be as funny as I am, so she knows better than to try and keep up."

"Ha!" I snorted, shooting him a glare.

"There's a notion!" Abe drained his beer and let out a belch. "Sounds like someone's afraid of a little competition, eh, Benny? You gonna take that, Nina?"

"He can talk all the shit he wants to, Abe. Deep down, Ben knows he can't hold a candle to my five-alarm comedic blaze."

"Hear, hear!" Abe shouted. "Another Tall Tale, Carrot Top, and screw you, Benny boy! The girl's sharper than English Cheddar."

"Anyway," Abe continued after I set down another beer and he'd had a swig. "You don't worry one bit about some silly high-school reunion, Nina. You pick out the cream of all those fellas you got and let him show you off."

"All what fellas, Abe?"

"Come on, Red. A pretty thing like you's got a million beaux lined up halfway down the block!"

"What universe do *you* live in, Abe?"

"Are you saying you ain't got a fella?"

"That's what I'm saying."

"Crying shame, that is. Benny, why don't you take this girl out and show her a good time?"

"Abe, Ben wouldn't know what a good time is from a hole in the wall. In fact, his idea of a good time *is* a hole in the wall."

That one broke up the whole bar. Even the comic onstage paused and squinted through the stage lights to see just who was stealing the laughs from him. Come on, dude, there's nothing to steal. Amateur.

"Nice, Nina." Ben rolled his eyes. "So now I'm a perv."

"Just now?"

I cracked a sarcastic smile at Ben and went on polishing the bar. A few drink tickets came in and I poured them with ease, traying glasses of merlot and Budweiser tallboys before handing them off to our decaying cocktail waitress, Betty.

When I finally looked up at Ben, he was buried in my reunion booklet again, shaking his head in disbelief once in a while before pausing and cocking his head.

"You're not in here."

"Yes I am."

"Where?"

"Right there."

"It's a gray question mark."

"Have you talked to my mother today?"

"Why didn't you send in your picture?"

"I don't know."

"Don't you want people to know what you're doing?"

"You mean making you miserable?"

"Nina."

"Oh, you mean making *myself* miserable."

"I'm serious! Are you going to go to this thing?"

"I don't know."

Ben looked thoughtful, stirring his beer with a finger before tossing the booklet back on the bar.

"Do you still keep in touch with anyone?"

"From high school?"

"Yeah."

"No," I scoffed, "why the hell would I?"

"I don't know. Why *wouldn't* you? I mean, I still talk to most of my buddies from school."

"You do?"

"You seem surprised."

"I just never hear you talk about them."

"Why would I? They're boring. Married. Kids. Hateful jobs. You know the story."

"All except the married and kids part."

"You don't really hate this job, do you?"

"Well, I *was* voted 'Most Likely to Work in a Comedy Club.' "

"Get out."

"I'm serious! I don't think this is exactly what everyone had in mind, though."

"You were funny in school?"

"Yeah, Henry, turn to the last page of that booklet."

He obliged, flipping through the pages, now sticky from being handled so many times and lying in a puddle of beer.

"Nina Kurtz: Class Clown. Wow, Kurtz, I have to admit, I'm a little surprised."

"Why?"

"You know."

"No, I don't know. Enlighten me, please."

"Because you're a girl."

"I am?"

"Shut up. I just meant, usually it's the *guys* who get voted Class Clown. Because they're goofier, in general."

"Ah, yes. Well, I guess I just lucked out and got lumped in with a graduating class of exceedingly bland boys. Good thing, too, or I never would have made an impression on anyone."

"Who were your friends?"

"What do you mean?"

"I mean, in here; show me who you were friends with."

"Why?"

"I don't know. I'm just curious. And if I'm gonna be your date to this thing, I might as well know ahead of time who I can expect to talk to."

"Who said you're going to be my date? Who even said that I'm *going*?"

"Of course you're going, Kurtz. And come on, who else are you going to take. Abe?"

"At least he'd treat me like a lady."

"That guy there? He'd have three beers and try to play pinochle on your ass."

"Shows what *you* know. He's a three-card-stud kinda guy."

"Come on, show me your friends. This girl? How about this one? No, she's a tiny little blonde thing, so you must have hated her."

"I resent that!"

"What?"

"The implication that I'd hate a tiny little blonde girl simply because she's tiny and blonde. I'm not a jealous girl."

"So you were friends with her? With . . . Chrissy Di-Nardo?"

"Ooooh, *no*. I hated that little bitch."

"Ha! Next. Let's see . . . Serena Carlson?"

"Eh."

"Lynn Wilkins?"

"Eh."

"Joanna James?"

"Why are you only naming girls?"

"I don't know; I thought girls were friends with girls."

"Have you met me?"

"OK, well, what about the guys?"

Ben flipped around some more, clucking his tongue for a minute. "Let's see . . . let's see . . . Jason Turner?"

"Eh."

"If you're just going to keep saying 'eh,' I really don't see a point to this."

"You're the one who started it!"

"Nina!" Hal called from down the bar. "You've got drink tickets, love."

I busied myself pouring drinks while Ben, still determined to prove that I had at least one friend before I met him, kept calling out names.

"Chris Reynolds."

"Eh."

"Cut that out. Mark Murphy."

"Ew!"

"What? He's a stud!"

"He was the biggest cokehead in school."

"Not necessarily. He could just be skinny."

"Look at his nose."

"Ooh, you're totally right. OK, moving on. Seth Heinz."

"Eh."

"Paul Sylva."

"He was OK."

"Jacob Ryan."

The pint glass I was cleaning slipped out of my hand and hit the tile floor with a *CRASH*, shattering into a million tiny shards.

"Ooooh. Did I hit a nerve?"

"The glass was wet."

"Who's Jacob Ryan?"

"Nobody. Move on."

"There's no way I'm moving on from this one. Let's see. Jacob Ryan. President, Outdoors Club. President, Rock Climbing Club. President, Orienteering Tribe—hey, this is a guy to get lost in the woods with, huh? Vice-President, Key Club. A do-gooder, too."

Ben kept rattling off the profile, but I didn't listen. I didn't need to. I'd spent most of that afternoon staring at it, mesmerized.

JACOB RYAN
Boulder, CO

Activities
President, Outdoors Club
President, Rock Climbing Club
President, Orienteering Tribe
Vice president, Key Club

College
UC Berkeley
Double major, political science and environmental
  engineering

Occupation
Wilderness Guide

Marital Status
Single

"A professional dirty hippie, huh?"
I blinked. "What?"
"This guy, Jacob. A 'wilderness guide'? What the fuck is
that? A sherpa? He doesn't look Nepalese."
"He's probably like an Outward Bound leader or some-
thing."
"You say that with conviction. I didn't think you even
knew what Outward Bound is! Have you ever even *been* in
the woods?"
"Shut up."
"I'm serious! Your nose gets itchy if anyone even men-
tions bugs or snakes."
"Shut up!"

Dammit, he said "bugs." I rubbed my nose with the heel of my hand.

"See?"

"Itchy. Anyway, I only know that because he always talked about wanting to move to the Rockies and work for Outward Bound or some other orienteering organization."

"So you *did* know him."

"Of course I knew him, Ben, our high school wasn't that big."

He looked at me thoughtfully.

"Did you like him?"

"You mean, did I like him or did I *like* like him?"

"Ha! Did you *like* like him?"

I didn't answer.

"You did! Ooooooh, Jacob Ryan, Nina's number one! I'll have to remember that. Well now we're definitely going to this reunion."

"Who is this 'we' you keep mentioning?"

"Obviously you have to bring me with you, if you want to make this guy jealous."

I snorted. "You think that *you* would make a guy jealous?"

"And why not? I'm handsome."

"Ha."

"I'm charming."

"Ha."

"I'm terribly funny and successful—"

"Ha!"

"And I can say 'Where's the bathroom?' in six different languages."

"Well, I'm sold. I can't imagine why you're single."

"Now you're starting to get it. Jacob Ryan. So what happened? You had a huge crush on him and he wouldn't give you the time of day, right?"

"Fuck you, Ben. Nice how that's the first thing that comes to mind, ass."

"Well, you seem pretty touchy about him."

"So you think he wouldn't give me the time of day?"

"So what is it then? You guys got drunk and made out at prom?"

"I didn't go to prom."

"What? Why?"

"I thought it was stupid. Why, did you go?"

"Of course! Top hat and tails!"

"Didn't get laid, did you?"

"How did you know?"

"Top hat and tails."

"Ouch."

Ben checked his watch and stroked his chin.

"I only have six minutes before I go onstage, so why don't you just tell me."

"Tell you what?"

"Who this Jacob guy is. You're obviously touchy about it, so—"

"So I should, obviously, tell you all about it."

"Come on, I tell you everything."

"And most of the time it's more than I want to know!"

"Fine." He sniffed, taking a final swig of his beer before pushing the half-filled pint across the bar toward my collection of dirty glasses.

Jesus Christ. Ben can be such a *girl* sometimes. He gets all touchy if he thinks I'm keeping something from him.

"We went out, OK?"

"You and Jacob Ryan?"

"Yes."

"For how long? A long time? Like, six months?"

"Nope."

"Less or more?"

"More."

"A year?"

"Nope."

"More than a year?"

"Almost two."

"Holy shit. I didn't know you were capable of such commitment."

"Shocking, right?"

"Completely."

Hal waddled past the bar and clapped Ben on the shoulder.

"Come on, Ben. Time ta quit yer yappin' and get ta work."

"Yeah, Hal, crack that whip!" I hooted. "Get your lazy ass onstage, Henry, and leave me and my pathetic high-school romance alone!"

"I want to hear more about this when I'm done." Ben jabbed a finger at Jacob's picture before heading for the stage.

Good Lord. I rolled my eyes at his back as he made his way onstage and grabbed the microphone, greeting the rejuvenated crowd. How does he get the room all energized like that? I find Ben *so* annoying when he doesn't have a microphone to hide behind. I swear, it's like a magic wand.

Abe scooted down to take his place.

"All right, Carrot Top. What are you really afraid of? No more teasing; let's get serious."

"You wanna get serious with me, Abe? What's your wife gonna think about that?"

"I mean it, Red. You look like you could use a good chat."

I stared at him, this ruddy-faced regular who spends 70 percent of his time with his nose in a pint glass, flirting with a girl who could be his daughter's daughter.

"OK." I put down the glass I was cleaning and rested my chin in my hand.

"So what's on your mind?" Abe asked.

"Nothing, really."

"Aw, come on now. Not exactly yourself tonight, sweetheart. You think us old farts wouldn't notice?"

I couldn't help but giggle; Abe has a really thick Boston accent, so that came out as 'Nuawt exactly yaself tonight, sweethaht. You think us old fahts wouldn'ta notice?' It cracks me up. *Good Will Hunting* renewed my appreciation for Boston-talk.

"I'm fine, Abe." I chuckled. "You ready for another beer?"

"In a minute. Gonna let that last one swim around a little."

A wise idea, since Abe's eyes were already threaded with capillaries and it wasn't even eight o'clock.

"So," he continued, "you're really all bent out of shape over some reunion, huh?"

"It's dumb."

"What, the reunion, or dumb to be bent out of shape?"

"Both."

"So don't go! What's the problem?"

"I . . . I don't know!"

Honestly, I'd been asking myself the same thing since I got the stupid invitation in the mail. I would never have thought twice about it if my mother hadn't asked me about the very same boy that Ben had grilled me about. Until I heard his name, I wasn't planning on being anywhere *near* Boston Harbor or the Long Wharf on November 9.

Abe was watching me intently, clearly waiting for me to spew a better answer than "I don't know."

"I heard you talking with Benny," he said, "something about an old boyfriend?"

"Yeah. Jacob."

"What's the story, Carrot Top?"

"Not much to tell."

"You're a terrible liar."

True.

"OK," I sighed, "what do you want to know?"

"How did you meet the lucky fella?"

"Spanish class, junior year."

"No kiddin'! You can speak Spanish?"

"I didn't say that."

"Ah. For a second there I was impressed."

"Let's not get crazy, Abe. So yeah. We met in Spanish class. He was a new kid, and it was his first day. I was showing off, telling some stupid joke as usual, and I smacked him in the face."

"Sheesh. What for?"

"It was an accident. I was waving my arms around to punctuate, and he was sitting at the desk next to me."

"I knew you were dangerous, Red. So it was love at first smack?"

"Kind of. I turned to apologize and that was that. He was the finest thing I'd ever seen. Black spiky hair, huge green eyes, the cutest little freckles on his nose. Why am I telling you this? Sorry, I'm starting to ramble."

Abe wrinkled his own ruddy honker and shook his head, signaling for me to pour him another beer.

"So get to the good stuff, Carrot Top."

"Hmm. Well, he was the first guy that ever treated me like a girl. Shit. Come to think of it, he may be the *only* guy that's ever treated me like a girl."

"How do you mean?"

"I don't know. Even back then I couldn't get beyond a high five with a dude. But then Jacob showed up and . . . he didn't care that I was loud. And made stupid jokes all the time. Most men are completely turned off by that. It wasn't just in high school; it's still going on."

"Really?"

"Are you kidding? I've perfected the fine art of pinpointing exactly when I make the transition from cute redheaded romantic prospect to new best buddy. It's usually right around the salad."

"The salad?"

"You know, at dinner. The waiter shows up with salad right around the time my date has decided that our evening will be strictly platonic and a little bit awkward."

"That can't be true."

"Why not?"

"Don't get offended, Red, but you're a cute young thing. I can't imagine that any young man wouldn't at least want to . . . um . . ."

"Wouldn't want to what, Abe? Wouldn't at least want to stick it in?"

He threw his head back and let out a great big laugh, drawing stares from the rest of the bar and a stern look from Ben, who was onstage trying desperately to capture the attention of the lukewarm crowd. Hey, can't win 'em all.

"I was going to be a little more tactful." Abe chuckled, wiping the tears from his eyes with the corner of his tired flannel shirt.

"No you weren't."

"You're probably right."

"Well, nobody does. Nobody wants to stick it in. I've tried for years, and the only action I ever get is a handshake."

"You know, Red, now that we've gotten to talking about

it, it makes sense that none of those idiots wants to take you on as their lady friend."

"I know. Apparently I'm intimidating."

"I'll tell ya, Nina, men your age are such thickheads."

"No shit."

"It'll change as you get older."

"A girl can dream."

"No, it's true." Abe drained his beer and swallowed slowly, breathing a long *aah* and pointing to the tap once again.

"Men are stupid when they're young," he continued. "They convince themselves they want a woman with big brains and big tits, but really it's just the tits that they want. Because, between you and me, men are fragile."

"Really?"

"Oh, you bet your sweet face. Much more fragile than the fairer sex. Can't handle it when a lady has an edge on them upstairs."

"But that changes with age?"

"Somewhere around thirty-five you start to figure out that the tits will droop long before the brain does. So this Jacob character, he treated you like the lady that you are. And as a teenager, bless his heart. What happened?"

"We were together for a long time and then we graduated."

"And that was that?"

"Pretty much. He moved out West to start his life, and I stayed here to start—procrastinating."

"And you haven't spoken since?"

"Nope."

"Ever think about him?"

"Sometimes."

Lies.

I've actually found myself thinking more and more about Jacob as the years have passed, usually in the immediate wake of yet another failed first date.

It's totally sad that the only romantic success I've had was when I was a teenager. And it's even sadder to keep dwelling on it. But I can't help but compare all of my amorous failures to the one actual success that I've experienced.

He was an amazing guy, Jacob Ryan. Not just mind-numbingly gorgeous but smart and kind and always up for some kind of adventure. We used to kill ourselves laughing, hopping backyard fences to "borrow" somebody's barbecue for a midnight snack, early-morning skinny-dipping in historic (and historically smelly) Walden Pond, taking spontaneous road trips to anywhere but Ashford. Our whole relationship was like a young adult novel, until we started doing it, but man, that was the most fun I've ever had with a man. Well, he wasn't a man then. He was a kid. Oh my God, ew, I'm drooling over a kid.

"Wheels are turnin', Red. I can smell it. What's on the brain?"

"I was just thinking that I must have done *something* right ten years ago. It would be nice to know what that something was."

"And . . ."

"And?"

"And you miss this fella. I can see it in your face."

"You can?"

"Sure. Your eyes have gone all gooey."

"Probably just the conjunctivitis."

Abe chuckled again, plunking his pint glass on the bar and reaching for his back pocket.

"Another beer?"

"Naw, thanks. Gotta get home to the missus."

"Yeah, what are you doing here anyway? It's Saturday night. Shouldn't you be resting up for the big Sabbath?"

"I'm terrible, eh? Nah, the wife's out with her girl-friends for somebody's birthday, so here I am. But tomorrow's service will be twice as long with a hangover, so here I go."

"Well, say hello to Jesus for me."

"Will do. So you still confused about this reunion of yours?"

"Kind of. It's complicated."

"It's supposed to be."

"What, reunions?"

"No, love."

"I don't love reunions."

"Good night, Red."

" 'Night, Abe."

"Man! Tough crowd tonight. Where's Abe? He take off?" Ben finally finished his first set and slid into his usual perch at the bar, looking mentally weary, like a hobo with a Harvard degree.

"Yeah, you just missed him."

"Where's my beer, slowpoke?"

"What? Oh, sorry, your highness. Coming right up."

"Aaaaaah. Thanks. So you look more serious than usual. Abe rattle your chain or what?"

"No, we were just talking about the reunion."

"That whole time? Damn. So did he convince you to go?"

"No."

"Did he convince you *not* to go?"

"No."

"Hmm. Pros?"

"Reconnecting with a man I'm possibly still in love with."

"Cons?"

"Looking like a disastrous loser because it's been ten years and I still haven't done a single progressive thing with my life, including changing my hairstyle."

"Really? I thought chicks did that every few months!"

"Not this chick."

"Hmm," Ben mused, popping a cocktail stirrer in his mouth and chewing on it thoughtfully. "Sounds like you have a dilemma, Kurtz."

No kidding.

Five

"Yep. Oh, that's gorgeous, love. Now lean over a little so I can see yer . . . beautiful!"

Seven o'clock, Sunday morning, and I was stuck holding an umbrella over Hal. There's nothing worse than starting your day next to a fat man with a chubby.

"Can you pull that strap down a little? There's a good girl. Nina, hand me that flash."

"Uh, the what?"

"The flash, the flash, love, that square jobby that lights up all pretty like a Christmas tree? It's in the camera bag."

"I thought it was built into the camera."

"Does this look like a disposable underwater Fuji, love? It's a bloody Nikon! The flash goes in the hot shoe."

"The huh?"

"Just hand me the pretty light, Nina, and I'll stick it in myself. There's a good girl, Bridget, just hang on a tic and we'll get you bent over that scaffolding there."

Super.

Hal is one of the horniest men I've ever met. Astonishingly, he's managed to manifest his perverse impulses into an artistic endeavor. He somehow convinces gorgeous women to pay *him* so that *they* can take their clothes off and pose for photographs. Really, it's astounding.

The nymphet du jour was Bridget Gates, a brunette with enormous boobs and sparkling white teeth. Buck teeth. Bridget, an aspiring model/actress/restaurant hostess, had hired Hal once before to take portfolio shots, but needed new pictures since she had just upgraded her breasts from a B to a DD. From the looks of it, the surgery was fairly recent, since poor Bridge was having a hard time keeping her balance.

"Hal, it's freezing," she breathed. "Are we going to move inside soon?"

"Sure, sure, but Bridget, I've got to tell you, the lighting out here is fantastic! Really, the contrast is stunning. And her nips look sensational."

I'm not sure if I was supposed to hear that last part.

Horse-face was right; it *was* freezing. Charcoal clouds had been drooling on us for half an hour as Hal snapped away. We were shooting her at a construction site in Waltham—a skeletal parking garage that boasted lots of jagged metal beams and concrete slabs. Hal kept instructing her to pick up abandoned drills and wrenches and do sexy things with them. If ever the man made me shudder. Hal thinks he's an artist, but, as I've tried to point out to him, his artistic vision combines the two things that men get the most excited about: women and tools. Throw in a keg and a BMW, and I think you've got yourself a solution to erectile dysfunction.

Every so often, Hal hires me as his photographer's assistant. The first time he asked me to do it, I was totally confused. I know *nothing* about photography. I'd never *pretended* to know anything about photography. Two years of doing this and I still haven't *learned* anything about photography. I'm not even that *interested* in photography! But he offered me a hundred bucks, cash under the table, so I couldn't turn him down. After a few shoots, I began to figure it out.

He never asks me to come along on anything that actually requires help, like a wedding or a bris or something. He has another assistant, Pedro, for that. Pedro is a graduate student at the Massachusetts College of Art, studying photography—more specifically, the *camera obscura*. (So he says. I don't know what the hell he's talking about.) But I'm always the go-to girl when it comes to one-on-one shoots with near-naked ladies. At first I concluded that Hal was actually being a gentleman, that he wanted to make his models feel more comfortable by bringing a woman to the shoot, and I thought that was pretty admirable. But upon further reflection I came to understand that that assumption, in fact, gives the piggy wiggy too much credit. The truth is, Hal does indeed want these girls to be more comfortable, but only because when they're comfortable, they're more likely to take their clothes off. And so, my presence practically guarantees that Hal will get to see breasts, take pictures of breasts and keep the negatives of the pictures of breasts. Genius. Evil, perverse genius.

I'm a sucker for it, though, every single time. Whenever Hal offers me a shoot I'm so blinded by the prospect of making extra cash that I forget how disgusting I find this whole experience to be. I'm usually reminded within the first three minutes of the session.

"All right, got the flash popped on there. Now, Bridget, what are you wearing under your clothes? Have you got a thong on?"

"Yeah."

"Brilliant. Could you hike the skirt up a bit, show me yer

bum? There's a good girl. That looks gorgeous. Now, wrap yer leg around that pole there. Uh-huh. Can you lean back on the scaffolding a bit? Yeah, now climb up a notch or two. I'm not going to shoot up yer skirt, love, it's just that your breasts look fuller from down here. Nice. Yes. Brilliant. OK, Nina, let's move it along. Location two."

Bridget wrapped herself in a coat while I followed Hal around with the umbrella as he packed up his camera. For a fat man, Hal is very vain, especially concerning his hair. He's proud to boast, to anyone who will listen, that he hasn't had a haircut since 1979. He wears his graying curls slicked back in a low ponytail that swishes ("like the blade of a musketeer!" he claims) when he waddles, but is quick to frizz, hence, my stint as the personal umbrella holder. Really, I could give P. Diddy's guy a run for his bling.

Hal gets visibly nervous at the threat of excessive moisture, be it rain, humidity, or the room temperature in the club. He keeps the Bellyaches' thermometer at a comfortable 67 degrees, and the slightest bead of sweat on a comic's brow prompts a further decrease in temperature.

"All right, all packed up, got me lenses, me light meter. Nina, have you got the filters? You don't know, do you? Well, have you got all the little bits and pieces? That's all right, let's pile in the car."

"The car?" I hate driving with Hal. For all the years he's spent in this country, it's never quite gelled with him that in America we drive on the right. I've found it's best to avoid road travel with a displaced Englishman, or else refuse to sit in the passenger seat and cower in the back with your hands over your face. "I have my own car, Hal. How about I just meet you there?"

"Not much parking where we're going. Best to take one car."

"Where are we going, exactly?"

"*Location two.* Come on, Nina. I haven't got all morning."

"Really? Where exactly are you supposed to be? Don't we have the same work schedule?"

"Not that it's any of yer business, but I have a very important meeting at an art gallery this afternoon." He shot a sly glance at Bridget, who had joined us under the umbrella and was looking interested.

I knew he was lying, or at least exaggerating, but I said nothing.

"I've got to discuss which of me models look the *best*," he continued, "which of them has what it *takes* to have their photograph on *display* for hundreds of *people*."

"Hundreds?" Bridget breathed.

"Dozens," I muttered.

"*Hundreds*." Hal shot me a death glare and looked pointedly at Bridget's rack.

"Hmmm," Bridget breathed, clearly doing her best to sound like Marilyn Monroe. (That, or she needed to quit smoking.) "What exactly does it take to get your photograph displayed in an art gallery?"

Jugs.

"Courage." Hal beamed when he said it. "And poise. The conviction to recognize yer own inner beauty and the confidence to let it radiate through the lens."

Oh come on.

"I can do that!" Bridget straightened up a little, allowing her coat to fall open and reveal the V-neck of her soaked, cut-off NASCAR T-shirt.

"Of course ye can, love." Hal looked at me again, a "blow this wank for me and I'll wring your Yankee neck" kind of look. "Now, let's all hop in the car and head to our second location. Nina, hold the Nikon in your lap, please. Bridget, my dear, let me get the door for you. No, Nina, don't get *in* yet, it's still drizzling and I need the umbrella."

Hal always manages to make me feel like the most putrid, androgynous lump on the planet whenever I come along on these things. Usually, he's very nice; he's been almost like a second dad since I started working for him. OK, maybe not a dad; more like that creepy uncle that you only see once a year on holidays who always gives you ten bucks but makes you feel dirty about it. Anyway, other than when I help him out on shoots, he's great. Kind, understanding, a good boss, the whole bit. But when I'm cock-blocking him from exploiting his artistic credibility and sticking it in an eager young thing, he gets a little cranky. Jesus, I know I'm not a supermodel, but come on; I don't have hairy tentacles growing out of my forehead either.

Hal took extra special care with buckling Bridget into the passenger seat, then snatched the umbrella from me and waddled to the driver's side. Of course he didn't unlock my door first, so I was left to be drenched in the freezing rain while he tucked his fat butt into the bucket seat and fumbled around with the keys. Eventually it was Bridget who reached around to unlock my door.

"Where are we going?" I asked as I shoved newspapers and empty (I hope) take-out containers from the backseat. No, really, Hal, no need to clear out a space for me.

"I told you, Nina, location two."

Hmph.

I knew exactly why he was trying to be discreet. Two months ago, Hal took me on what was a seemingly normal (for him) shoot at an abandoned mill in Lowell. Some of the old equipment was still there, so he draped his models, blonde twins named Candy and Brandy (I wish I was kidding), over gears and machinery, pretty much old hat.

Then, as the sunlight faded, he announced it was time to move to "location two" and that I should wait until the moon rose and then take my car and meet him at the oldest tombstone in the creepiest cemetery in Sudbury, one of those towns where every standing building dates back to the seventeen hundreds and is haunted by the ghosts of drunken colonials.

I refused. Hal was pissed.

So now, he, as an act of vengeance, always refuses to reveal "location two" to me beforehand, and I'm forced to ride with him in his crappy LeBaron (why do fat men like tiny convertibles?) to additional locations, or forfeit my payment.

"Hal, you've got us trapped in a moving vehicle, OK? There's no escape, so you may as well tell us."

He glanced at Bridget, who was peering at him with as much curiosity as can be expected from a woman who counts peppermint gum as a significant portion of her daily caloric intake.

"Fine," Hal said, "we're going to Metropolitan State Hospital."

"What? Stop the *fucking* car!" I screamed.

Bridget jerked in the middle of lighting a cigarette, letting the Marlboro Light fall to her lap at the sound of my shriek.

" Wh—what's Matropilin State Hospital?"

"Nina, would ye calm down, please? You're making Bridget nervous. There, there, love, have yer ciggie."

"She should be nervous, Hal. Bridget, *Metropolitan* State Hospital is an abandoned mental institution."

"What's that?"

"A *nuthouse*, Bridget, a creepy, eerie old loony bin where they used to torture patients until they retreated as far into their psyches as humanly possible. It's been closed for years. Condemned by the state because of all the appalling shit they used to do to people."

"It's just a building, love."

"It's a building haunted by schizophrenic poltergeists, Hal, and you'd better turn this fucking car around pronto."

"Aw, what's the matter Nina, afraid of a few ghostie wosties? Scared the bogeyman will get you?"

"It's not funny, Hal. You didn't grow up around here. Kids I went to high school with would sneak in on a dare and come out . . . changed."

"Bollocks."

"It's *true*, Hal!"

"I'm not givin' up a gorgeous shot with a gorgeous girl because you're like to wee yer pants, Nina."

Bridget looked as nervous as if someone had just told her that Marlboro Lights have six thousand carbs a puff. "I don't think this is a good idea," she whimpered. "That sounds scary, and I can't pose sexy when I'm scared."

"You can't help but be sexy in this joint, love. There's this one shot I'm dying to get, of you in the boiler room; oh, it's wicked. Have to wade through an old water pipe to get there. Anyway, when I was scouting I found this rickety wheelchair that looks like it's been sitting around for a century. Fantastic visual. Picture this, right? You're strapped in with all these buckles and things, right next to a wall of dials and gadgets. Brilliant. Oh, and you're in some black, lacy knickers, right? Gorgeous."

We were silent for a minute, I trying desperately to calculate just how hard I'd hit the pavement if I opened the car door and dove into a barrel roll. Death, maiming, or permanent aesthetic scarring by asphalt was pretty appealing, given the alternative. Ghosts are one thing. Raving, schizo, demented ghosts I do not want to fuck with.

"Oh get off it!" Hal burst out laughing, spraying the steering wheel with spittle and hawing like a fat donkey.

"You don't really think I'd take you *there*, do ya, loves? To Metropolitan *Hospital*?"

Huh?

"I'd have to be bloody *wonky* to set foot in that booby hatch! Really had ye going for a minute, didn't I?"

"You're an asshole, Hal," I said. Son of a bitch. I really did almost wee my pants.

"What?" Bridget looked confused again. "You mean we don't have to go to the Metripolitopilan hospital?"

Honestly, I don't remember "metropolitan" being an SAT word.

"Naw, love." Hal was still choking on his own comedic brilliance. "I'm just taking the piss."

"You're taking a piss? Right now? Don't you want to pull over?"

"Taking the piss," I piped in. "It's the totally crude and disgusting way that British people say they're making fun of you."

"Aw, you're one to talk about crude and disgusting, Red." Hal laughed again. "The fellas won't come *near* ya with that mouth of yers."

"Shut up."

"Hoo. Really had ye going there, didn't I? Metropolitan State Hospital. I'd a crapped me pants before we'd walked past the parking lot."

Hal really does know how to talk around the ladies, huh? All this about wee and piss and crap and, frankly, I'm surprised Bridget hasn't hopped in his fat lap already.

"Anyway, do ye want to know where we're *really* going?"

"No!" Bridget and I spoke at the same time.

"Sure ye do. We're going to the drive-in pictures, gals."

Boobs McGee cocked her head, confused once again. "Driving pictures? But I don't have my license."

"I'll take this one, Hal," I said. "Movie theater, Bridget. The drive-in movie theater."

"Ooooh!" Bridget squealed. Probably her old tramping grounds.

"See? No harm done." Hal reached over and squeezed Bridget's thigh. Ick. "Just a coupla shots of Bridge in front of the big screen and we're good to head home. Metropolitan State Hospital. Hoooo, I'll have ta remember that one, Nina. Ben's going ta hear about this first thing tomorrow night!"

"Splendid. Which drive-in are we going to?"

"The Starlit Screen, offa Route 95. Ya been there, girls?"

"Actually, I used to go there all the time," I said.

"I bet ya did!" Hal hooted. "Gave the fellas an earful when they tried to stick their hand in yer britches, I reckon."

He tickled Bridget's leg again, higher this time, and she squealed, slapping it away with a giggle. I can't believe Hal gets away with touching these girls; they all put up with his flirting and inappropriate touching because they think he's going to get them somewhere with his photographs. I'm sure if I weren't here to supervise, the only place they'd find themselves is the damned women's clinic.

Hal and Bridget began gabbing away about drive-ins and make-out sessions, but I tuned them out, stuck on the Starlit Screen.

In the nineteen eighties a retired firefighter by the name of Norman Huckleberry came to a wistful realization. Gone were the days of coaxing kittens from trees, rushing to the scene of a burnt potpie, rescuing teenage girls from getting pregnant in the back of a Chevy. The post-Woodstock period had hustled in a wave of decadence, of crime and drugs and disco fever, dissolving the innocence that had encased the most pure and perfect era Norm had ever known. How he longed for the nineteen fifties—the sock hops, the casseroles, sharing an egg cream with his sweetheart. His thirst for nostalgia haunted him; he would perch on the stoop of his Granddaddy's farmhouse, passed down to Norm by his mother with her dying breath, and start each day with a steaming cup of Folgers Crystals, staring at the endless cornfield to the left of his barn and wondering, wanting, wishing for the days of blissful ignorance.

Then, it came to him.

A drive-in. A drive-in movie theater!

And so Norman Huckleberry scraped together every penny he could, raiding the savings under his queen-size mattress; cashing in stocks and bonds; selling his most prized possession, a baby blue 1966 Cadillac Fleetwood. And when he finally had the money, Norman built that theater from the ground up, clearing the fields with his own two hands, hiring retired farmhands and their brothers and cousins to hoist the gigantic movie screen, erect an authentic snack shack, install a hundred speaker poles. It was a gesture of cinematic proportions. Norman built that drive-in on his Granddaddy's cornfield, and they came. By God, they came.

That's what Sony would have you believe, anyway. Truth is, the Starlit Screen Drive-in sits on a lot that was originally supposed to be a shopping mall, until The Gap pulled out at the last minute and the contractor was forced to sell to the highest bidder. That Huckleberry crap was a marketing ploy. But it worked; to this day, the drive-in is a huge success, and the nostalgia of it all elicits the same behavior it did fifty years ago; sneaking cigarettes and extra buddies in the trunk, scampering from car to car to catch up on gossip, steaming up the windshield with your panting date. The only big difference is that by the nineteen eighties, all the girls were on the pill. No Gen Y baby boom for us.

My parents took the family to the Starlit quite a bit when we were kids. We'd pile in the maroon Dodge Caravan, the five of us slapping and pinching and scratching over who would have to sit in the third row middle seat. It took half an hour from Ashford to get there, so Mom and Dad would pop in a Linda Ronstadt cassette and crank that puppy up in an attempt to drown us out. Never worked, but it didn't really matter; the first sight of neon pink sky rendered us dead silent, as jaws snapped closed and we sniffed deeply, deeper, deeper, until our nostrils were crammed with the gorgeous smells of buttery popcorn and sizzling grade-triple-F hamburger.

The Starlit Screen Drive-in is nestled at the end of a skinny country road lined with weeping ash trees, just wide enough for a single-file line of cars to kick up the powdery turf. Hal maneuvered the LeBaron awkwardly, cursing the damage each dip and bump was doing to his tires.

"State-of-the-art treads," he mumbled as we were jostled again. "Bloody American roads. Shoddy crap."

The lane tumbles into a meadow, demoted from a road to a crudely mowed path. During the summer the tall grass is speckled with flowers: pink, violet and cool blue polka dots scattered about like a spilled sack of playground marbles. Once the season is over the flowers shrivel up and the grass fades to olive and then brown, as it was now. Still, against the October leaves the meadow looked crisp and cidery.

We wove through the grass and came out at the foot of the theater, a few neatly trimmed acres scored by rows of speaker poles. Two cars could squeeze between each pair of poles, which, in the summer, sported portable avocado-colored speaker boxes that you could hang from your window if you were feeling particularly nostalgic. Most kids chose to tune in on their radios instead, so they could keep the windows up and shield the world from steamy and inept make-out sessions.

"Bringing back memories, Nina?" Hal chuckled as we jerked to a stop. "Had yer knob turned a bit in these parts, I imagine."

"Hal, if you mention my 'knob' one more time, I'm sending my brothers after you with a handsaw and a box of industrial garbage bags."

"Easy, old girl. Why don't ya hop out and see how bad it's drizzling while I prep Miss Bridget for this shoot here."

Ick. Fine by me.

I got out of the car and took a look around. The place hadn't changed since the last time I'd been here; I still felt tiny among the hundreds of speaker poles, at the foot of an enormous yellowing screen that, from a few acres away, still looked as big as ten thousand moons.

Tucked in the back of the lot is the snack bar—a shack with a counter, really. A factory of tantalizing smells and greasy, cathartic joy. The menu still hung by rusty chains, crudely painted on scrap wood, thick red letters that trickled and clotted like Heinz 57. Beer-battered onion rings, it coaxed. Rippled Idaho french fries. Tiny hamburgers, two for a dollar. Black-and-white shakes, thick as mashed potatoes. Malted milks, egg creams, Coca-cola in green glass bottles. And the candy . . . Bit-O-Honeys, Necco Wafers, Goobers, Zagnuts, candy buttons, wax bottle miniatures oozing with liquid. In the peak season, fat hot dogs sizzle as they laze on the grill; the glass-encased popcorn machine syncopates, bursting with airy Redenbacher's kernels. Paul and I used to share a striped paper bag of the stuff, the biggest they had, bathed in butter and salt.

"All right, Nina? Still raining out there?"

"No, Hal."

"Ye going to make it, love? You're foaming at the mouth. I'll buy ye breakfast when we're through."

"I'm fine. Just thinking."

"I thought I smelled something burning. Well, come on, stop yer starin', and let's get the shot set up."

Hal led Bridget by the hand and posed her in front of the movie screen, while I grabbed the camera bags from the car.

"This'll be so unbelievably sexy, love, you with yer chest thrown out and a huge silhouette projected on the screen behind ye. We'll have to play with the lights a bit, but it'll be worth the time.

"Where do you want these, Hal?"

"Jest bring 'em here, Nina, and I'll show you how to check a light meter. No, Bridget, I know it's nippy out here but top off, please. There's a good girl. Now, arch yer back a little, and—"

"Excuse me," a voice came from behind me. I spun around, to find that a trollish creature with cottony white hair and thick, pink lips had sprung up behind me. Probably crawled out from under a bridge somewhere.

"Um, can I help you?" I asked.

"The question is, can *I* help *you*?"

Help me what? Toll some church bells, Quasimodo?

"I'm Sherman Schlessinger, the manager of the Starlit Screen"—he drew himself up to full height (almost to my chin) and puffed out his chest—"and right now, you and your friends are trespassing."

"Oh. Shit. Um, didn't that guy call you?"

"Regarding?"

"He's a photographer, and we're doing a shoot here. Or, we'd like to. I guess."

"A photographer?" Sherman looked interested. "And he's taking pictures of . . . oh. Oh my. Is *she* the model?"

Who, that chick who just took her shirt off and is standing in the mist wearing nothing but chain metal ass floss?

"Yeah."

"Nina, what the devil are ye—oh. Oh hello there!" Hal noticed that I had company and huffed his way over. It took a minute for him to reach us; he's that out of shape.

"Hal Rickenson, mate," he grabbed Sherman's hand and began pumping it enthusiastically. "Photographer, entrepreneur, lover of ladies. What ye think of my girl, there? Ripe one, eh mate?"

"Sherman Schlessinger. She's . . . she's . . . uh . . ." Sherman stammered.

"Precisely what I thought first time I saw her. Wicked set, eh?"

"Y—yes."

"I knew ye'd agree, Sherm. Listen, here's the thing. I meant ta give ye a call regarding using the space, but I plum clean forgot, didn't I Nina? I'm a pretty busy fella, what with the models and the club and all. I own a comedy club, downtown Boston. Bellyaches. Heard of it, mate?"

"I don't think so."

"Don't get outta the sticks too much, eh mate? The redhead here, she's my bartender. Top form. Listen, I hope it's no problem to take a few quick shots in fronta yer screen there. It'll have to be quick; Bridge, she's not gonna have her clothes on, ye know?"

"I can, uh, see that."

"Bit chilly out. Don't need the help catchin' a cold!

Course, ye want ta stick around and supervise, make sure I don't mess the joint up, of course yer welcome to."

Sherman looked uncomfortable and exuberant at the same time. "Yeah. Yeah, that's probably a good idea."

"That's the spirit," Hal thumped him on the arm. "Want ta get a little closer, mate? Nina, grab the tripod outta my trunk, would ya? We're gonna have ta play with the light a bit if I want to get her silhouette on screen."

"Her silhouette?" Sherman looked confused. "But it's completely overcast."

"Aaah, a man who knows his way around key lighting. Yeah, I have this vision of puttin' er up on the silver screen, jest the shadow, of course, but I'll have ta do it in Photoshop or something, since the weather leaves a little ta be desired. Not the same effect with a blank screen, I'm afraid."

"Well, what if we projected something on the screen behind her?" Sherman offered. "I could run an old film if you like."

"Could ye, really?" Hal stroked his chins. "Something real Hollywood, right? Old glamour, right? Big red lips, pointy tits and the like? Got any Marilyn? That'd be something."

"I came by to clear out the projection booth today." Sherman dug in the grass with his tiny little dwarf foot. "So there's still a few films lying around. You could come take a look, if you want."

Hal clapped him on the back, nearly knocking him over, and the men strolled toward the projection booth, leaving me to struggle with the camera equipment and poor naked Bridget standing around, looking like a lost lamb. A lost shaven lamb.

"Oy, Nina?" Hal called after a minute. "Could ye set up the light meter?"

"The what?"

"The light meter. The *light meter*. The little thing with the . . . Jesus. Never mind. Jest put everything down back by the snack bar. I think I'll shoot her from there."

I did as I was told, and waited. Every minute or so the overcast silence was punctuated by a liquid snicker from the projection booth; Hal was probably spitting all over poor Sherman in his quest for the perfect tit flick.

"Ha! Ha-HA! That's the one. That's the one, old Sherm. Throw it on. Bridge!" Hal came huffing from the booth. "Bridge, got yer ciggies on ya?"

"They're in the car."

"Nina? Go get her cigs out the car. This'll be brilliant."

Really, this fetch-and-carry shit is starting to get old. But of course, I did it anyway, cursing the fat man through clenched teeth.

I was digging through the heap of clothes on the passenger seat when I heard the whir and click of a kick-starting projector.

"Nina?" Hal called. "Got the keys with ye?"

"Yeah."

"Turn the ignition, would ye, love? Tune inta 97.7 so we can get some sound."

It took a minute to tune Hal's ancient stereo, but once the needle caught the frequency, there it was, crackling with static.

"I was just fixing some iced tea. Would you like a glass?"

"Yeah, unless you've got a bottle of beer that's not working."

"Gorgeous. Now run up there and light her a cig, huh? Her hands are shakin'. Bridge, pull on tha cig and put yer hand on yer hip. I'll start shooting in a minute."

"What is that?" Bridget whined at me through pursed lips, a fleshy vise clamped around her precious cancer stick.

"Double Indemnity," I muttered.

"Double what?"

"Double Indemnity."

"You've seen it before? How can you stand to watch movies with no color? It's like Web sites with no pictures." Einstein turned toward the camera and stuck out her chest, flicking the cigarette with her pearly pink talons and narrowly missing my elbow.

"Actually," I sighed, "I saw it here. On my first date."

"Oh my God! Your first date was here? That's soooo cute!"

"Yeah."

Actually, cute is probably the last word I would use to describe that night.

Terrifying. Exhilarating.

Those are more like it.

"I think it sounds soooo romantic," Bridget continued, "having your first date at a drive-in movie theater. What was his name?"

"Jacob."

"Jacob? Not Jake? That's sexy. Did you do it with him?"

"What, at the drive-in?"

"Yeah."

"Isn't that a little cliché?"

"I think it's so sweet. My favorite movie is *Grease*."

What?

"OK . . . what does that have to do with doing it at the drive-in?"

"Well, Danny and Sandy do it at the drive-in!"

"Um, no they don't. Sandy won't put out and she leaves Danny by himself. That's why he sings that song about being alone at the drive-in."

Bridget scrunched up her face, clearly trying to remember that pivotal scene, the ultimate cinematic blue-balls. "Oh!" She giggled. "You're right. I'm thinking of *Gone with the Wind*."

I wanted to believe it was hypothermia that would motivate her to make a statement like that. She was shivering and her lips were blue. (Of course, that could be from the pack and a half of cigarettes she'd plowed through since the beginning of the day, and that was only two hours ago.)

"Bridget. *Gone with the Wind*? *Gone with the WIND*? Honey, there aren't any cars in that movie."

"No, silly! I'm thinking of what was playing when *I* did it at the drive-in."

She took another long pull of her cigarette. "Too bad it wasn't a better movie."

"Better than *Gone with the Wind*? Reconstruction isn't sexy enough for you?"

"No, I mean, too bad there wasn't a better movie playing on your first date."

"What are you talking about? *Double Indemnity* is a classic!"

Bridget wrinkled her nose. "Really? Why?"

"Well, it's a detective story, and it's *film noir*, so it just looks really cool. Lots of Venetian blinds and shadows and smoke everywhere."

"Huh. Is that why it's called 'black film'?"

"Excuse me?"

"'Black film'"—she examined her nails—"because of, like, the smoke and the shadows?"

"I suppose so," I began slowly. "But how did you know that?"

"Know what?"

"That *film noir* translates to 'black film.' I mean, the 'film' part is easy, but—"

"Oh, I speak French."

"You do?"

"Yeah. I majored in romance languages."

"You did? Um . . . *where?*"

"Well, I guess I didn't technically, like, *major*. My dad's a professor at Harvard, so I got to study for free. A few years ago my modeling career wasn't really going anywhere, so I just took a bunch of classes to, like, pass the time. And my agent says that speaking lots of languages is, like, really good to put on your acting résumé."

"You studied French because your agent made you?"

"Well, he's not really my agent. He's my stepmom's cousin, and he used to be an entertainment lawyer. Now he represents a few people in the biz, so he gives me free tips."

"OK, but you speak *French*?"

"And Italian. And Spanish."

But . . . but the girl didn't even know how to say "metropolitan"!

"Wow, Bridget." Completely floored, I motioned for her to pass me her cigarette and I took a long, contemplative drag. "That's, um, surprising. And impressive. Really impressive."

"A lotta people are surprised. But, you know? It's already been, like, so helpful. Guys *really* like it when I talk French to them in the sack."

"I bet they do."

"What's that about you in the sack, love? Are you *smoking*, Red? I thought you didn't do that anymore." Somehow Hal had managed to sneak up behind me—strange, because I can normally hear his wheezing and clodding halfway across the city without having to strain my eardrums.

"Just when I'm stressed."

"Whatcha got to be stressed about? Sounds like yer

havin' a fine time over here. The convo's gettin' a bit raunchy, eh? No, now, Bridge, don't ye blush on *my* account, love. I'm happy to hear ye talk about the sack till the cows come out to pasture. No, love, there won't actually be any cows here; it's just an expression. Want to fill me in or shall we get started?"

"It's just girl talk, Hal," I said.

"Fair enough. I managed to charm that cranky wanker into sticking around to run the projector."

"*You* charmed him, huh?"

"Don't look so surprised, Red! I can ooze charm if I have to."

"Yes, Hal. You certainly do ooze. What? I thought it was funny!"

I shrugged off the death glare from Hal and the quizzical squint from Bridget and made myself look busy. As best I could without actually knowing what any of the equipment was.

"All right, Sherm," Hal called, after spending an inordinate amount of time fiddling with Bridget's chain mail, "while this one's rolling can you get that Jayne Mansfield pic ready to go? Perfect, Bridge. Now just tip your head back and take a big pull off that ciggie. Gorgeous. Nina, get the magazine ready. The goddamned magazine, Nina, it's sitting next to the mat box. It's the square thing with the— you know what? Never mind. It's starting to drizzle again, so just grab the umbrella. Oh, that's gorgeous, love. Yeeeeah. Very nice. Now tip yer tits back and give me a wink."

Six

Jacob Joshua Ryan was six foot two and played a dirty game of eight ball. Above Seattle espresso eyes his dark hair sprouted in manic spikes. His body rippled with sex; smooth butterscotch skin stretched taut over concrete, unabashed muscle. And if I'd ever described him that way to my neurotic, Communion-crunching mother, my teenage lovebox would have been under padlock and solitary key until the very last millisecond ticked down to my eighteenth birthday.

He wandered into Spanish class, junior year of high school. I took one look at that tall drink of agua and promptly popped the record-breaking, cherry-flavored bubble I'd been slowly inflating over the course of class.

Typical third-period language class; Señor Zahowski was scrawling verbs to conjugate on the blackboard. Asian girls were scribbling notes. Jocks were passing them.

The only thing that ever got me through Spanish was the golden opportunity to goof off. Señor Zahowski often kept his back turned to the class for a half hour at a time, jabbing enthusiastically at vocabulary words while he grilled us, most of the time not even bothering to turn around as he blindly barked out the names of hapless students. He had a sixth sense, though, that mysterious man. He was one of those teachers who knew you were about to pass a note even before you'd finished drawing the check boxes for the questions about liking and *like* liking.

"Give it here," were the only words he ever spoke in English, whipping around in a frenzy to catch you red-handed *every single time* you tried to play Cupid between your neighbors. He would take the notes, crumple them in his hand and slip them into the pocket of his chalk-encrusted seersucker—probably, I later realized, to have a good laugh at his horny students with the rest of the teachers in the faculty lounge. That's what I would do if I had to spend my days teaching a bunch of punk-ass kids who thought their perms were hot shit.

I never had a knack for languages, so I dreaded being called on in class. Señor sensed this, and, being the masochist that he was, always called on me for the toughest vocab questions.

"Señorita Kurtz, *como se dice* 'blush'?" he'd asked that day. " 'To blush.' *Como se dice* 'to blush'?"

I didn't have a chance to answer.

"*Poner rojo.*" A textured baritone revved from the doorway.

A new voice. Unfamiliar. Intriguing.

I spun around in my seat and looked up. Way up. What towered above me was six pubescent feet of a new, strange glory, a cocky Blackboard Jungle grin crinkled around his midnight eyes like papery sex.

I think every girl in school saw a chiropractor that semester. We all threw our backs out at one point or another, whipping our necks around at impossible speeds, straining and contorting to get a better look a the mysterious transfer student who roamed the halls so zealously, as though searching not for classrooms, but adventure.

Word had spread pretty fast that Jacob had a thing for redheads, so right from his first week of school I heard rumors that he had his eye on me. Of course, said rumors were always accompanied by guffaws and elbows to the ribs, peppered with cries of confidence boosters like, "He's into *you*? Does he know you're not a chick?" or "Come on, Kurtz. Don't go getting your hopes up."

Jaws dropped at hyper speed when a Jeep full of jocks caught us together at the Starlit. It was my very first date, and I was nervous enough about totally blowing it (without Devon Moore, Chris Grasso, and Steve Summers making slurping noises at me while I stood in line at the snack bar), thanks to three hours of etiquette coaching courtesy of my best friend Jenny and my mother. Between listening to Jenny screech through the phone about how I probably shouldn't act like my normal, sassy self, and *definitely* shouldn't let him go under-the-shirt on the first night, and my mother peering over my shoulder while I sifted through the clothes in my closet, offering tidbits about keeping my jokes to myself and playing coy before letting him hold my hand, I had been ready to throw up by the time Jacob pulled into the driveway.

It turned out fine. I was too terrified to remember anything Mom or Jenny had advised, so I just acted like myself and made Jacob laugh. Jesus, it worked so well that we were basically inseparable after that, until we graduated and Jacob moved out West to do some crazy mountain shit, like live in a tree house and teach cougars how to tap birches for syrup, or something.

No dramatic breakup; we just went our separate ways. I haven't seen him since.

It's pretty pathetic to be twenty-seven years old and boast such a sparse relationship résumé.

OBJECTIVE: To find a man who wants to move beyond date one.

EXPERIENCE: Jacob Ryan. 1.5 years. Developed and implemented guidelines for an exciting and successful romance. Responsibilities included event planning, management of emotions, and close collaboration with partner department.

SKILLS: Upon request.

Huh. Either I'm completely incompatible with every single human male on the planet Earth except for Jacob, or I really did something right with that guy. Something that I haven't done again, but should. I wonder what it was.

I wonder how he's doing.

I wonder if he'll be in town for the reunion.

I probably won't have to wonder *that* for too long. My mother is like captain of the Ashford Gossip Squad; she gets all of her inside info from people she runs into at the grocery store, and it's usually pretty accurate. She likes to flap the yapper, though, which is why I stopped telling her about any feminine mishaps I might be unfortunate enough to have had. It wasn't exactly a comfortable moment when Mrs. Fracilliardi showed up at my apartment with an economy-size tub of yogurt and coupons offering thirty cents off of some contraption called the "Yeastinator."

If I put the word out through Mom that I needed a location on Jacob, she'd get back to me in a week's time with his whereabouts, upcoming travel plans, and whether or not there's been any activity on his social security number in the last month.

"Nina? There she is, Gideon, she *is* working tonight. Nina! Nina honey!"

Speak of the devil herself.

It would have to be on our busiest night of the week in the middle of our most popular comic's best rant that my parents would burst into Bellyaches like the Osmonds would into song, dressed to the nines and recoiling from the stench of cheap beer and cheaper jokes.

"Excuse me! Excuse me. Oops! Sorry. Oh, Gideon, that's Ben up there! Excuse me. Sir, could you move your . . . thanks. Excuse me. Hi honey!"

"Hey Mom. Hi Dad."

Hearing me greet the parents, each of my regular bar perches tossed out a wave and a garbled greeting, a chorus of drunken well wishings that made my mother's grin skydive, twisting into a transparent Cheshire half smile as she scooted closer to my father and clung to his elbow tightly.

"Well," she chattered nervously as she made it to the bar, twisting the pink, flower-shaped costume brooch that was pinned to her filmy black shawl, "we haven't been to visit you at work in quite some time. Hasn't changed much, has it? Same signs, same tables and chairs. Jesus and Mary, are those the *same* men who sat at the bar every night when you first started working here? Do you have someone to walk you to your car after work?"

"Usually one of these guys."

"The drunk ones?"

"They sober up by the time I get out of here."

"You're cutting off the circulation in my arm, dear." Dad winced while he peeled at my mother's death grip, one finger at a time. "Could you knock off the human tourniquet routine? Really, M.A., it's starting to get numb. How's tricks, Jellybean? Raking the bread in this evening?"

"A few crumbs."

"Keep plugging, kiddo. Chin up—you could be wearing a three-piece monkey suit."

"True. And it's early anyway, only—hey. Guys, it's eight o'clock on a Friday night. Shouldn't you be passed out in front of the TV?"

My mother and father are rarely seen outside their living room post dinner hour, even on a weekend. They watch sitcoms together, or medical dramas, or cop dramas, or legal dramas, or political dramas, or military dramas, or baby's mama dramas, or they play canasta. Sometimes Mom knits cozies. Just cozies. I don't know why she's convinced that the inanimate objects that live in her household are in need of tiny sweaters, but they've all got winter wear; from the tissue boxes to the picture frames to the plastic Jesus that bobs piously on the dashboard of her Volvo station wagon.

Mom forgot that she was terrified and lit up like a Marlboro man. "Your father and I are having our date night!"

"You two have a date night?"

"Oh yes. I got the idea from one of the sisters at church."

"Mom, you're not black. You're not allowed to call other women sisters."

"Mary Grace isn't black. She's a nun."

"You're getting romantic advice from a nun?"

"Mmm-hmm."

"Don't you find that vaguely ironic?"

"I tried to argue that point myself." Dad rolled his eyes and patted my mother on the arm. "But she said something about *The Sound of Music* and I tuned out."

"Speaking of musicals," Mom said proudly, "tell Nina where you're taking me tonight, Gideon."

"Ooooh," I teased, "yeah, Pops, where are you taking the lady on your big night out? Gonna take her to the pictures? Load her up on bathtub gin and slip her the tongue?"

"That's not a bad idea, Jellybean. It's at least an improvement."

"Oh stop it, Gideon!" Mom rolled her eyes but was clearly charmed. "He's taking me to the theater!"

"No kidding? The *theeeeatah,* huh? I'm impressed. What are you going to see?"

Silence. I looked from one parent to the other and then back again, trying to interpret their vastly different facial reactions to my question. Mom looked pleased as punch; Dad looked punched.

"Go ahead, honey," Mom said, "tell her!"

"We're going," Dad began slowly, painfully, "to see . . . *Cats.*"

"*Cats*?" I sneered.

"*Cats!*" Mom beamed.

"*Cats.*" Dad hung his head.

"No. *Cats*? Dad!"

He threw up his hands. "My wife wants to see some theater. So I'm taking her to see some theater."

I swallowed a snicker. "Well, I think that's really nice. You two will have a terrific time. Want a beer, Dad?"

"Oh Lord, yes. My only hope of keeping my own brain from strangling itself with my spinal cord is to keep it liquored up."

"Come on. It's not a bad show, is it?" I handed him a draft. "It should be fun. I mean, it *could* be fun."

"It's *Cats*! Cats singing about how they're cats! And your mother loves it." He took a healthy gulp of lager. "Son of a bitch, I'd better be getting a canoe for my birthday this year, M.A. No, two. Singing cats is worth *two* canoes. I can strap them to the car like skis."

"Chardonnay, Mom?" I'd better interrupt before he gets going. One thing about DJs; they can talk, talk, talk without needing any feedback. My brother Paul figured out that he could trick Dad into shutting up by waving his hand around in a circle and mouthing, "Wrap it up!" but none of the rest of us ever got away with it.

"Thanks, honey, but I'd better not. I want to be absolutely fresh for the show."

"You sure?"

"Well . . . I suppose half a glass will be fine. Just a touch more. That's good."

"The thing about cats," Dad began before examining his beer and pulling another swig, "Aaah. The thing about cats is that I hate them."

Me too. Must run in the family.

"Dad, it's two hours out of your evening. Stop complaining."

"Two and a half. Not counting intermission."

"Did you come in here exclusively for sympathy? Because you're not getting any from me, Dad. I happen to think it's great that you're sacrificing a Friday night so that you can do something nice for your wife. Suck it up."

"Yeah, suck it up!" Uh-oh. I had given my mother a pretty healthy glass of wine despite her instructions, and she was apparently taking her own advice to heart, since most of her drink had already disappeared. She's not a big woman, so giving her a glass of wine can be the equivalent of pumping a hummingbird full of liquid cocaine and then taking it to a Yankees/Red Sox series opener.

"All right dear. Didn't we have a reason for coming in here, M.A? Or was it just to watch my darling daughter get you schnockered?"

"Oh heavens, thank goodness you reminded me, Gideon! Nina. Have I got a surprise for you."

Oh no, I hate it when she begins conversations like this.

The last time my mother had a "surprise" for me, she presented me with twenty dollars' worth of Dunkin' Donuts gift certificates *and* a coupon for a three-month membership to the Somerville Health Club. She makes no sense. She makes *no sense*.

"This isn't like the time you 'surprised' me with a root canal, is it? Because that surprise still hurts."

"What do you mean, it still hurts? That was sixteen years ago!"

"It hurts emotionally."

"Well, you'd better get over that before tomorrow night."

"Any particular reason?"

Mom broke into a huge smile. "Because you've got a date!"

Oh no. Oh no, no, no, no, no.

"No you didn't. Please tell me you didn't, Mom."

"Didn't what?"

"Please, please tell me you didn't set me up with another one of your friends' loser sons."

"I think I'll go outside and check on the dog," Dad said nervously.

"Dad, we don't *have* a dog!"

"I'll find one." He threw a few bills down on the bar and took off like a shot. Dammit.

"Goody! Girl-talk time. Pour me another chard and I'll give you the dirt."

"Mom, one: you can't have another glass of wine. Two: I'm *not* going out with some dude that my *mother* has set me up with."

"Why can't I have another glass of wine?" she hiccupped.

"Because you're drunk."

"Oh, big deal. I have to go sit through a musical about cats, for pete's sake. Hit me again."

"Mom! I thought you *wanted* to see it!"

"Better to let your father think that, honey. He went through a lot of trouble to get those tickets and he thinks he's making a huge sacrifice for me."

"So neither of you wants to go tonight but you're both pretending to be thrilled?"

"I'm the only one pretending to be thrilled, honey. Your father's miserable and making a huge show about it. That's what men do. It's much easier to let them think you're pleased as punch that your big, strong man is forfeiting an evening for you."

"I don't believe what I'm hearing. Gloria Steinem is rolling over in her grave."

"Gloria Steinem's not dead, dear."

"She's not?"

"Nope. Married, but not dead."

"Hmm. Hey, don't you need to get going?"

Mom opened her purse and pulled out her cell phone to check the time. "I still have a few minutes. Let's talk about Rex."

"Excuse me?"

"Rex Brandon, the man you're going out with tomorrow."

"I told you, I'm not going out with a man that my mother sets me up with."

"Don't be silly, Nina. That's never stopped you before."

It was true; I *had* allowed my mother to fix me up with a few—in her words—"choice young gentlemen," and after the last one I vowed up and down and sideways and diagonally and multidimensionally that I would never, ever, ever let her play matchmaker again.

The very first courtship she talked me into was Derrick, her best friend's nephew and a "hardworking Catholic boy." My father about choked on his matzo when she announced that one, but to his credit, kept his mouth shut. Much like I wish I'd had, instead of agreeing to go.

Derrick was an underwhelming five foot three, prematurely balding and, as he whispered to me over a plate of calamari, secretly tattooed in all the wrong places. Ick. He was wee, weer than me, a pocket-size man, with tiny little doll hands and nail beds lacquered with grease. He worked as a benefits consultant, and wasn't allowed to have unconventional haircuts, tattoos, body piercings, or any other expression of individuality that would distinguish him from his fellow corporate robots. So he thought it was, like, totally balls-out awesome that I worked in a comedy club, and, like, wanted to know if I had any naughty body décor, because that was, like, soooo sexy. I hated to disappoint the little guy.

Over an excruciatingly long dinner, Derrick rambled on and on and on about his beloved weekend passion: race cars. Apparently, he worked as a pit technician on the side, for some motorsports club in New Hampshire. He was totally out of town all the time for races, and it was totally friggin' awesome. Sometimes, if it wasn't an important race, the club even let him drive a few laps. It was totally balls-out awesome. He could hug a curve tighter than a thirteen-year-old girl. (I held my tongue in a half nelson.)

Someday, when he was done with the office bullshit, he was going to get another tattoo, a big one, a big number three, right on his forearm. A number three for Dale. R.I.P., dude.

He got all weepy after that, the wee little race-car driver, so we sat, in awkward silence, until I burped, a big, fat, bestial garlic *uuuuuurp*. I wanted to laugh. He wanted to leave.

After that there were two Marks in a row, one an old college buddy of my brother Paul's, the other the son of the sister-in-law of the organist at Mom's church.

Mark One could have been the product of one too many lonely nights for the Birdman of Alcatraz. He had a peckish appetite, a screechy turkey laugh, facial features that were dwarfed by a crooked Durante beak. Even his eyes were birdlike—beady little peepers that stared at me intensely, unblinking, throughout an uncomfortable cup of coffee at the 1727 Coffee House. He, in fact, watched me like a hawk.

Mark Two turned out to be a medical student at Harvard. (It's a good thing my mother isn't Jewish, or she'd have already called a calligrapher about wedding invitations before I'd even met Doctor Moneybags. *Oy*.) He also turned out to be inexorably boring. I spent the longest evening of my life at a sushi bar hovering between nodding blankly and nodding off, while he droned on about cyclitol nomenclature and hydroxyl groups and other things evocative of high-school chemistry that made me want to jab a chopstick into his Adam's apple. At the end of the night I was in the middle of mumbling a polite good-bye when he ambushed me with his unnervingly squishy lips and shoved a hand in my crotch. After I batted him away he began to wail like a wet toddler, and spent another forty-five minutes sputtering about his ex-girlfriend, who had recently left him for a plumber.

On deck in the loser lineup was Michael, a baby-faced lambykins who worked as a high-school drama teacher. Mom found *him* at a yard sale—they were both rooting through the same bin of sweaters. Michael was *really* excited about his upcoming theatrical season; the school board had *expanded* his budget, so he could *finally* afford to put on *Showboat*. After getting all starry-eyed about that for a good three quarters of our meal, he monopolized the rest of the conversation with talk about the Fall Fling. It's the traditional autumn costume ball! He gets to chaperone! The senior class used his theme idea! It's Andrew Lloyd Weber characters! Yippee!

Granted, these dates were all intensely awkward—complete disasters—but I don't count the discomfort and incompatibility as the worst part of the evenings. The worst part was that each one of these men told me, before the night was over, that they could tell that I wasn't their type, and that we'd probably make better friends. The consistency was astounding—by the time Michael was up to bat I could practically mouth along with the "friends" speech. "I think you're great, Nina, really great. You're *so* funny and *so* intelligent and just an *awesome* woman. And that's why I think we'll make great, great friends. But I don't think anything beyond that is in the cards. I just . . . don't want to lose your friendship. So, I don't think we should date. But, you're *great*. Friends?"

Insert noncommittal hug, complete with obligatory masculine back-patting, here.

Unbelievable. And they all used the phrase "in the cards." Who *says* that? Even Mark Two blubbered about friendship after I finally pried my lady parts out of his vise-like grip. And, come *on*; I couldn't even entice a closeted homosexual employed by the public school system into using me for a smokescreen?

I'm cursed, I swear it. Not that I wanted to see any of those bozos again, but it would have been nice to have had the *option* of crushing the amorous hopes and dreams of at least one of them. Jerks.

I'm so, so tired of being the "friend." I have enough friends, dammit. I need to get me some lovin'. Hard lovin', sweet lovin', slow lovin', fast lovin', whatever. I'm not too picky in the lovin' department.

Some wining and dining wouldn't be so bad, either. And maybe a movie or two—hell, even some hand-holding. Followed, of course, by some lovin'.

"Where'd you meet this one, Mom? Digging through the discount bin at the Victoria's Secret semi-annual bra and panty extravaganza?"

"He's Eammon's stepson, Miss Smarty Pants."

"A-min? Who's A-min?"

"*Eammon*. Eammon O'Shaegon. My bagpipes instructor."

"Your *what*?"

Since the twins left the nest, my mother has become somewhat of a joiner. Can't really blame her—she was a full-time mom for more than thirty years, so when she dropped the last of her brood off at college this past fall, I think it hit her that the last time she had the house to herself, polyester was cutting edge. So she *has* gone a little crazy with the extracurricular activities. Church groups, sure. Pilates classes, why not? But bagpipes? Mom stands proudly at an ominous five foot one. In heels. She's a tiny, tiny lady. Tough for me to imagine her casually hoisting a sack of pipes over her shoulder and strolling through the mystical forests of County Tipperary, soothing all of the Emerald Isle with musical melancholy magic.

"Since when do you play the bagpipes, Ma?"

"Oh, I started a few months ago. I haven't told your father yet. I want it to be a surprise."

"So, what, you pass off your practice sessions as a family of geese that you're raising in the basement? You might only get away with that until Christmas."

"I practice when he's at work. So, you're meeting Rex at Medea's Garden tomorrow night at eight."

"Mom, tomorrow night is Saturday. I work. Remember? I work *here*."

"Did I just hear ye call someone 'Mum,' Nina?"

How did he do that? Hal is unbelievably good at catching me off guard. He magically appeared behind me at the bar and leaned over toward my mother, resting his chins in a palm. How can a fat man be so sneaky?

"This can't be the missus," he continued. "This is yer sister, right, Red? Not yer mum. Can't be."

"Good one, boss man. Did you come up with that charmer all by yourself?"

Hal was smiling, but I could see annoyance in his squinty eyes. He hates when I rib him in front of women.

"Ooh, touchy tonight, are we?" He smirked at me. "Hullo, Mrs. Kurtz, I'm Hal Rickenson, proud owner of this establishment and even prouder employer of yer hard-workin' daughter here."

My mother's gaze flickered toward Hal's outstretched hand before taking his grasp. Can't blame her; he was probably having a wank in the office not five minutes ago.

"Hello Hal, I'm Margaret Ann. I think we've met once before, actually, when Nina first started working here."

"Oh, that's right!" Hal mused, still holding my mother's dainty hand in his own meaty paw. "I met you and the hubby when Red was still barbacking for me. She's moved up a bit in the food chain since then."

"I have? I thought I was still classified as algae. So I'm like a turtle now? A frog? Or am I higher? Hey, can I be a rhinoceros?"

"So I guess it's you I should thank," Hal continued to my mother, "for Miss Nina's delightful cheek."

"Cheek?" Mom asked, withdrawing her hand from Hal's grasp and touching the side of her face.

"Cheek, like sarcasm," I said, "like my boss is insulting your daughter right in front of you."

"Cheek is a compliment!" Hal protested. "It's sassy, it's adorable! The lads love it!"

"Really?" Mom looked interested.

"He means *these* lads, Ma." I swept my arm grandly, gesturing to the line of drunk and withered grandpas who were slumped at the bar, belching a symphony of lager. "*They* love it."

"Oh good. So no competition for tomorrow night, then."

"*Mom*, I told you I'm not going."

"Tomorrow night?" Hal looked interested. "What's tomorrow night?"

"Saturday," I said through clenched teeth.

"Nina's got a date!" Mom sang, draining her wineglass.

"A date!" Hal grinned broadly. "Ye didn't tell me ye had a date, love. Who's the lucky fella?"

"I don't have a date. I have to work. I have to work *here*. Why has everyone suddenly forgotten that I work here? In fact, I'm working right now. Here. I'm working here. Now."

"Hold on a minute, Red. I think we can afford ta give ye a Saturday night off every once in a while. If it's in the name of romance, then anything's possible. More chardonnay, Mrs. Kurtz? Pour yer mother a snort, Nina, on the house a'course."

"There's no romance, Hal, and I don't need the night off. And she definitely doesn't need more wine."

"And why not?" Mom asked rather grandly, holding her head higher than normal even though it looked like a struggle.

"Because you've gone all squinty and—Mom, take your hands off of that gentleman's beer, please. No, Mom, put it down. I'm sorry, sir. Dad? Where's Dad? Of course—outside, averting disaster. Put the beer down, Ma. Here. Here's a splash of wine, OK?"

Does anyone make liquor-flavored pacifiers for anxious

adults? Maybe I can patent that shit and sell the idea to the makers of Paxil.

"So where's this young lad taking ye tomorrow night, Nina?" Hal clapped me on the back and I swear I saw him toss my mother a wink.

"Medea's Garden," Mom said before I could protest.

"Mom," I sighed, "you know how uncomfortable this makes me."

"Well I already told Eammon you'd meet his son at the restaurant, honey! You can't back out on me or I'd never be able to face him again. And he's the *only* bagpipes instructor in the Metrowest area!"

"The pipes?" Hal looked impressed. "Now that's a skill ya don't encounter often. Normally I'd make a crass joke about knowin' how ta give a good blow, but there's a lady present."

"Hey." I rolled my eyes. "Don't hold back on account of *my* virgin ears."

"I was talkin' about yer mother. And remind me later to make an inappropriate joke about you and yer virginity."

"Gross."

"Hey, Mrs. Kurtz!" Great, Ben was done with his set. He'd appeared behind my mother and draped a casual arm around her shoulders, causing her to blush and giggle like a schoolgirl. Mom has a bit of a harmless crush on Ben. Not like she wants to do him or anything, but, rather, she wants *me* to. That thought is even grosser than what I anticipate Hal will chortle to me later about my redheaded flower.

"Ben!" she said, a little too warmly, shooting me the eye before twisting in her bar chair to give him a hug. "We were just talking about the *date* that Nina has tomorrow night."

"*Really?*" Ben pursed his lips and swung around to look

at me, eyebrows raised nearly to the top of his precarious hairline.

"Yeah, I've got a scorching night on the town planned tomorrow night. Jealous, Henry?"

"Depends on where you're going."

"Medea's Garden," Mom chirped.

"Nope. Definitely not jealous." Ben laughed.

"Can we please stop talking about this?" I pleaded. "I have work to do, and I don't want to waste any more time standing around and emphatically reinforcing that I *am not going*. End of story, here's your purse, Mom, have a good time."

Silence. Even some of my customers down the bar were leaning in, I guess to see if I was going to throw a tantrum. Hey, I'll admit, sometimes my moods are more exciting than what's going on onstage. It keeps customers coming back.

Mom, Hal, Ben and four drunk, indistinguishably old men, each of whom could have been either my grandfather or Strom Thurman, were staring me down with an intensity that made me squirm.

"The glaring game won't work, guys. I'm not going."

Still, not a word.

"You're all going to give me a hard time about this, aren't you? Anyone? . . . Anyone?"

Sigh.

"What time am I meeting him?"

Seven

"Is this too tight in the chest?"

"I'm not going to ogle your chest, Ben."

"Maybe I should go with the red one."

"The red made you look washed out."

"Really?"

"No, not really. Come on, they all look fine."

"You're the chick, Kurtz. You're not supposed to tell me I look fine. You're supposed to tell me the difference between fabrics and colors and shit. I can't figure this out on my own."

"So I'm a chick now? I was wondering when you'd notice."

I know that look. The "I'm totally masculine but am feeling fragile light now" look.

"OK, OK. Sorry. Put the red one on again."

Shopping for clothes with Ben is dizzying and kind of pitiful, like watching a baby lab rat scramble through a maze, too desperate for cheese to notice its dismal predicament.

I don't know any men who even own full-length mirrors, much less have extensive experience gaping at the sallow, warped reflections produced by a bath of fluorescent light. Dressing rooms are such vortexes of anguish for women;

there has to be a correlation between self-esteem and time spent trying to find a pair of pants that doesn't make your ass look like two biscuits swathed in cheesecloth. It's always mystified me, anyway, the lighting in department-store dressing rooms. Shouldn't it be soft and flattering, not morph my body into a cesspool of radioactive cellulite?

The dressing-room phenomenon seems to be alien to most men. Whenever my mom took the kids back-to-school shopping, my brothers would never have to try anything on that couldn't be slipped over their T-shirts in the middle of a store. The twins would scramble around the mall making everyone crazy, swatting at each other with fingers that were pink and sticky from food court strawberry milkshakes. Paul stuck by me dutifully while my mother trailed Jeremy around the Young Men's departments of stores like Filene's and Brooks Brothers. My oldest brother, the Alex P. Keaton of tenth-grade Bostonians, would slip his scrawny arms into navy blue blazers and knot bland neckties into Windsors while Paul thumbed through racks of jeans, ultimately grabbing a few pairs of stone-washed and being done for the year.

It's never that easy for girls, is it? I suppose it would help if women's clothing were sized by actual measurements, not arbitrary numbers starting at zero, but I've never, not once, purchased a single piece of clothing without first scrutinizing it from every angle in the close confines of a dressing room.

Ben, being the exception to every rule about heterosexual masculinity, can turn a simple search for a new sweater into a grueling decathlon, wanting only for endorphins and high-protein energy bars.

He'd spent the last hour trundling in and out of a changing stall at Abernathy and Tate, one of those uppity bullshit retail stores that associates elitism with stuffy British last names, and puts out a quarterly catalogue showcasing Frisbees and freckles as trademarks of the hip and beautiful. I sat uncomfortably on a slip-covered folding chair, chewing alternately on my fingernails and a stale granola bar I'd located at the bottom of my backpack. Ben, Cuse and myself had initially come to the mall so I could shop for a new outfit for my lukewarm date with the bagpiper's kid, but Ben, as always, managed to make the afternoon all about him. He'd snakily staged a shopping mutiny and dragged me from wistfully fingering frilly negligees, while Cuse tried to pretend he wasn't interested. Now I was sitting on my ass playing fashion consultant. Lucky Cuse managed to wiggle from Ben's tyrannical grasp—I would bet he was either playing video games at Best Buy or getting a massage from one of those space-stationy kiosks.

The dressing room smelled the way I imagine a dead old lady would after being embalmed in liquid cardboard. Every once in a while, Ben would emerge, modeling multicolored versions of the same cotton turtleneck.

"OK, here's the red one again. Thoughts?"

"It looks fine." I chuckled.

"Goddammit."

"Sorry. What I meant was, it looks gay."

"Jesus, Nina!" Ben huffed. "Can't you be serious for two seconds?"

"I *am* being serious, Ben! Turtleneck sweaters are gay! And aren't we supposed to be shopping for me?"

"We *were* shopping for you, but you've done nothing but bitch about everything you've tried on."

"Well, I can't find anything!"

"Why do you care so much, anyway?" He spun around, I assumed to face me for the remainder of our conversation, but instead swiveling his neck back over his shoulder so he could check out his butt in the mirror. "I thought you were only going out with this guy to appease your mother?"

"True, and thanks so much for backing me up last night, by the way. Honestly, Henry, if you were any farther up my mother's ass you'd need to leave a trail of breadcrumbs to find your way back out."

"That's so gross."

"Yeah? Well, I'm gross. What time are we meeting Cuse at the food court?"

God, I can't believe I just spoke those words out loud. Am I seventeen?

"He'll be there around three."

I checked my watch. "That was ten minutes ago, Ben."

"Shit. Well, let me change, and you run and meet him while I buy this."

"You're going to buy the gay sweater?"

"It's not *gay*; it's hip."

"Hip?" Chuckle. "Hip?" Snicker. "Hi . . . hip? Aha. Ahaha. Ahahahahahahahahaha!"

"It *is*!"

"Ben," I sputtered through a juicy, liquid laugh, "you are the furthest thing from hip that I could possibly imagine. I can't even conceive of a fictional image of a caricature of a man who is less hip than you are. You are to hip what the planet Earth is to the closest star in the universe. Light years and light years away. You couldn't even reach hip in a spaceship. I'm going to write a poem about that. 'Ben Henry, Ben Henry, he's so far from hip, he couldn't be trendy if he had a spaceship!' "

"Are you done?"

"Not quite. 'Ben Henry, Ben Henry, the biggest of nerds, to describe his squareness, there aren't any words!' "

"Did you just say 'squareness'? Who are you, Alan Ginsberg?"

"I'm your token chick friend, bitch, and I'm telling you that turtleneck sweaters are not going to get you laid."

"What do you know about getting laid?"

Ben knows all the buttons that sober me up.

"Anyway," he continued, wriggling out of the sweater to reveal a Wilco T-shirt and hair spooked by static, "I bet you ten bucks your date shows up in a turtleneck sweater tonight, and you'll think it's sexy."

"I rue the day I think one of my mother's matchmaking victims is sexy."

"Go meet Cuse. I'll catch up in a minute."

"I'm going to get food. Want anything?"

"Grilled cheese," he said, "but not from the food court, though. Will you get it from Johnny Angel's?"

"That's all the way on the other side of the mall! And the singing waiters are *so* annoying! Can't you just suck it up and find something fast? . . ." Ben shot me a wounded puppy look. "Fine." I sighed. It's not that the look is cute, but rather that it's usually followed by incessant whining. Ben's somewhat of a grilled-cheese snob—he needs orange cheese on white bread, period. I once took him, starving, to a cozy pub in Cambridge, one that serves incredible gourmet eats. It was heaven to me, but Ben's personal hell. He sneered at the white Vermont cheddar that bubbled over thick crusts of seven-grain freshly baked bread, took one audibly savory bite of his delicious-looking sandwich, and flung it back on the plate as though it tasted like a backed-up garbage disposal.

I ate the rest of it. Make that mauled. Mauled like a wolf would an abandoned Eskimo baby slathered in barbecue sauce and the blood of a thousand gazelles. Mmmmm.

The thought of that grilled cheese awakened my slumbering stomach.

"Fine, Johnny Angel's it is. But I'm getting my food first, so just meet us there and we'll have ordered it for you."

"OK."

I couldn't get out of there fast enough, leaving Ben to debate his spectrum of sweaters for what I estimated would be at least another fifteen minutes. Poor Cuse. He always gets dragged along with the two of us like a reluctant kid out with his parents on a summer Saturday.

He was waiting for me at the food court, one knee bouncing in time to the rhythmic whizzes and dings coming from the nearby arcade, the other balancing a heaping cardboard dish of spicy-smelling curly fries. Whenever Cuse eats spicy food his cheeks leak briny sweat and glow even redder than his hair; judging by the clammy brow he was mopping, I'd say Cuse was working on his second order.

"Hey Cuse. How're the fries treating you?"

"Oh, hey Nina," he panted, wiping his forehead with a dingy corner of his long-sleeved T-shirt. "Where's Henry?"

"Still trying some stuff on. What do ya got on there? Tabasco?"

"They're Five Alarm Suicide Fries. *Breeeeeech*," he belched. "Could you hand me a napkin?"

"They sure make your breath smell like death." I reached to the table behind me and grabbed a fistful of paper from the dispenser.

"They're pretty good."

He burped again, a visceral growl of gas that nearly took my eyebrows off.

"Damn, Cuse. Don't light any matches for a few hours, OK?"

"*Brrreeeeeeeeeeeccccch.* Jesus. I hope my stomach calms down soon. I've got two shows tonight."

"Oh yeah? Where?"

"At the Chuckle Barn. It's in Somerville."

"Yeah, I know. It's not that far from my apartment."

"Oh yeah. Well, if your date sucks you should come check it out. I'm up toward the end, so probably for the second run I'll go on around eleven, if you wanna come. I think it's, like, five bucks at the door."

"Eleven? Are you kidding? My date starts at eight. I'm expecting to be home eating fistfuls of cheese puffs by eight forty-five."

"*Breeeeeech.* Damn. You don't know that. Maybe it'll go good this time."

"That's brutally optimistic of you."

"I don't know," he shrugged, belching again and twisting his lips to blow it to the side. "I mean, you never know. You know?"

"Wise words, oh great and powerful Oz. Maybe you should ditch this comedy pipe dream and pursue a career in academia. Or at least write a self-help relationship book. I bet there are thousands of desperately lonely women who would pay top dollar to devour that invaluable knowledge."

"*Breeeeech.*"

"Ah, and chapter one is off to a strong start."

"Man. You want any of these before I toss 'em?"

"No thanks."

Cuse shrugged, and dumped the offending spuds into the nearest bin.

"Where's this dude taking you tonight?"

"Medea's Garden."

"That's that Greek place, right? The huge one out offa I-95?"

"That's the one."

"*Breeeeeeech.*"

My sentiments exactly.

By the time I got home from the mall it was nearly five o'clock. Ben ended up sending his grilled cheese back to the kitchen twice before the poor line cook at Johnny Angel's got it to precise Ben Henry specifications. That left me about two and a half hours to get ready for my date— plenty of time to relax, primp, and doll up before making a leisurely drive to the restaurant.

At seven-fifteen I happened to glance at the clock on my cable box. Goddamn you, *Law and Order* marathon! Goddamn you for once again sucking me in to your bewitching vortex of compelling legal drama!

With fifteen minutes to throw myself together, I slapped on some lip gloss, nearly took my eye out with a mascara wand, wiggled into the only "date dress" I own (a swingy blue number with spaghetti straps and a 1920s-style hemline) and almost punctured Kitty's paw with a teetering misstep in four-inch stilettos. Oops.

Ben's right—I shouldn't care. My dates are more predictable than the romantic resolution in a Meg Ryan film. As sure as Meg will succumb passionately to the man she spends most of the movie love/hating, my date will end in a friend speech and a handshake. *Maybe* an awkward hug.

Still, at least a date, any date, is an excuse to wear something besides my work uniform or my pajamas. Although considering where I'm meeting this dude for dinner, I have a feeling that three minutes into the evening I'll wish I were either at work or in bed. Alone.

For one thing, it's never a promising sign when a man takes you to Medea's Garden. I suspect that no good can possibly come from an evening spent in a restaurant named for the place where a vengeful Greek sociopath murdered her own children to spite a wandering husband. I'm just saying.

Amazingly, I arrived at the restaurant with two minutes to spare. A man with a gigantic erect penis strapped around his forehead greeted me as I pulled into valet. I nearly peed myself, and was about to peel the hell out of there when I remembered something I read in high school mythology class about satyrs, servants of the Greek god of wine (who was, as you'd imagine, somewhat of a partier). I handed the poor bastard my keys, plus a five-dollar tip.

The owners of Medea's Garden have put all other Greek restaurateurs to shame. Let me rephrase that. All other Greek restaurateurs are ashamed of Medea's Garden. It's like the flamboyantly gay illegitimate half-cousin that everybody has but nobody talks about.

Clearly, the architect who conceived the restaurant's design was no stranger to the phenomenon that is the Rainforest Café, a restaurant chain that redefines the meaning of "taste." Not because of the food. Characterized by over-the-top aesthetics and an atmosphere devoted to plaster-of-Paris talking jungle beasts, a Rainforest Café is by no means an epicurean wonderland. People don't go there for the grub. At least, I don't. A girl can stuff only so many coconut-encrusted chicken fingers down her craw.

No, a Rainforest Café draws crowds of families for its magically kitschy imitation of that dense, tropical paradise that liberal arts college students have been rallying to save for decades. It's a tacky, feeble shadow, the Rainforest Café, crawling with masses of faux greenery housing plastic snakes and robotic monkeys. Every sixteen minutes a fountain in the middle of the restaurant lights up with pastel laser lights, flickering in time to the jaws of plastic elephants that lip-synch to "The Lion Sleeps Tonight."

While not a chain, Medea's Garden is loosely modeled after the Rainforest Café. Instead of jungle vines and evergreens, the walls are crawling with plastic grape leaves and ivy. Enormous white columns divide the dining room into different sections, each named for a Greek island. Imposing ceramic statues of mythological figures are scattered among the tables; they seem to supervise the diners, making sure patrons clean their plates from *tzatziki* to baklava. One entire wall comprises an aquarium, home to exotic-looking fish that glide lazily around an eerie, barnacled Poseidon clenching a trident in his raging fists.

Just in case that's not enough eye candy, the entire debacle is choreographed around what might be the most atrocious eyesore ever to be crafted by human hands. At the center of the restaurant towers a plastic Mt. Olympus. Monolithic it's not; the thing looks like it was crafted haphazardly by a half-baked preteen campaigning for extra Earth Science points. The thing could pass for a three-stroke hole at a Myrtle Beach Putt-Putt course.

Every half hour or so the lights in the restaurant dim and the plastic mountain quakes while a faux marble bust moves its mouth in time to such ominous utterances as, "I am the mighty Zeus, king of all gods! Kneel before my awesome presence, lest ye be struck unto Hades by my formidable bolt of thunder! Happy fourteenth birthday, Kara Steinberg!"

"Mt. Olympus" doubles as a dessert display. Shelves of them shimmy in time to the plastic mountain's comic trembling.

As a kid I thought this place was tasteless. As an adult I

hope nobody I know spies me skulking through the front entrance.

"Good evening, madam." An impossibly skinny woman greeted me as I entered the lobby. She was wearing a metallic lamé toga and flashed a matching gold tooth when she grinned.

"Hi . . . I'm supposed to be meeting someone here?"

"Ah. Do you have a reservation?"

A few.

"I don't know. I don't think so. Well, maybe we do. I don't know."

"Uh-huh. And the name, please?"

"Name? Um . . ."

"Are you Nina?" came a nasally male voice from behind me.

I turned around to find myself faced with a decent-looking guy, not too much taller than myself, with carefully messy hair and watery bedroom eyes, clutching a highball glass filled with ruby liquid and plastered with a grin that said "plastered."

"Ah," I said, "you must be my date. I can tell by how nervous you smell."

"What does that mean?" he asked, taking a sip of his drink. He kept his middle finger extended as he lifted the glass to his lips. Hmmm. Questionable etiquette, or a subtle bird flip? Either way, not a good start to the evening.

"Nothing," I said, "just making a joke. That's what I do."

"Make dumb jokes?"

"I said I make *jokes*, not dumb jokes."

"Your table is ready," the hostess interrupted, concerned, perhaps, that a rumble was about to ensue. "Right this way, please."

"After you," my date mused with an awkward sweep of his arm.

We followed our sparkly leader to a table in the corner of "Crete," nestled between an ornate piece of pottery and a statue of Medusa, replete with wiggly fiber-optic snakes sprouting from her head like wild grass.

"Your server tonight is Achilles," she informed us, "and he'll be with you in a moment. Can I start the lady off with a drink?"

"I'll have a Manhattan," I said.

"That's a manly drink." My companion smirked, draining his glass and sliding it toward the waitress. "I'll take another Malibu and grenadine. And could you add a splash of pineapple this time?"

Trying to compensate for my manliness by being tragically hip and sensitive?

"Perhaps you'd like a tiny umbrella as well?" I smirked in return.

He eyed me—I couldn't tell if it was with amused interest or deadly caveman poison.

"And we'll start with some hummus, please," he said to the hostess, never taking his eyes from mine.

"Certainly, sir. I'll have Achilles bring it over with some bread and olive oil."

She couldn't get away from us fast enough.

No-name leaned back and crossed his legs, stroking his fashionably stubbly chin contemplatively.

"Now, Nina. Nina, Nina, Nina."

Shit. I still don't remember his name. Must choose my reply carefully.

"Yo."

"My stepfather tells me you work in a comedy club? That's interesting. What do you do there?"

"Oh, you know."

"No, I don't. That's why I'm asking."

"I . . . work."

"Fascinating."

"I think so."

The silence that followed was an awkward eternity. Achilles finally showed up six centuries later, drinks in hand, flexing his glistening muscles in silent greeting. Both the nameless date and I immediately started knocking them back.

"So . . . what do *you* do?" I finally asked.

"I'm a psychotherapist."

Awesome. No wonder my mother loves him.

"You look pretty young to be a doctor, Doc."

"My degree is in psychology. I can't prescribe medication. I don't feel it to be a necessary element of psychological rehabilitation."

"Oh."

"Mmm. Of course, I don't feel that behavioral science is my life's true calling," he continued, draining his glass again and leaning way back in his chair. "Ultimately, my pipe dream, fantasy, plan B kind of thing, is to be a rancher."

"A what?"

"A rancher. Of course, that probably has something to do with my penchant for authority and control."

Yikes.

"Do you want to raise cattle?" I asked. Better keep Freud talking about himself before the tables turn and he tries to pick me apart. God, I hate therapists. They make me nervous.

"No, no, no. I'd want to have a ranch out West somewhere, and spend my days taming wild horses. At night we'd sit around a campfire, eating stew and singing folk songs."

"Who's 'we'?"

"Myself, and my wife."

Oh my God. "You're *married*?"

He rolled his eyes. "My *hypothetical* wife. Visualization of goals is the first step towards actualization."

"I see. And where would you get these horses?"

"I don't know," he shrugged, signaling to Achilles to bring us another round. "There's just places where you go in the wild where you can find wild horses. And then you round them up, bring them back to the ranch, and tame them."

I mimicked his observational pose, leaning way back in my chair and cocking my head. "So what you're saying is that what you really want to do, in a perfect, fantasy world, is to spend the rest of your life breaking the spirits of otherwise healthy and carefree animals."

He shrugged. "Sure. You could put it that way."

Check, please.

The evening didn't get any better. The only exciting moment was when we were chatting awkwardly about our hobbies and he mentioned King's bowling alley in Boston.

"Rex! Your name is Rex!" I blurted out before I could stop myself.

"Yes . . ." He looked at me strangely.

"Oh . . . I just . . . you know. King. Rex is Latin for 'King.' "

"Yes . . ."

"I just . . . um . . . get excited. About Latin."

"You get excited about Latin?"

"Yeah."

We skipped dessert. Not because there was achingly tangible sexual chemistry wafting over our table. In fact, the minute I stabbed at my last forkful of lamb, Rex looked at his watch in a manner that reminded me of a Broadway actor trying to express his concern for the time to the very last row in the very highest balcony of a theater.

"Whoa, it's already past nine! I hate to cut this short, but I've got a big morning tomorrow. I hope you won't think it's rude if we grab the check."

Rude? Why would I think it's rude that he's been jiggling his leg anxiously since the moment he choked down his fifth and final roasted potato? Five is an estimate, actually. The man chowed so goddamned quickly I barely had time to identify the slab of meat on his plate before bare blue china was staring up at his chin.

"No, Rex, that's fine. I have a jam-packed Sunday morning myself. Lots of sleeping to do. And TV to watch. I can completely understand your predicament."

He sighed and leaned forward, reaching across the table. For one perplexing second I thought it was to take my hand, but instead, he grabbed my knife and tilted it upward, using the reflection to check for food in his teeth.

"Look, Nina," he began. "I think you're great, really great. You're so funny and so intelligent and just an awesome woman—"

"And that's why you think we'll make great, great friends?"

Rex chuckled weakly and tipped back in his chair again. "You'd make a good therapist. It's like you can read my mind."

He waved a gold credit card in Achilles' direction, mouthing, "Can we have the check?" and making the appropriate motion with his other hand.

I was still gnawing on my dinner, little lamby bits that wedged themselves between my molars and tasted richly of salt and mint and premature baby sheep death.

I sucked at my teeth for a minute.

"No, Rex."

"No what?"

"No, Rex, we're not going to be friends."

He shifted in his chair. "There's no need to make this uncomfortable."

"I'm not making this uncomfortable. Are you uncomfortable? I'm not."

"Come on."

"I'm serious! Let's cut the bullshit here; I don't want to be your friend any more than you want to be mine. Why is that uncomfortable? I'm just being honest. You don't want to actually be my friend; you just want to avoid shattering my delicate feminine ego into ten million heartbroken shards. Not because you care, of course, but because you don't want me to make a scene in the middle of dinner, because abandoning a crying woman mid-meal is tackier than all of the Formica tabletops and pitiful plastic artifacts in this entire place. And believe me, I can see five Dumpsters' worth of tacky shit without having to even turn my head."

"Do you have to do this here? Thank you." Achilles had slipped our check onto the table and seemed intrigued by my reddening cheeks and Rex's increasingly slinky posture. Rex threw his credit card down and shot our poor waiter a Trojan look of war. He got the hint and scampered away, toga flapping in his hasty breeze.

"Seriously," my date continued, "can we just give each other a hug and call it a night?"

"You're stuck listening to me until you get your card back. You might as well shut up and listen. Consider this a free lesson that will undoubtedly plump up your lackluster date skills."

"Lackluster?" he smirked. "Why, because I haven't tried

to make out with you? Believe me, Nina. If I wanted it, it would happen."

"I'm going to give you the benefit of the doubt and assume that by 'it' you don't mean my lady parts."

"Your what?"

I ignored him and continued. "You know what really gets my goat?" Jesus Christ, I'm starting to sound like my octogenarian Irish grandmother. "Men seem to think that offering their friendship in the wake of a crappy date is like a fabulous consolation prize."

"Nina, I'm sorry if I'm hurting your feelings—"

"You are not hurting my feelings, dimwit! You're missing my point. I'm not consoled by the thought of your friendship, because I don't *want* it. I'm not so smitten with you that I feel compelled to cling to some superficial olive branch that you're extending because it makes you feel like a nice guy! Honestly, that is so fucking presumptuous! How dare you assume that I'm so desperate for your company that I'd treasure your friendship as a precious commodity?"

Rex looked at me as though I'd just sucker punched him in the gut in front of all of his varsity football teammates. He tried to take a gulp of his dainty fairy cocktail, but, finding nothing but ice, he pushed the glass to the edge of the table and tapped his fingers nervously.

"I'm sensing," he began, "that you're very angry."

"Wow," I snorted, "you must be top of your field."

"And there's definitely a deep-seated resentment towards men. That's been obvious since the minute I met you."

"Oh yeah? This should be good. Let's hear why I'm resentful."

"Well," he mused, "we didn't delve much beyond small talk tonight, so I can't say for sure, but the fact that you're so quick to make snide jokes really speaks volumes of your psyche. I'd imagine you grew up with mostly boys?"

Hmm.

"Four brothers," I grumbled.

"That makes sense. And I suspect that you attract a lot of men, but never get beyond the first few dates? Just what I thought." Rex smiled at his own genius when I mumbled an affirmative response. "You see, Nina, the fact of the matter is, you probably think that when you joke around, you're being witty. But your jokes are more like sharply aimed barbs. Like your first line of defense. I'd say you don't have a lot of experience with men, and you keep yourself well guarded."

"Am I supposed to be paying you by the hour or something?"

"See what I mean?" Rex smiled. "I've hit the nail on the head, and you don't like it. You're quite insecure. You don't want me to be right about you, so instead you've tried to deflect the focus of the conversation by making a joke. Usually that's a male personality characteristic, but since you were raised with four brothers, you've developed some social mechanisms that most women don't pick up. Don't get me wrong," he continued, "you're very smart. But I have to warn you that most men don't like having to go head to head with the fairer sex, especially on the first date. Tone it down a little. Ah, thank you." Achilles had finally returned with Rex's credit card, which he set down along with a complimentary dish of little round things drowning in honey.

"*Loukoumades*," Achilles trilled. "Deep-fried puffs. Like Greek doughnut."

We thanked him, and he gave us an awkward little bow before disappearing again.

Rex signed his name in rigid script, crossing the "x" in his first name with a flourish, and pushed back from the table. "Ready?"

All I could do was blink. Was this guy for real?

I chose my words carefully. "So, if I'm to understand you correctly, because I was raised with boys I have a tendency to be defensive about my insecurities."

"Yes."

"And the fact that I make jokes all the time is really a reflection of those insecurities."

"Yes."

"And so, if I want to be more successful with men, I need to 'tone it down' and try to act more like a typical girl instead of constantly trying to assert myself?"

"Precisely."

"Nina. Nina, calm down. I can barely understand what you're saying. Is my hearing finally starting to go, or did you just scream something about balls?"

So mad. So mad! After leaving my date speechless in a pool of honey I'd nearly maimed the valet in my haste to motor the hell out of Medea's Garden. His forehead penis bobbed furiously as he scrambled to match my ticket to the sets of keys hanging from a pegboard behind his podium, while I screamed indecipherable obscenities to nobody in particular.

I made the drive home in less than ten minutes, and burst into my apartment like a DEA agent on a drug bust in Colombia, which sent both Jaime and Kitty scrambling for cover. It took me a minute to locate our cordless phone—I finally found it underneath the couch—but when I did, I was on number-punching autopilot.

"Is that all you heard? Because I don't think I can bring myself to repeat the whole story, Ma."

"Let me get this straight." For the first time in my life, I could hear fear in my mother's voice. We're talking about an Irish-Catholic woman with five children; the only thing that scares her is God. She usually giggles dismissively when I call her post-date to bitch about the awful time I'd just had with yet another loser she's set me up with. "This man put his balls in your face? Honey, are you all right?"

"MOM, that's not what I said at all! Are you listening to me?"

"I'm trying."

"I said that I threw balls in his face. Honey balls. Little Greek doughnuts. I threw them in his face after he psycho-analyzed me."

"Oh," she sighed in relief. I could hear the unmistakable clink of ice cubes in the background, and there was a pause while she took an audible slurp. "Oh, that tastes good. OK, so no balls in your face. Well, come on honey, he's a doctor—you have to expect that his mind is in 'analysis' mode at all times. Poor man is probably completely overworked."

"He's not a doctor, Ma."

"What?" her tone shifted. "What do you mean, he's not a doctor?"

"He doesn't believe in medication. He's just a therapist."

"No MD?"

"Nope."

"No PhD?"

"Nope."

"Son of a—" she gulped her drink again. "Eammon told me his stepson was a doctor! If I'd known he was just a therapist I'd have *never* set you up with him! Picking apart *my baby* like that! The sheer nerve! What exactly did he say? I need verbatim so when I rip into Eammon I can be precise."

"Verbatim? Um . . . he said that I'm insecure and I make jokes to mask that because I was raised with four brothers and developed male social mechanisms. And that I need to tone it down if I want to be successful with men because they don't like to go head-to-head with girls."

"Oh that is such *poppycock*!" my mother fumed. "You make jokes because you're funny, not because you're insecure, and you have bad luck with men because you haven't been out with anyone who's smart enough to keep up with you! Those goddamned—pardon my French—monkeys I've been setting you up with are intimidated by your brain."

"But, Mom, you've said the same thing about toning it down."

"I'm your mother; I can say whatever I want to you. But *no man* has the right to analyze *my* little girl. The nerve! And what does having four brothers have to do with anything? As if I have any control over what flies out of my uterus. You know, it's *just* like a man to make this about reproductive rights."

"OK, Ma? Now you're talking crazy."

"Ooh, I've got call waiting. I bet it's Eammon, calling to get the dirt. Boy, am I going to give him a piece of my mind! Hang on a sec, dear, OK? Hello?"

"Still me, Ma."

"Darn it, I can never get the hang of this thing. Hello?"

"Still me."

"Darn. Hello?"

"*Still me*, Ma. Are you on the cordless? Press the 'flash' button."

"The what?"

"The '*flash*.' "

"Oh, 'flash.' OK, hold on . . . wait, there it is . . . Hello?"

"Just call me back, Mom."

It was less than a minute when . . . *Riiiiiing*.

"Hello?"

"That was just your father calling. He's on his way home from a night shift he picked up for one of the new DJs and he wanted me to make him a sandwich. Can you believe that? Just like a man. I told him to make his own damned dinner. I'm a wife, not a slave! Why do men have to be such oppressors?"

Oh Jesus. I may have created a militant feminist.

"Mom, Dad is not an oppressor. He's just hungry. Why don't you go call Eammon and take your anger out on him, not your husband? And shave your legs before Dad gets home, OK?"

"You're absolutely right, dear. I'm going to call him right this minute. If that man ruins my marriage I'll never pick up the bagpipes again."

"OK, Ma. Just call me when you're off the phone, OK?"

"OK, poppet. Talk to you soon."

I wonder if there's any booze in the apartment.

We used to keep it on top of the fridge, until I came home from work one night to discover a howling Kitty, stumbling around in circles and looking a little cross-eyed. Turns out one of us hadn't completely screwed on the top to a bottle of tequila, and Kitty had knocked it over in one of his many vindictive missions designed to entrench his scent into every crevice of my home. That cat and I are going to battle to the death; I can feel it.

So Kitty got schnockered and Jaime got nervous. Personally, I think a little snort here and there would calm his nerves, but my roommate didn't agree. She hid all of the liquor, and goddammit, I can't remember where.

I'd just begun to rifle through the kitchen cabinets, when . . . *Riiiiiing*.

"Oh for God's sake, Ma. Just make him the sandwich."

"Um, hello?"

It was not my mother, but rather, a butterscotch baritone.

"I'm looking for Nina Kurtz," the man said. "Is this the right number?"

"Oh, um, yeah." I fumbled. "This is Nina."

"Good!" he sounded relieved. "I was afraid I wouldn't be able to track you down."

"I'm sorry, who is this?"

"Oh right. I'm sorry. This is Jacob. Jacob Ryan. Do you remember me?"

Eight

"So, Mountain Man called you completely out of the blue?"

"What the hell *is* that, Ben?"

"It's a sandwich. Where did he get your number?"

"It looks like radioactive plastic. Where did you *get* that?"

"I don't know, some market. Come on, what did he say?"

"Did you *sit* on it?"

"*Nina.*"

The grilled cheese Ben had produced from a misshapen swath of foil was making my stomach watusi. A double, crumpled trapezoid of blackened bread that barely restrained its mucousy filling, orange cheese that shimmered like art deco plastic. New Englanders don't eat orange cheese; I've tried to explain to Ben. It's unnatural, like drinking juice that's blue. Ever seen orange milk?

I'd been waiting all night to get Ben's take on my Saturday-night phone call. Monday nights at Bellyaches attract large crowds, mostly corporates from the nearby financial district, so I hadn't had more than three minutes to chat with him since my shift started. Suits are big drinkers; they seem to like to prepare for a tough week of negotiating by chugging American beers and listening to spiky-haired greaseballs rant about homosexuality and the lack of elbow room on airplanes.

I stare at the backs of their impeccably groomed heads while they sip on Coors Light, chortle in unison at the same off-color jokes and try desperately to forget their wives for an hour or two. For the most part, these happy hour groups are boys' clubs, but occasionally a woman will tag along. Most that I've seen have had mannish haircuts and a Thanksgiving's worth of breasts. None are particularly attractive, which never even matters; their coworkers hit on them anyway, drunk and merciless.

The act onstage was Larry Palladino: twenty-one years old, fresh out of art school and far too fond of pop-culture jokes about decades that passed in concurrence with his stint in an ovary. Gets most of his material from those kitschy nostalgic shows on VH1. Comedy about as organic as a Fruit Roll-Up.

"Man, this kid sucks," Ben sighed. "Are you going to tell me what Jacob said or not? Otherwise I'm going to talk about *my* love life."

Oh Lord. Ben was in a decent mood for once, on cloud nine and a half because he'd finally summoned the courage to approach the mysterious bouncy-haired girl. He'd been acting like a goon all evening. Jerk.

"What love life? You said, like, two sentences to her."

"I asked her on a date!"

"*You* asked a complete stranger out on a date?"

"Yep."

"What happened to Ben Henry, social retard extraordinaire? How the hell did you summon the balls to do that?"

"You really want me to talk about it?"

Hmmm.

"Brief synopsis," I said, "then I get to talk about my serendipitous phone call."

"I wouldn't really call it 'serendipitous,' would you?"

"Why not?"

"Jacob didn't call you out of the blue, and the proximity of the phone call to your mutual ten-year reunion isn't a coincidence."

"So?"

"So that's what serendipity *is*. It's discovering something meaningful or useful in an accidental way."

"Jesus, Ben, did you swallow a dictionary as a kid?"

He took a bite of his poor excuse for a sandwich. "I'm just saying."

"Ben, how long has that sandwich been in your backpack?"

"Hmmmm?"

"It's like, all congealed. Ew, you're *eating* it!"

"Nina," he said through a mouthful of cold cheese, "tell me about the phone call. I've got less than ten minutes before I go onstage, so it's either now or in about an hour."

"OK, OK! So, he called . . . and I was surprised . . . and I think I'm going to the reunion."

Ben blinked. "That's it? 'He called, I was surprised, I think I'm going to the reunion'? That's all you have to say about it?"

"What else am I supposed to say?"

"Well come *on*, Nina; you've been gooing about this man ever since you got that invitation in the mail and now all you can say is 'He called, I was surprised, I think I'm going to the reunion'?"

"I have *not* been 'gooing.' "

"Like hell you haven't been gooing! Oh my God, you've been talking about him so much it's annoying!"

"What the hell are you *talking* about? I've maybe mentioned Jacob to you three times."

"Yeah, that's two times too many."

"I can't believe this. I've listened to you talk about the bouncy-haired girl three *hundred* times. You begrudge me a little reminiscing about who, so far, has been the most important man in my life, romantically speaking?"

"I'm a man. I have a short attention span for this shit."

"Fine," I bristled, "then I won't talk about him anymore."

"Come on," Ben sighed, "that's not what I meant."

"No, it's fine. I didn't realize I was talking about him that much. The last thing I want is to be annoying."

"Dammit, Nina, you can't hold back now. Tell me what he said!"

"Why do you want to know?"

Ben threw up his hands, nearly smacking a bar patron in the face with his dilapidated dinner. "Because I want to know! Jesus Christ, this is going to turn into a cliffhanger in about"—he checked his watch—"three minutes, if you don't spill *now*. You know I can't stand going onstage with something nagging at the back of my mind."

"Fine."

So I told him.

After recovering from my initial shock Saturday night, when my mystery caller had revealed his identity and my stomach nearly smothered my toes, it took me a minute to remember how to string two words together.

"This is Jacob. Jacob Ryan. Do you remember me?"

"Remember . . . you? Do I . . . yes!" I had to pinch myself on the thigh in order to jumpstart my cerebrum. "Yes, of course! Of *course* I remember you, Jacob. Oh my God. Oh my *God*. How are you? *Where* are you? Why are you calling me?"

Jacob had laughed, the same sweet-cream-buttery chuckle I remembered from high school, except leagues deeper—much more substantial.

"Which question should I answer first?"

"Um . . . random order is fine. Surprise me."

"Sure. Well, I'm doing really well, I'm living in Seattle—"

"Jacob," I interrupted, "there's only one answer left, and so far you've answered in the same order that I asked the questions."

"But you told me to surprise you!" he laughed again. "So I thought I would answer in the least predictable way, which would be to *not* answer in random order."

Damn. He's still good.

"Nice work," I said.

"Do you want to hear the last answer? Or are you going to keep interrupting?"

Oh good Lord, you could bet your pants I wanted to know why he was calling.

"Do you want me to answer those in random order?" I teased.

"Ha! You haven't changed one bit, Red."

"Yeah, as obnoxious as ever."

"Good. I should have known you'd be exactly the same."

"I'm not *exactly* the same," I said. "I have Doctor Epstein to thank for that."

"Who's that?"

"My plastic surgeon. Kidding. I'm kidding!" I exclaimed when Jacob didn't say anything.

"Jesus. For a second you scared me. I was picturing you with huge breasts and a tiny nose, or tiny breasts and somebody else's nose."

"Stop picturing my breasts, sicko."

Man, was I on fire! Take that, Rex Brandon. Some men *like* my sass!

"I still have one more question to answer." Jacob laughed again.

"What was it again?"

"Why I'm calling you."

"Oh yeah. Why are you calling me, Jacob?"

He paused; my heart beat double time to the metronome click of the kitchen clock.

Maybe he's getting married.

Maybe he's getting divorced.

Maybe he's dying.

Maybe—

"I miss you, kid."

"He *misses* you?" Ben cut in. "But that's absurd. You haven't seen each other in ten years!"

"So?" I huffed. "That's a long time to miss somebody!"

"Do you miss *him*?"

"I don't know."

"Liar."

"I'm not lying."

"You ain't truthin' either."

I forget sometimes how well Ben knows me.

"I've only had one boyfriend, Ben," I said, trying to keep the whining to a minimum but probably not having much success. "*One* boyfriend, and that was in fucking *high school*. Don't you think that's weird?"

"Why is that weird?"

"Because I'm twenty-seven."

"You *do* miss him."

"Yes. No. I don't know."

"But you don't actually miss him," Ben took another thoughtful bite of his sandwich, chewing for a minute before continuing, "because you haven't talked to him in ten years. So, really, you miss his memory. Like, your memory of Jacob as a teenage boy."

"I guess."

"That's sick."

"Shut up. Don't you ever wonder about your ex-girlfriends?"

"Not really. I'm confident that they're all devastated without me."

"That's awfully healthy of you, Henry."

"Hey, you know? What can I say? The ladies love me."

"Sure they do. Do you think we can get back to *me*?"

"Hey, by all means, Narcissus."

"That's better. Anyway, I guess I *have* been thinking about Jacob since I got that invitation—"

"You guess?"

"—and then when he called . . . I've been thinking about how great it was with him, and how I haven't found a guy since then who's been as . . . into me."

"Lots of guys have been into you!"

"Like who?"

Ben didn't answer.

"Right," I rolled my eyes. "All *those* guys."

"There have been guys!"

"You're missing my point, Ben."

"You haven't made one yet."

Jesus. Sometimes I want to tear my best friend's tongue out and cram it up his nose.

"My *point*, Ben, is that clearly, this guy saw something in me that nobody else has. And I want to know what it was."

"And *do* him."

"Excuse me?"

"And you want to do him."

I thought about it.

"OK, that too, but—"

"Ha! I knew it!"

"Shut up. But mostly, I just want to know what the hell I did right when I was a teenager, so I can do it again."

"You mean, do *him* again."

"You are such a child," I snapped. "And what makes you think I *did him* in the first place?"

Ben's mouth twisted into a sinister pain-in-the-ass grin. "Because you've torn up that cocktail napkin into a million pieces, Miss Sexual Frustration, and every time I say the name Jacob, you get all red and fizzy."

"I do not!"

"Come on, fess up. It's obvious, anyway. Hal and I have been talking about it since the night you brought that invitation in."

"What the fuck, Ben?"

"So far, we figure you guys probably did it more than ten times, and *definitely* in your Dad's car."

"Benjamin!"

"Ha! Hey, great timing, boss!" Hal had joined us at the bar, looking unusually somber. "Nina just called me Benjamin!"

"What?" Hal asked weakly. "Oh. Well, you know what that means, chap!"

My face could have reheated Ben's sandwich. "And what *does* that mean, exactly?"

"It means I'm right," Ben said. "Girls never call me Benjamin unless I've hit the nail square on the head and they're embarrassed about it. You want to date him again!"

"I do not want to *date* him, Ben."

"You want him to take one look at you at that reunion, sweep you into his strong, mountain-man arms, and make sweet, sweet monkey love to you, right on the buffet table."

"EEEEEEW!"

"Don't deny it." Ben laughed. "You loooooooove him."

"Grow up, Henry. What are you, twelve?"

"You *loooooooove* him!"

"I just want to see how he's doing!"

"Nina *loooooooooves* Jacob Ryan!"

"*Benjamin!*"

Shit.

"Ha!" he laughed. "Oh wait, *shhhh*. Better hide the cherries and cocktail onions, Kurtz; Larry's about to launch into his big punch line."

"Which?"

"The Crystal Light joke."

Oh brother. Larry Palladino tells this tired Crystal Light joke every goddamned gig he takes. He needs to start watching better TV.

"You guys remember that drink? Crystal Light?" Larry queried the audience, who murmured in agreement. "Came in all those pastel colors, right? You know, there was the yellow one, a couple of pink ones. OK, OK, so remember how, in the commercials, there was always that stream of the drink, that waterfall, and a gorgeous, scantily clad woman would kind of pass underneath it and pause, like she's suddenly serene and refreshed, and start smoothing her hair back under the cascade? OK? So she's now *bathing* in the drink, in this waterfall of sugar water. Sexy, right?"

Oh my God. Yes, you're right. You're right, OK? Stop asking us. Nobody's arguing your right-ness.

"Here's my question, folks. How attractive is it to be with a woman, as soaking wet as she may be, who has just completely drenched herself in a stream of sugar water? I mean, think about it; you're all making your move, got your arm around her, you go to run your fingers through her hair, and *wham!* Your fingers are now enmeshed in the sticky rat's nest that is plastered to her head! Appealing, right? Or how about this, folks: You're all kissing up on her, right, and she tastes pretty good. No arguments there, I mean, she tastes like a freshly glazed cruller, which is, frankly, what I look for in a woman. But then you're all kissing, and touching, and trying to slide a hand up her shirt, when you start to hear it: the buzzing. Just subtle at first, just a little, but then louder, more insistent."

This joke never ends. I wish I was as drunk as the audience. Or as hopeful that this rambling monologue will turn out to be funny.

"Suddenly"—Larry swept his arms across his chest dramatically, bulging out his eyes for full effect—"suddenly, you see them; you see them *everywhere*. Flies, moths, ants, bees; this girl is like a living, breathing, bug magnet! I mean, forget Jeff Goldblum, OK? This girl has more flies than the Lord himself!"

Bugs. Nose itchy.

At this point I can never tell if the crowd titters because of the obscure high-school literary reference (or poignant coming-of-age movie starring Balthazar Getty), or because they're relieved that dude finally delivered a punch line, as flat and bland as it is. I'm betting on the latter; this place has seen a lot of pity laughs.

Well, the Crystal Light bit is Larry's big joke, so the rest of his set was downhill from there. I tuned out rather than continue to watch him ham awkwardly about more products from the eighties that made women sexy in a repugnant way. I guess I should be more annoyed with the eighties for that misogynist phenomenon than this poor, barely post-pubescent kid, but hey; he's sweaty and I don't like his shirt.

I was distracted by Hal's wet cockney whisper. "Love, could you hand me that bar rag?"

I looked up at him and noticed that he looked . . . *different*. His usual Bellyaches uniform, greasy blue jeans and one of various Boston sports jerseys had been replaced. Not that I'm complaining; it is NOT pretty to see a fat man wear mesh. Tonight, however, Hal sported a three-piece suit—cheesily cheap and about to fall apart, but three-piece nonetheless—with a Hawaiian print ascot and snakeskin wingtips.

"Wooow." Ben whistled. "Nice ensemble!"

"What's the occasion?" I teased. "Oh God, you didn't convince some poor girl to go out with you."

"No, love, not yet."

"Ew, you're not going to try and convince *me* to go out with you?"

"Come on, love, if I was goin' ta do that, I'd be wearing body armor and wielding a bloody light saber."

Ouch.

"Then what's the occasion?" I asked.

"Just hand me the bleedin' rag!"

"Why are we whispering?"

"The *rag*, Nina."

"OK, OK."

I handed him my cleanest towel and he promptly wiped his forehead with it.

"That's it?"

"What's it, love?"

"You're wiping your forehead with my dishrag? First of all, that's disgusting; do you know what I mop with that thing? Second, why the hell couldn't you find a napkin or something?"

"A what? Oh." Hal looked genuinely surprised that there was indeed an alternative source for brow mopping.

Ben and I exchanged glances.

"What's the problem, big guy?" I asked. "You look like you just got caught with your finger halfway between your nose and your mouth."

"Just nerves, I s'pose."

"Why?"

"You know how I hate getting up on that bleedin' stage."

It's true. Hal's stage fright far surpasses mine. I just get shaky; Hal sweats enough to power a grist mill and loses all ability to speak in complete sentences. Not that he was working with too much linguistic skill to begin with.

But wait.

"Why do *you* have to get up onstage?" I asked. "Is our emcee drunk again? Son of a bitch, I've *told* him to keep his hands off the merlot. Sorry, Hal—he must be snagging it when I'm not paying attention. Serves him right; that shit's cheaper than Spam. I hurl after one glass."

"Morty's fine," Hal said.

"So what—"

"Thank you so very much, ladies and germs!" Palladino was wrapping up his set, much to the relief of everyone in the room except one, enthusiastic table—probably his parents. "That's all *I* wrote, but hot damn, have I got a treat for you. Before our next comic gets up here and completely bombs, Bellyaches has a special guest that we'd like you to meet. He's big, he's mean, he's English, and I'm terrified. Ladies and gentlemen, I give you Hal . . . Rickenson!"

I whipped my head around. Hal gave me a shrug and a

nervous half smile before waddling toward the stage, taking his sweet, fat time.

He arrived onstage close to thirty seconds later and completely out of breath. Enough to make me think twice the next time I start to eat anything fried.

Larry handed him the mic and Hal paused for a minute, paralyzed, no doubt, by respiratory problems induced by fear and the treacherous fifteen-foot trek from the bar to the stage. Again, nothing but vegetables for me from now on. Shudder.

"Is this on? Uh, 'ello. 'Ello, everyone!"

The crowd replied, most of them in drunken cockney imitations.

"Uh, I'm Hal Rickenson, as Larry here was kind enough to point out, and I am the proud owner of this shitehole."

This time I chimed in with the crowd's cheers, mostly because it was the first time I'd heard Hal admit to Bellyaches being the "shitehole" it is.

"I usually leave the spotlight to these chaps," Hal continued, "but tonight I have an announcement to make. You know, we're not the grandest of comedy clubs, but we've got heart. And we've got a terrific band o' comics that come in here every week and put on a show for you folks. Some of 'em, like our Ben Henry—where are ya, Benny? Oh that's right, I left him in the back, there—are up where I'm standing nearly every night, always with new things to make you laugh, and usually with a smile on their face, unless they're being pelted with garbage. Oh, deservedly so, folks—God knows I can't tolerate a bad comic. It's hazing, really. Rite o' passage into the stand-up band o' brothers. And sisters, I guess. Well no, we never have any birds get up here. Pity. Anyway, I'm up here because I am a big believer in giving people a chance. So tonight, and I'll be post-

ing this by the door and in the papers, I'm pleased to an-
nounce Bellyache's first annual Wet Behind the Ears contest. We want to give rookies a chance to get up here and
give it a shot, just like I did with Mr. Henry back there,
who's not doing too badly now. Well, I know, Benny, it's not
exactly the bloody Apollo, is it? Just as well—you're whiter
than a vampire's arse. Oh, got a bit o' a laugh with that one,
didn't I? That's unusual. I'll be here all night! No really, just
in that back corner over there."

For crying out loud, now I've seen it all. The fat man is
red hot and I'm still yellow.

"So, first prize"—Hal was smiling now, looking like a
fourth-grader who'd reached the home stretch on his oral
book report—"is five-hundred quid—sorry, *bucks*—and a
month-long regular gig, publicity included. Well, it won't
be in the bloody *Globe* or anything, but, you know, we'll run
off some posters, put it in the *Phoenix* and the like. So that's
all I have to say, really. I hope to get some fresh faces in here,
hopefully who have a lot of supportive friends and cousins
to pack the place. Oh, and it's November ninth, yeah? Yeah,
the ninth, it's a Saturday. If you want to enter, just show up
at the door at seven with an ugly shirt and some original
jokes. Thanks, folks. Oh, and I'll be one of the judges, but
just to keep it fair we've got a few seasoned comics and
some fellow club owners thrown in the mix. It'll be great,
like reality telly, yeah? And I promise, I *promise* I won't be a
bit like that nasty git on *American Idol*. Really, he's a national
disgrace. All right then, enjoy the rest of yer evening.
Who've we got up next? Oh, it's our Mr. Henry. Give him a
hand, folks—he deserves it."

Hal exited to enthusiastic applause. Nothing like a
messy British accent and the promise of cold hard cash to
get a crowd going. He and Ben exchanged a quick high five

as they passed each other, and Ben took the stage to begin his act.

"How'd I do, Nina?" Hal gasped when he'd made it back to the bar, sinking onto a stool and signaling for me to give him some water.

"Fine," I said, handing him a glass, which he immediately drained. "Funny. You did a good job up there."

"Ah, thanks, love," he sighed, "I think they liked that bit about the vampire's arse."

"Yes, very good, boss man. You have a bright future in funny."

"I get so nervous up there, under the lights."

"I know."

"All those people staring."

"I know."

"Judging."

Boy, did I know.

"Anyway"—I refilled his water glass—"you'll probably get a huge response. There's a million fledgling comics out there, looking for a break."

"You included, I hope."

"What? Who? Me? No."

"Aw, come on, love! You're a funny bird! It's eighty percent of the reason I'm still open! Well, that and yer tits."

"Hey."

"Sorry. That and yer boobs."

"That's better. Anyway, I don't do the stage."

"And why not?"

"For all the things you just said. Lights. Judging. Et cetera."

"Scared, are ya?"

"You know that."

"Yeah. But I don't know why."

"Well, that makes two of us."

"That can't be true. Everyone knows exactly why they're afraid of anything."

"Who are you, Freud?"

"Bit of a Jungian myself, actually."

"Figures."

"So, I'll sign you up, then? Put you on somewhere in the middle o' the lineup?"

"Don't even think about it, Hal," I warned.

"Fine, I won't even sign ye up, just call yer name out so yer forced ta get up there."

"I will quit on the spot."

"A likely story. You've been threatening that fer years."

"Fine. Then I'll maim you with a corkscrew."

"Now, *that* I believe."

"Besides, I can't do it, Hal, that's the same night as my reunion."

"What, that wonky thing? Thought ye weren't goin?"

"I may have changed my mind."

"Another fish tale."

"I'm serious! I've been thinking about it, and I think I want to go."

A light went on behind Hal's eyes. He rested his chins in his hand and nodded, creating a mesmerizing ripple effect— flab quivering like fleshy layers of Christmas gelatin.

"Want ta see that fella, I reckon?"

"Who in the hell told you that?"

"Well, it's fairly obvious, isn't it? Got all gooey on that shoot at the drive-in, and Bridge told me ya had yer first date there. Young Mr. Henry filled in the blanks."

"I'm not gooey! And by the way, I *didn't* do it with him in my father's car, thank you very much."

"Ah," Hal scoffed, "and the Pope doesn't shit in the woods."

What?

"Don't quit your day job, Hal."

"Admit it, love, ye want to rekindle an old flame. Nothin' wrong with that."

"Yeah, well, it would be nice to see an old friend."

"Still a bit starry, eh?"

"No."

"Really?"

"No."

Hal chuckled. "Didn't think so, love. OK, so go to yer reunion. You officially have the night off."

"You're giving me *another* night off? Really?"

"Really. I'll hold down the fort."

"You think you can?"

"A one-handed chimp coulda done it the last time, love. All I did all bloody night was pull beers and uncork wine bottles."

"That doesn't speak well of my job security, Hal. You make me sound so useless."

"Well, yer a woman, love. Kidding! I'm kidding. Jesus and Mary, don't hit me. Help! Anyone! Protect me from the wrath of the Great Red one!"

"You're a jerk, Hal."

"And then some, Miss Nina." He chuckled breathlessly as I swatted at him with a dishrag. "OK. Uncle. Uncle! I'm goin' fer a Scotch."

"We don't have any, Hal, you know that."

"We don't have any behind the *bar*, Carrot Top." He winked. "I'm talkin' 'bout me own private stash, in me desk upstairs. See you in a few hours. I'm hittin' the bloody bottle."

With a great sigh, Hal heaved himself from the stool and made his way toward the tiny staircase leading up to his office, tucked behind a shabby curtain in a corner of the room. Don't know how he fits himself in there. Or gets up the stairs without kicking it on the way. I always have to remind myself to check the stairwell for a felled fat man if he's been absent for more than an hour.

Ben made his usual beeline for the bar when his set was over, but he didn't even glance at the beer I'd set out for him.

"Hal wasn't trying to talk you into that contest, was he?" he asked.

"A little."

"Well, you're not going to do it, are you?"

"My reunion is on the same night."

"OK, good."

Why is that good?

"Why do you seem so relieved by that, Henry?"

"Oh, you know"—he fiddled with his sleeve uncomfortably—"I just know how much you hate being onstage. Didn't want Hal to haggle you too much. Besides, I know how much you want to see Jacob."

Ben Henry, as near and dear as he is to me, is the most self-centered, arrogant, narcissistic man I have ever met in my entire life. No complaints here; it's why we get along so well. But, in all of the years of symbiosis, of banter, of giggling and collaborating, not once, not *once*, has he expressed concern at the prospect of someone giving me a hard time. He relishes it, actually. Likes to see what I'm made of. So this newfound concern is obviously of great suspicion.

"You're afraid I'll win, aren't you?"

"What? No. Not that you couldn't, I guess, but no, I'm not *afraid*. Why would I be *afraid*? That's stupid."

"You *are*, Ben. You're afraid that I'll win and suddenly you won't be the fresh-faced little darling of Bellyaches any more."

He muttered something that I couldn't hear.

"What was that?"

"I *said*," he grumbled, "that you couldn't win anyway, because you'll probably choke like you always do onstage."

"That's fucked up, Ben."

"What? It's true."

"And what do you mean, like I *always* do onstage? When have you ever seen me go onstage?"

"You must have, at some point, or you wouldn't be so adamantly afraid of it. What happened, anyway? Get booed? Did your pants fall off?"

"Why are you being such a bitter prick?"

"I'm not."

"You *are*."

"I'm sorry, I'm just trying to be honest."

"Well, it's terrific to know that my alleged best friend is so supportive."

"Supportive? I've been *so* supportive! I've been talking to you about Jacob all night! Why are you looking at me like that? You're not *actually* thinking of entering this stupid contest?"

"Well, I wasn't until about three seconds ago."

"You're not serious," Ben snorted. "You can't be. You're serious? You look serious. Oh man, Nina, that's just a bad idea."

"Why? Why is my entering a comedy competition such a bad idea?"

"Well, first of all, you said it yourself; your reunion is that night."

"So? Maybe this is more important."

"But I thought you wanted to see Jacob?"

"Who said that?"

"*You* did! And why else would you even dream of going? You don't care about how anyone else from high school turned out."

True.

"OK," I said, "but maybe I should forget about reliving the past and actually do something. You know, maybe it's time to get on with my life."

Ben snorted. "Get on to where? There?" He pointed at the stage. "You honestly consider *that* to be moving *on* with your life? That's kinda *sad*, Kurtz."

"I don't think you're getting it. But I can't explain it."

"OK," Ben sighed, "so you want to get on with your life, and you think that getting up onstage with a bunch of wannabe comics will help you do it. Fine, be my guest."

"I didn't realize I needed your permission."

"I just don't want to have to nurture you out of some deep blue funk because the night didn't go as successfully as you planned."

"Well, that's very thoughtful of you."

"You know what I mean."

"I do?"

"You're my friend. I don't want to see you be disappointed."

"I have a feeling that, come November ninth, I'm going to be disappointed in myself no matter what I choose to do."

"Why?"

"Well"—I let out a long, shaky breath—"let's say I enter the contest. If I don't do very well, I'll be disappointed. If I *don't* enter, I'll miss the only relatively comfortable shot I have at getting over this whole insecurity thing, and be disappointed. If I go to my reunion and see Jacob, and he doesn't want anything to do with me, I'll be disappointed. If I go to my reunion and see Jacob, and then we make out under the buffet table, I'll feel like I'm living in the past instead of trying to move forward with my life. And I'll be disappointed. There's no winning."

"Why don't you just stay home and skip everything?"

"Now that's just stupid."

"True. So why not do both?"

"Huh?"

"Come here, do the contest, leave for the reunion. Or, vice versa, go to the reunion for a little while, then come back here and do the contest."

"Can't."

"Why?"

"The reunion is a harbor cruise. It leaves from Long Wharf at seven, doesn't dock again until after midnight."

"Shit. Well, you've got some thinking to do, huh?"

"Everyone keeps telling me that."

"Serious business, Nina. Do you choose past, or do you choose future? Or do you choose nothing, therefore, choosing inertia? The present, forever?"

"My, you're terribly philosophical."

"Why thank you."

"I was being sarcastic. That was the cheesiest thing I've ever heard. Have you been watching *Passions*?"

"I make a good point, Kurtz. Think about it. Let's say you choose to come here and compete. Whether or not you win, you're still 'getting on with your life,' as sad as I think that is."

"Why is that sad? *You* perform here."

"We can talk about my issues another time. This is about you."

"Wow, Ben, I don't think I've ever heard you say that before."

He ignored me. "And say you choose the reunion? That *could* be construed as choosing the past, but it could actually help you move forward, too, right? You see the former love of your life, you reminisce a little, maybe you get back together, maybe you don't. Either way, he helps you see what you did right with him, just like you were hoping. Maybe he gives you the confidence to have a successful dating career."

"You can make a career out of dating?"

"I'm pretty sure Ben Affleck did it before he finally settled down."

"Oh yeah. OK."

Crap. Ben *did* make a few good points, though I'd never admit that out loud. One thing's for sure; I can't just ignore November 9. I'd be out of my mind to choose inertia. And my mother would throttle me with her rosary.

"Maybe I can get Hal to move the contest," I said.

"I seriously doubt it. That man is *desperate* to make something happen."

Hmm. Maybe I should be, too.

Nine

October flew by awkwardly; kind of an airborne ostrich. Autumn is my favorite season, and I'm never more satisfied with being a Bostonian than when the trees begin to blush vivid hues of crimson and tangerine. It's around this time of year that I relish my night job; I can spend the days strolling through the Public Garden, savoring the crunch of leaves beneath my shoes, filling my lungs with crisp, cold air and my belly with spiced apple cider.

This year, though, I'd been preoccupied.

Change had been swirling all around me; Hal hired a contractor to begin renovations on the comedy club. Two of my regular perches retired to the Carolinas, to condos right up the beach from each other. Ben was "seeing" the mysterious bouncy-haired girl on a regular basis, whatever that meant.

I had yet to make a decision about November 9.

Jacob had called once since the first call, to let me know that he was leaving on a month-long extreme backpacking expedition. Sounds extremely uncomfortable to me, but hey, I'm not a mountain man.

He said that he couldn't wait to see me.

Ben and I weren't spending much time together, besides

seeing each other at work and making some quick conversation. He was always on his cell phone; chatting away, I imagine, with his lady friend. He didn't sit for his post-gig beer anymore, but would shoot me a happy wink and a salute before heading out the door, leaving me with Hal, a few drunks, and a whole lot of free time. I missed the little bugger.

I did manage to con him into accompanying me out one Sunday night; I launched a sneak attack about ten days in advance, and guilted him into it.

On the first of November, I trudged in to work to find Ben roosting on a bar stool, daydreaming chin in hand, sighing poetically from time to time. It was sickening. I put up with it while I turned on the cash register, set up my bar, stocked my clean glassware and cocktail napkins. When I had no more distractions, I put a stop to his lovesick nonsense by pinching him on the arm.

"Ow! What was that for?"

"You look like a moping teenager! Go somewhere else if you don't want to talk to me!"

"You're working! You shouldn't be talking, anyway."

"Are you going to narc on me?"

"No," he sighed. "Oh. Hey, do you still want to go to Jaime's rock show thingy tomorrow night?"

"I guess. Why, change your mind?"

"No."

"Did you tell the mysterious bouncy-haired girl that you were free?"

"No."

"Really?"

"All right, I told her I *might* be free."

"Aaaaah."

"Well, I didn't know if you still wanted to go."

"Mmmmm."

"Obviously I'm not going to break my plans with you to go out with a girl."

"Oh?"

"I'm not like that."

"No?"

"No."

"She has bouncy hair, Ben."

"So?"

"And she's mysterious."

"So?"

"And you loooooove her."

"No I don't."

"Hmmmm?"

"I might love her a little."

"Hmmmmm?"

"Stop. I told you I'd go to this thing, so I'll go. But if you keep busting my balls I might change my mind. I'm not *that* hard up to see your roommate stuffed into pleather."

Oh God, I didn't even think about what she might be wearing.

For a mouse, Jaime's a weasel. She's got this crafty approach to sucking people into her weird little world. Like social quicksand. *Suuuuuuuck.* This time, she chumped me into attending some gig that her band is playing at a punk dive in Allston.

It was a stealthy attack; it gets an A+ for effort. I came into the living room on a weekend morning to find Jaime curled up in a fuzzy pink blanket on the couch, feet swathed in panda slippers and sticking straight out, à la Lily Tomlin's Edith Ann. Her favorite guitar (black Stratocaster, shaped like a skull) was perched in her lap, and she plucked at it listlessly.

"Hey Jaime," I yawned, fresh out of bed and itching for caffeine.

"Hiiii," she sighed.

Ignore her, I told myself. I know trawling for attention when I hear it. *Head for the coffee and ignore her.*

I nearly made it to the kitchen before I heard the first sniffle, then a tiny little mew, like a lonely kitty. At first I thought it *was* Kitty, so I went on my sluggish way. But the mew came again, then the sound morphed into banshee yowls.

Oh for crying out loud. I'm no good with emotions, especially in the morning, but I can't just let a girl sit there and cry. Damn my Catholic empathy.

"Jaime?" I backtracked cautiously into the living room. "Jaime, are you OK?"

"Oh," she choked, making a half-assed effort to curtail her wails, "I'm fine."

"You sure?"

"Really. Really, I'm . . . I'm fiiiiiine. *Waaaaahahaaaaaaaa.*"

"Jaime, you're not fine. Jaime, you're getting snot on my couch. Hold on a sec . . . um, here. Here, take this napkin."

"Thank *yooooooou.*"

She blew her nose. It bellowed, like the trumpet of a horny goose; the same honk my father's stuffy sinuses make. It's mortifying in quiet restaurants.

I waited to see if she'd start crying again, but she just stared at the guitar in her lap and hiccupped.

"So, uh . . ." I began, "do you, um, want to talk about it?"

That's what my mother always asks me when I cry. I tend to take my cues from her when trying to deal with other people's emotional crises. Mom seems to know what she's doing.

"Oh, it's no big deal." Jaime sniffed. "It's just . . . well . . . *waahaaahaaaaaaa.*"

Frankly, my brain was making the same noise, for lack of sweet caffeine.

"Well, if you're not ready to talk, I'm just going to grab a cup of—"

"*Ihaffagiganobudyshcooooomin!*"

What?

"What?"

"*Ihaffagigannobudyshcoooooooooooominnnnnnn!*"

"One more time?"

"*Ihaffagigan—*"

"Jaime. Jaime, slow it down for me, OK? I can't understand a goddamned word you're saying. Just breathe for a second. Ready? In . . . aaaaand out. Good, do it again. Innnn . . . aaaaaand . . . out. Better? OK?"

Jaime followed my lead for a minute, shaking a little but otherwise all right.

"Where's Kitty?" she gulped.

Probably hiding under my pillow, waiting for me to crawl back into bed and let my guard down so he can gouge a chunk out of my juicy flesh with his creepy little needle teeth.

"Kitty? I don't know. Hmm. Um. Maybe he's taking a nap in your room? We probably shouldn't bother him."

"Will you go get him for me?"

"*Me*? Go get the cat *now*? Shouldn't we let him rest a little? I'd hate to disturb him; I mean, he only got seventeen hours of sleep yesterday."

"Kitty always makes me feel better. I just want to hold him and snugglllle. *Waaaaaaaaaaaaaaaah.*"

"OK, OK! I'll go get Kitty. Just . . . stop crying, OK?"

I left my roommate in a heap on the couch and tiptoed cautiously toward the bedrooms, trying in vain to keep the ancient floor from creaking beneath my bare tootsies. *Heeeeere, you evil Kitty.*

No evil Kitty in the hallway.

Creak.

No evil Kitty in the bathroom.

No evil Kitty in the linen closet.

Creeeeeeeak.

No evil Kitty in Jaime's room.

I was running out of places to look. My hunt for the evil Kitty hit way too close to a horror flick—the kind where you *know* the jaded, knife-wielding mutant is hiding behind a door, waiting to feast upon the flesh of Jennifer Love Hewitt as soon as she retreats to the seemingly empty room and sighs with relief.

No evil Kitty in my room.

Creeeeeeeeeeeeeak.

No evil Kitty in my clo—AAAAAHHHHHHHHHHHH-HHH!

Evil Kitty! Evil Kitty in my closet! Evil Kitty clamped onto my toe! Let go of my foot, evil Kitty! LET GO OF MY FOOT, EVIL KITTY!

In a flash, I snapped my leg towards the ceiling, kicking frantically while the cat gnawed my big toe like a meatsicle. Son of a bitch, son of a fucking bitch, it wouldn't let go! I shook my leg faster, faster, faster, hopping toward the wall on my Kitty-less foot so I'd have something to hold onto, something to thrash the man-eating feline against if it came to that. Let. Go. Evil. KITTY!

"Did you find him?" I heard Jaime call from the living room.

"Uhh-hnnnnng." I could barely get a sound through my lips, the pain in my foot was so searing, otherwise I would have cried out for help, or perhaps, warned Jaime that her beloved pet was about to get its skull crushed in if only I could hop over to the cast iron candlesticks my mother had given me for Christmas two years ago.

"Kitty! Come see Mummy, wittle ittle Kitty boo!"

At the sound of Jaime's voice calling from the living room, Kitty's ears perked up, though by no means did the little bastard release my toe from his jaws of death.

"Kitty! Mummy has a treaty weaty for you! Come and see!"

"Yeah, you little shit monster," I managed to hiss, still trying to shake him off. I was starting to feel dizzy. "Go see your goddamned Mummy and get a goddamned treaty weaty."

"Mmmm, smell those liver treats! Wouldn't you like a nice wittle wiver tweat? What are you two doing in there? Playing? That so nice of Auntie Nina to pway with my wittle Kitty! Come here, wittle Kitty. Come see Mummy on the couch!"

Over the intense pounding of my heart and the hum of adrenaline hauling ass through my bloodstream, I could hear Jaime shaking a bag of treats. Kitty heard it, too, because with a pissy little howl he finally released my toe and scampered from the room, tail swishing.

Oh sweet Jesus. I looked down at my toe, gushing blood and already an angry shade of purple.

"There's my Kitty witty! There's Mama's big boy!"

Mama's big boy has some big fucking choppers. I wiped the blood from the surface of my toe and discovered two perfect puncture marks, an inch apart. Instantly, two bubbles of blood gurgled to the surface.

I limped back toward the kitchen, cursing to high heaven under my breath and averting my eyes as I passed by my roommate and her flesh-eating fluffball. I knew if I looked at Kitty anytime soon, I was likely to tie him to the ceiling fan by his tail and play Mexican Fiesta. Naturally, I nearly made it to coffee AGAIN when Jaime started crying. Again.

"Jaime," I gritted my teeth and tried not to pounce, "are you going to tell me what's wrong, or am I going to have to lose another toe?"

"*Ihaffagigan—*"

"Yes, Jaime, I got that part earlier. *Ihaffagigandnobuddysh-commin.* Now, could you translate that to English, please, because I have *no* idea what the fuck you're saying, and I *haven't* had any coffee, and it's *nine* in the morning, and now I'm *bleeding* from my fucking *toe.* Help me *out* here."

She took a deep breath and let it out slowly.

"I'm sorry. It's just that I'm playing a gig next weekend, and everybody in my band has a bunch of people coming, and the club is kind of a big deal for the cover-band scene—"

(There's a cover-band *scene*?)

"—and none of my friends can be there, and my family won't come near the place, and Wade is going to be at a tattoo convention in Cleveland—"

"Who's Wade?"

"My new boyfriend."

"You have a new boyfriend?"

"Yeah."

"That's cool. What does he do?"

"He's a fire-eater with that traveling sex circus that came to town in September."

Of course he is.

"Anyway," Jaime whined, "he's out of town, and I don't know if I can nail my licks if I don't have anybody in the audience, and it's really important to me, and Nina, can you please come, please?"

"Nina? Nina who? Nina *me*?"

"It would mean so much to me if you could be there. I just need to know that I can look out and see a friendly face."

"I don't know how friendly my face will be, Jaime, your cat just sucked half the juice out of my damn toe."

"Did you do that? You bad Kitty witty. Auntie Nina doesn't like to pway wike dat."

Kitty, very busy getting his chin stroked by his foolishly doting human parent, rolled on his back to expose his fat belly, which Jaime promptly began scratching.

"Anyway," she turned back to me, "I know you've probably got big plans—"

"I probably have to *work*, Jaime. It's something I do every night."

"But the gig is on Sunday. That's your night off, right?"

"When, this Sunday? Sunday I have plans with Ben. We haven't hung out in ages."

"Oh, Ben would love this kind of thing! He'll have a great time."

"Ben? At a rock show? I'm talking about *Ben*. You know, goofy guy, big ears, not a cool bone in his skinny body?"

Tears welled in Jaime's eyes again, and son of a bitch if she wasn't sticking out her lower lip like a five-year-old, or a sorority girl trying to flirt with a senior.

"I know we're not that close, Nina, but it would mean so much to me if y'all came, and I think it would be really special if we could start, you know, becoming a part of each other's lives!"

"Jaime . . . I'm not very . . . good at being part of people's lives."

"No, that's not true, Nina. I can tell, you're such a good friend to Ben, and . . . I'm sure you hang out with other people. I wish I had a close friend like that, someone who always wanted to spend time with *meeeeeeee*."

"Jaime. What about Wade?"

"*Waaadedoshnthavetimeformmeeeeeeee.*"

"Will you stop crying? For God's sake, will you stop crying if I say that I'll go? Oh my God, I'll go, OK? Just . . . calm down. You're soaking the cat."

Aaaaarg. My only night off down the tubes. At least this time there wouldn't be any thong-clad vixens draped over machinery. So I guessed.

I had to beg Ben to come with me, and I'm pretty sure he only agreed because, as I spent a few minutes *gently* reminding him, he forgot my birthday last year.

Ow. My toe still hurt, dammit. Maybe after Jaime left for the club that night, I'd dope Kitty up on catnip and invite Paul to bring his Rottweilers over for a visit.

"Nina? Earth to Nina."

"What?" Ben was snapping his fingers in my face and looking annoyed. "Oh, sorry."

"Thinking about me naked?"

"No, about exacting my revenge on Jaime's malicious voodoo toe-biter. What were you asking me?"

Ben rolled his eyes. "It's a cat, Nina. It's more afraid of you than you are of it."

"Could you let him know that, before I lose another digit?"

"You're such a wuss. Anyway, you haven't heard a damned word I've said, have you?"

"Just that last part. Ask me again."

"Where do you think I should take Samoa for our one-month anniversary?"

"Who?"

"Samoa. The bouncy-haired girl."

"Her name is Samoa?"

"So?"

"Why does that word sound familiar? Isn't that a kind of sled dog?"

"No, that's a Samoyed."

"Wait, no, it's a Girl Scout cookie."

"What?"

"Yeah yeah yeah, you know, those crispy ones with the coconut and caramel and chocolate stripey things. Man, those are the best."

"Nina, Samoa is a country. Two countries, actually, there's Samoa and American Samoa."

"Are you sure it's not a cookie?"

"Come on."

"So she's named after a country? Is she, like, a Hilton?"

"Is this what it's going to be like when you meet her?"

"You're going to let me meet her?"

"I don't know why I'm even asking you. You never even go on dates unless someone sets you up."

"Excuse me? That is patently untrue."

"I don't count."

"That wasn't a date, Ben, that was a disaster."

"Whatever, you totally fell victim to my smooth moves."

"If by smooth moves you mean the fact that I spent the next three days trying to dislodge chunks of your tongue from between my molars, then I guess you could say I was a victim of something."

"Fuck you."

"Besides, I've been out with other guys since then, thank you very much."

"Aaaah, yes. Rousing success stories, no? More charming princes Grimm could never conjure."

"Did you just make a joke without my help? That's not allowed."

He was right, though, dumb bastard. The few-and-far-between pathetic dates I'd allowed myself to be set up on had emblazoned themselves in the pages of global dating history as some of the most awkward, icky evenings ever experienced. Ever. By humans.

I shifted gears.

"Can you be at my place at six tomorrow? I thought we could grab dinner before Jaime's thing."

"Yeah, that's fine."

"Cool."

"Hey!" Ben snapped his fingers. "I thought of someone!"

"What are you talking about? Thought of who?"

"Remember, a little while ago, when we were talking about Jacob and you said that no guys are ever into you?"

"Yeah?"

"I thought of a guy who was into you!"

"Ben, that was a *month* ago! It's taken you *this* long to think of a man who found me attractive? Oh, come on. Why don't you just hang the noose for me?"

"I'm serious! My friend Bill, from home, remember? Tall guy, blond, lots of earrings? You guys went out. Whatever happened with that?"

"He stood me up, Ben."

"He did?"

"Don't you remember? We went out that one time, and then we made plans again but he never showed, and never called. You made up some lame excuse about how he had the flu, but then you slipped up about it."

"Oh yeah! I forgot about that. Yeah, you scared the hell out of that guy."

"Shocking."

"I keep telling you, Nina, intimidation factor is high with funny chicks."

"It's a curse."

"Eh, don't worry about it. You'll find someone."

"Are you kidding? At this rate, I'll never date again. One boyfriend every decade? I'll be lucky if I get to reproduce before the next cycle of evolution!"

Who needs to date, anyway, when you can take your khaki-addicted stand-up comic buddy to a dank, moldy pit of stench, sin and rock? Watching Ben twitch in the presence of greasy, shaggy-haired pincushions was better than any movie I've ever seen.

On Sunday night we arrived at the club, an underwhelming and incognito basement dump called the Sweat Shop, with an hour to kill before Jaime's gig started. It took us a while to find it; the street address was some alleyway smushed between a triple-X movie theater and a family planning clinic. The club was in the bowels of the alley; the only light came from the purple neon sign that buzzed above a graffiti-covered door. Half the letters on the sign were burned out, so it actually read, THE WE T HO . Nice.

The doorman looked me up and down for much longer than necessary, even longer than what would be an acceptably creepy amount of time, and waived the cover charge when I told him I was a natural redhead, chapped lips twisting into a jack-o'-lantern grin. He licked his chops. His tongue was forked.

I was halfway down the rotting entryway staircase before I realized that Ben was being held at the door.

"Oh my fucking Lord," he panted when he was finally allowed in a minute later. "Where are we? I mean, where the *fuck* are we? Are you sure this is the right place? Your nerdy little roommate is playing a gig *here*? This is hell. I mean, we are actually in the pits of hell right now."

"Shut up, Ben," I muttered.

"What's that smell?" he continued, jackass that he is. "Is that roasting flesh? Do I actually smell *roasting flesh*?"

"Shut *up*, Ben."

"Do you know, I actually had to bribe that doorman to let me in? He told me I was dressed like his grandmother's demented old man, and there was no way he was gonna let a chump like me hone in on that fine piece of red ass. He called you a *fine piece of red ass*. I had to slip him twenty bucks! Plus the cover! Un-fucking-believable."

"He thought my ass was fine? Maybe I should go talk to him."

"If you leave me alone again, I will cut you. I will carve you like a goddamned turkey. Don't even think about it, Nina. If you leave my side, you are absolutely, unequivocally dead."

"Stop using big words. You'll scare the punks away."

"Is that what it takes? Repugnant. Fallacious. Inexorably execrable."

"Do you want a drink before Jaime's set starts?"

"Indubitably."

I took my sheltered best friend by the hand and started to squeeze past two mohawked biker babes who were making out in the middle of the staircase.

"You mean we have to go downstairs?"

"That's where the club is, Ben."

"Further into the depths of Hades?"

"Are you going to whine all night, or do you think you could try and get through this like a big boy?"

"Will you buy me a beer?"

"Will that shut you up?"

"Probably."

"Then yes. Come on. Mind the lesbians."

"Believe me, I don't."

"See? There's something here for everyone."

We made it through the Sapphic gauntlet only to wind our way through a series of beefy, denim-vested giants that lurked at the bottom of the stairs, comparing tattoos and brandings while slamming down cheap domestic brews. Beyond them, a dimly lit hallway plastered with decrepit posters stretched into the darkness. I could hear a band starting to warm up, so I picked up the pace, Ben trembling at my side with each and every step.

"Are you *scared* or something, Henry?"

"This place is a fucking madhouse."

"What tipped you off? The fact that patches of the floor are on fire, or the dude back there with a bottle opener hanging from his cheek piercing?"

"Actually, I think it was the guy with the word 'skull-fucker' tattooed on the side of his head."

"That was a chick."

"Get out."

"Didn't you see her boobs?"

"Who could look at her boobs? I was too busy trying not to snag my shirt on the safety pins shoved through her arms!"

The hallway opened into a cavernous area featuring a shaky-looking bar on the right, sundry platforms and railings, a few rickety chairs (that were likely for bashing, not sitting) and a teeny-tiny stage. That took me by surprise; the performance space wasn't much bigger than the one at Bellyaches, and there's not a lot of movement involved with stand-up. Don't most musicians like to rock out? Move a little? Kick things, lick each other, bound around the stage like newly freed lab monkeys?

The band up there wasn't Jaime's, so I led Ben to the bar. Maybe if I poured a few drinks down his throat, he'd calm down a little. My God, can he be lame. Not that I'd care to spend every waking minute at "The we t ho ," but I wasn't going to pee my pants about the fact that the bartender had more holes in her face than there are freckles on an Irishman. She was also bigger than Dublin.

"I'll take a Pabst, please, and my friend will have a . . . Ben?"

"What? Oh, I'll have a Guinness."

The portly pincushion snorted. "None of that fancy shit here. Domestic or nothin'. Or we got whiskey."

"Irish whiskey?" said Ben.

"What the fuck you think?"

"I think I'll take a double."

"Rock on, cutie." She looked at him with new appreciation and, dare I say, a bit of a crush? I gave him a nudge when she turned her back to pour my beer, and he blushed.

"Looks like Samoa has some competition, *cutie*," I teased softly.

"Shhh," he hissed.

"Who are you guys here to see tonight?" The bartender turned back to us, twirling the whiskey bottle around in her porky fingers a few times before tossing it in the air, catching it behind her back, and shooting an amber stream into a rocks glass.

"My roommate is in the Bowie cover band. How'd you learn how to do that?" I watched her flip the bottle from behind her back and catch it with her index finger, allowing it to balance for a few seconds before tossing it into her other hand and replacing it under the bar.

"Oh, once you've been bartending for a year or so, you get the hang of it. A fucking quadriplegic bunny could do it."

Ben nudged me this time, snickering into his drink. Ass. Sure, a quadriplegic bunny could do it if it worked at a *bar* with *liquor*. That came in liquor *bottles*. Then it could *practice*. Sheesh. I hate my job.

"The Bowie cover band. Which one is that? Oh, Ziggy and the China Girls. Right on. They're pretty rad."

"Really?"

"Didn't you say it's your roommate's band?"

"Yeah, but I've only seen them play once before."

"So you know what I'm talking about."

"I guess."

"The lead guitarist kicks some fucking ass, man! I'd totally have her kids if she had a cock."

Niiiice.

"Um, I'll pass that on. How much do we owe you?"

"On the house, Red."

"Oh. Thanks. Are you sure?"

"I like your dork friend."

"Who, this guy?" (Where the hell did he go? Oh, there he is, halfway across the room, watching the band onstage.) "Uh, that guy?"

"Yeah. He your old man?"

"Oh no."

"Got a lady?"

"A couple."

"Yeah he does. Catch like that. I bet under all that khaki he's got abs like a fucking toboggan."

What does that even mean?

"Um. Well, thanks for the drinks."

"Rock on, sister. Tell your roommate she's the shit. And tell your friend there I think he's something special."

"Way to skip out on the tab, butt munch," I muttered to Ben when I joined him in the middle of the club.

"What? Oh, sorry, I was just checking these guys out. What do I owe you?"

"Just get the next one."

We bobbed our heads in silence while four dudes in purple hoopskirts ripped a hole in the atmosphere with terrible, terrible music. It took me a minute to realize that the distorted slop pouring from the tiny amp on the edge of the stage was actually a hard-core rendition of "Afternoon Delight." We were the only people in the club, though, who weren't thrashing and jerking around like freshwater salmon on the sun-soaked deck of a pontoon. I guess musical talent is only a small fraction of the highly specialized craftsmanship that is the cover band.

Of the songs I could recognize, the band managed to butcher "Turning Japanese," "Groove is in the Heart," "Fly Me to the Moon" (what the?) and "Kiss the Girl" from *The Little Mermaid*. That's right, *The Little Mermaid*. Agony. The rest of the shit they played could have been experimental Russian pop music for all I could tell, but these guys seemed about as cultured as fraternity pledges. All the while they stood, skirt to skirt on the tiny stage, cramping each other's ironically fem style while trying to earnestly rock.

It took four shots of whiskey to get Ben to tap his right foot; two more and I suspected he'd actually begin enjoying himself. Ben's a pretty happy drunk, but I'd have to cut him off soon if I didn't want him to pass out Elvis style in a bathroom stall by the time Jaime got onstage. He's been known to do that after a few spirits.

The hoopskirted men finally gave our ears a break, and there was a minute or two of bustle on the stage while tech dudes in black T-shirts fiddled with wires and things. One of them hauled a basket of coconuts to the already cramped platform, followed by a palm tree fashioned from green plastic soda bottles and rusty scrap metal.

"Did we stumble onto a low-budget production of *South Pacific*?" I whispered to Ben.

"I don't know," he giggled drunkenly, "but if some fat lady starts singing 'Bali Hai,' we're outta here."

The truth turned out to be far more aurally painful, as we discovered when the next band took the stage; dubbed Sloop John Apathy, they had, according to the lead singer, combined their penchant for beach music with a passion for all things goth and created a bitchin' new hybrid of sun, fun and destruction.

"Are you cats and kittens ready to GET the fuck DOOOOOOWN?" the frontman screamed at the top of his lungs, his gritty baritone the only thing in the room louder than the orange Hawaiian shirts the band was sporting.

"I'll be at the bar," Ben slurred, off like a shot before I could stop him. I was about to follow when—

OOOF!

Something slammed into my stomach.

I staggered backward, nearly knocking over a crowd of spiffy-looking mod kids (probably BC students trying desperately to unearth their inner hipster) dressed to the nines in what had to be pseudo-vintage Urban Outfitters. One of the girls shrieked as I bumped her elbow and the can of Schlitz she was clutching spattered a few flecks of foam onto her striped off-the-shoulder shirt.

"Oh my God!" she sputtered, "like, watch the fuck out!"

"Chill, Vanessa," said a boy in Buddy Holly glasses and a velvet stovepipe suit. "Are you all right, miss? That coconut came from out of nowhere."

That . . . what?

I looked at the ground.

I'll be damned. There *was* a coconut lolling on the floor

by my feet. And, son of a bitch, another was whizzing toward my head.

I dove sharply to the left, narrowly missing another snooty mod bitch who was screaming into a tiny cell phone with one hand and clutching a pack of French cigarettes in the other.

It took me a minute to recover, and as I turned toward the stage to figure out what the hell was going on, I heard a thud and a yelp from a few feet to my left. Then the same thing, this time from the front of the club.

The singer from Sloop John Apathy was crooning into the mike, swiveling his hips and reaching into the basket at his feet.

Wait, wasn't that thing overflowing before with—

Aha.

I followed the tropical ammunition with my eyes, and watched as it clocked some dude in the side of the head. Surprisingly, he didn't get knocked unconscious, or even seem to mind. Instead, he threw his hands into the air, fists pumped in victory, and let loose a rebel yell.

"YEAH!!" the pelting victim screamed. "I'm COCO LOCO!"

The singer threw back his head and laughed, a wicked, guttural Kris Kringle laugh. "That's what I'm talkin' about! Let's get KAH-RAAAAZY!"

He chucked one more coconut into the crowd and smoothed his ratty blond hair back with one hand, closing his eyes and drawing in a deep, cleansing breath.

"When some mothafucker tries to put me down . . ." he began.

The crowd erupted with cheers.

"And says his school is great. I tell him right away, FUCK

YOU BUDDY, ain't you heard of my school? It's numba one in the state!"

Mark my words, Jaime will pay for this. Pay for this in blood. The blood of a kitty.

"So be true to your SCHOOOOOOOOOL . . ."

"RA RA RA RA SIS BOOM BA!" came a drunken cry from the right side of the club. Oh fantastic. Audience participation. My favorite. Where the hell is Ben when you need him? I could use a partner in mockery right about now.

"RA RA RA RA SIS BOOM BAAAAAAAAAAAA!" the goon cried again. OK, OK, we get it! You like this song, you, too, are true to your—

Oh sweet Jesus. It's Ben. It's Ben making the cheerleader noises.

He was leaning against the bar, being fawned over by the fat bartender, who kept pouring streams of whiskey directly into his mouth.

"Ninaaaa!" he caught me staring and straightened up, whiskey dribbling down his chin. "Nina, comeonovahere and meet my new buddy—whashournameagin?—Pepper. Come and shay hi ta Pepper."

I scurried over to the bar as quickly as I could, shoving leering punks from my path so I could prevent my idiot best friend from letting Pepper put anything else down his throat—namely, her tongue.

"Ben." I finally made it over there, a few ass grabs later. "Ben, I'm getting tired. Let's just get out of here, OK? No, no, no, you don't need another shot of—could you stop spoon-feeding him liquor, please?"

"Pepper'sh my buddy." Ben's head was lolling against Pepper's beefy breast, his chin in hand as he closed his eyes and swayed, unsuccessfully, to the music.

"Yes, Pepper's a very nice lady, but it's time to go home now."

"I'm not drunk. You think Iiiiii'm drunk. I'm not. Be-sidesh, Jaime'sh band hashn't played yet."

Damn, he was right.

"OK, Ben, but as soon as they're done, let's go."

As if on cue, Sloop John Apathy screeched to a halt, and the singer hocked a huge loog into the audience, followed by the rest of the coconuts.

"All right, dudes," he screamed hoarsely, dodging a co-conut that was hurled back at him from the bowels of the crowd, "we're outta here, but you should stick around, be-cause up next is, quite possibly, the most righteous cover band in Boston. I hope you mothafuckas are ready to Rock. Out. Give it up, cats and kittens, for the fabulous Ziggy . . . and the CHINA GIRLS!"

The lights went out, and the room seemed to stand ab-solutely still. Suddenly, a single note resonated from the front of the club, then wavered, slowly at first, but then up and down, louder, louder, louder.

"Ground Control to the Sweat Shop . . ." came a raspy whisper, and the club was flooded with purple light.

The stage was dominated by four overwhelmingly awe-some creatures.

Each was clad in intergalactic sex clothes; silver miniskirts, moon boots, spangles, skin hanging out every-where. The lead singer had two yards of tangled, purple curls, ratted out in a gothic halo all around her head. Their keyboard player was seven feet tall, tapping a gigantic plat-form shoe as he prodded the keys with talons to rival an American eagle. To the left, the bassist grooved in her own little world, barefoot and blinding in reflective false eyelashes. The drummer beat his kit with sticks shaped like lightning bolts.

"Where the fuck ish Jaime?" Ben slurred in my ear. "I thought thish wash her band?"

"It is." I whispered back. "But I don't see her. Maybe she decided not to . . . holy shit."

Don't ask me how the Sweat Shop managed this, but suddenly the ceiling opened, and down from the rafters floated a glorious creature, swathed from head to toe in blood-colored rubber replete with millions of rhinestones and orange mullet woven with tinsel, shimmering under the hot stage lights. She panned her head from left to right, snarling while she surveyed the crowd and plucking one luscious note at a time from her guitar; a black, skull-shaped Stratocaster.

It was Jaime.

"No way!" Ben yanked his head from Pepper's pillows and stood at attention in more ways than one.

"Ew, Ben, put that thing away!"

"I told you she was righteous," Pepper smiled, patting my horny friend on the head before moving down the bar to help another customer.

Nobody breathed until Jaime touched down, then the entire crowd went coco loco.

Ziggy and the China Girls proceeded to rock the fuck out.

They launched immediately into "Space Oddity," and I couldn't take my eyes off Jaime. She was tossing out riffs like it was nothing, fingers flying over the frets at the speed of a thousand angry bumblebees. Every once in a while she'd glance at the singer and they'd share a private smile, fueled by each other's energy.

The club was beyond rejuvenated. Punks and mods alike

were jumping up and down, crashing against each other in that universal celebration of musical awesomeness.

Son of a bitch. My roommate is a rock star.

And she *was*. Jaime's playing just got better with every chorus of every song, and she moved around that tiny stage like she owned it, owned the club, owned the very souls of every tattooed drunkard within a ninety-mile radius. She was pouring sweat, the tangerine fright wig whipping around her head in a frenzy.

"Dude," Ben poked me clumsily in the ribs and leaned closer; his breath alone could have gotten me plastered.

"Whoa, Ben. Don't let anyone with matches come within ten feet of you, OK? Damn."

"Shaddup. Dude, that'shyour roommate."

"No kidding."

"Dude."

"Since when do you call me 'dude'?"

"Dude. Shaddup. Dude, Nina. That'shyour roommate."

"We've established this."

"She's fucking awesome."

"I know, Ben."

"She'shsooo hot."

"What? Ben, no, that's the whiskey talking."

"No. No, your roommate ish hot."

"Whatever."

"You're jealoush."

"Shut up."

Ben waved his hand to dismiss me, nearly taking off the nose of the girl standing to his left.

"No, nonononono, you're jealoush becaush your room-mate ish hot, an she can get onstage and you can't."

"Shut UP. I'm not kidding."

He was hitting a nerve, a big, fat, super-sized, pissy, perpetually premenstrual nerve. And, wasted or not, he knew it.

Humph.

I decided to ignore him, turning back to the stage just in time to catch Jaime, still cavorting around, leaning down to slap the outstretched hands of admirers while never missing a note.

She melted into a rich "Ashes to Ashes," and I watched the crowd as it simmered on the brink of going nuts but apparently waiting for some unspoken particular thing, for just the right moment. A delicious tension was building. The band played on.

"Heroes" whet their appetite, "Changes" took the edge off, but it wasn't enough for this bunch of drooling, Bowie-thirsty scavengers. It seemed they needed more.

The singer knew it, too. She was teasing the hungry masses, taunting them, licking her lips in anticipation of satiating the desperate throng.

"You know," she growled to her adoring audience, cocking her head for two or three endless seconds. Jesus, even I was sucked in.

"You know," she said again. "You remind me of someone."

We do?

"You remind me of . . ."

Screams of ecstasy shattered my eardrums.

Well, no wonder.

"Ben, could you back up a few feet if you're going to scream like a little girl?"

"Wooooo!" he shrieked again, oblivious to my pain. "WOOOOOOOOO!"

"Honestly, Ben, it's not Christmas. Tone it down."

"You remind me of . . ."

"THE BABE!" the entire club was on its feet now, all as worked up as Ben, but none quite as drunk.

Am I missing something?

"You remind me of the babe!"

"WHAT BABE?"

"The babe with the power!"

"WHAT POWER?"

The power to hit a homer for the Red Sox? I'm confused.

I turned to Ben, whose eyes were shining like a cocktail of liquid diamonds and sunshine and happiness. Pathetic.

"What is this?"

"Labyrinth." He didn't even look at me, keeping his eyes on the singer as she cooed and swayed.

"What?"

"Thish ish from *Labyrinth*. Let me lishen."

Oh. Oh right! That movie with puppets and Bowie in those alarmingly sexy stretch pants. I saw that. When I was eight.

As I looked around, though, I noticed that every single person in the room, male or female, underage or over the hill, punk or goth or mod or square, was staring at Ziggy and the China Girls just as mushy and starry-eyed as Ben was. Hmm. Did I miss something? Maybe *Labyrinth* was like *Star Trek* for cool kids.

"That's so fucking aweshome," I could hear Ben whisper.

I hated to admit it, but he was right. Jaime's gig was un-believable.

But instead of being uplifted to musical Nirvana with the rest of the crowd, I was depressed, discouraged, dejected, every "d"-word there is. Deliriously dismal.

Obviously, I'm sensitive about the fact that my nerdy, bank-teller roommate lives a secret, double life, moonlight-ing as the hottest thing the Boston underground cover-band music scene has ever witnessed. Obviously, I'm not proud of the fact that I haven't lived up to the expectations of anyone in my family, circle of friends, cache of coworkers or graduating class. Obviously, Ben is right, and I'm jealous of my ass-kicking, superstar roommate. But he doesn't have to keep pointing it out. Shedding light on my petty envy and sheer cowardice certainly isn't going to make me take a flying leap toward doing something with my life. No sirree.

But I'll tell you what it does make me want to do.

"Hey Pepper," I called down the bar. "Give me a triple of whatever this kid is sauced up on."

"You got it, Red," she handed me a shot. "Hey, pumpkin here was telling me that you might be going to your high-school reunion next week. You gonna look all those cheerleader bitches in the face? Stare 'em down? Tell 'em what's what?"

"Frankly, Pepper," I tossed the shot back with a grimace, "I don't know how I'm going to look anyone in the face. I'll take another."

Ten

Naps are underrated. There is no single moment more delicious, more exquisitely feathery and scrumptious than closing your eyes and watching the Technicolor fuzzies dance on the back of your eyelids as sleep creeps in and swaddles you in fleecy happiness. Sometimes, when my head is filled with pudding and my belly still sloshes with late-night cheese dip and backwashed hops, a twenty-minute rendezvous with my squishiest pillow is all I need, and I can face an evening shift with the pluck of a naked chicken.

Of course, it's impossible to snooze when your ears are leaking blood and liquid sanity because your brain is being scraped with an aural cheese grater.

"A-ha make me tonight! Tonight make it right! ATOMIC!!!!!"

"Mrrrreeeeeooowwwww!"

"Ooooh, yeah, sing it you bad kitty! *ATOMIC!!!!!!"*

"MRRRRREEEEEEOOOOOWWWWWW!!!!"

"Yeah! Bad kitty!"

You know, if I didn't know any better, I'd swear up and down there was a sadomasochistic bestial fetish ball being hosted in my bathroom.

Twenty minutes. Twenty minutes, that's all I'm asking.

It was four o'clock on Tuesday, and I had to be at Belly-aches in a little over an hour. Jaime, barely in the door after a long day of fondling other people's money, was completing stage two of her daily shower quota, and so far, the entire seventeen minutes of it was jam-packed with karaoke kitty action.

It was impossible to drown out. By now, I knew from experience that no amount of pillow burrowing could obscure the penetrating sound waves of a hard-rockin' feline and a screechy bank teller.

My respect for the roommate had certainly increased since watching her grab a club's worth of punks by the balls the other night and rock out with a handful of manhood, but quite frankly, I was feeling a little pissy about Jaime's local superstardom. Jealous? Yes. Going to admit it? Hell no.

But hark, what's that? What's that I hear? Could it be that sweet, sweet sound, the sound of silence? Oh good-fucking-glory be. Paul Simon would drop his guitar in a fit of ecstasy.

The singing had stopped.

Sleepy time at last. Here come the fuzzies.

"Tommy used to work on the dooooooocks. La la la . . ."

Enough.

I was out of bed and across the room in two seconds, and threw my door open.

"JAIME!" I bellowed.

The screeching stopped. I heard the water valve shrick to a close.

"Um, yeah?"

"Could. You. Please. Shut. Up. Please? Please just shut the fuck up?"

The latch clicked and the bathroom door opened a smidge, releasing huge wafts of steam and the smells of a two-for-one body-wash sale at CVS.

"I'm sorry, Nina, I didn't—quiet, Kitty! I didn't realize you were home."

"Where else would I be?" I snapped. "I don't go to work for another hour."

"Well, you weren't making any noise."

"That's because I was trying to *sleep*, Jaime."

"Why are you sleeping?"

"I don't *know*, why are you *showering* for the second time in ten hours?"

"I'm sorry," she said again. "I'm done in here anyway. Let me get Kitty to use the potty and I'll make us both a cup of tea, OK?"

"Tea?" I snorted, grumpy. I want a nap! I want a naaaaap!

"I've got a terrific jasmine blend. It'll pep you right up. You go and nap for ten, fifteen minutes, and I'll wake you up when the water's done, OK?"

Humph.

"Fine."

With no more kitty serenade I managed to drift off for thirteen minutes—not an ideal sleep cycle but enough to take the edge off. When Jaime's soft knock came at my door the apartment smelled like springtime in Beijing.

I settled on the couch and let Jaime serve me tea in one of her clunky Garfield mugs. It just didn't seem right, drinking fragrant Chinese tea from anything but the curve of a lady slipper, but I slurped at it anyway.

"Good, huh?" Jaime smiled encouragingly. "This blend has incredible healing powers and cleansing capabilities. It can do for your well-being what no Western medicine could in a hundred years."

"Do you have any sugar?"

"Sugar? Well, yes, but adding that would kind of defeat the purpose."

"It's a little bitter."

"Yes, but can't you taste the essence of purity and restoration?"

"Is that the bitter part?"

Jaime sighed.

"At least use honey in it. I'll get it for you."

The essence of purity and restoration was much more bearable with three squirts from the honeybear.

"So," Jaime smiled again, "I didn't get a chance to thank you for coming to my gig on Sunday! I really appreciated having an audience."

Ah, that explains the essence and the niceness. Reciprocal. Well, one cup of hot flower juice ain't gonna cut it, missy.

"Oh. Yeah, I mean, you seemed to have an audience anyway. You didn't really need me there."

"Yes, but," Jaime took a sip of her tea, "there's something so reassuring about having a familiar face in the audience, even if it's just one. You know, I've had experiences where the crowd just wasn't happy with the songs the band was playing, so we kind of get harassed. Does that happen at the comedy club?"

"All the time. Last week one of the comics nearly lost an eye."

"Really? What happened?"

"Some dickhead in the audience was throwing loose change, and quarters pick up more speed than you'd imagine."

Jaime laughed. "No, really! What really happened?"

"Um, I wasn't kidding."

"Oh. Quarters. Sure, that's pretty terrible."

"You don't look impressed."

"Well," she took another thoughtful slurp of tea, "the last

time we really had any trouble, I ended up losing half my hair. See? I still have a bald spot on the underside here. But that was definitely one of the worst episodes."

"Holy shit!" Jaime had flipped her head upside down and I could see that underneath the top layer, her hair was thin and patchy. "What the hell happened?"

"We were in the middle of 'Heroes' and I guess some guy got really offended by our version. We found out later he used to be in the military. Very sensitive."

"What did he do?"

"Lit a chair on fire and chucked it at me."

"Whaaaat?"

"Yeah. Wouldn't have been too much of a problem, but that night I was trying out a new wig woven mostly from peacock feathers. Very flammable. Pity. Terrific piece. It was on back order with the catalog for*ever*."

"Oh my *God*. Jaime! You could have been killed!"

"Yeah," she sighed. "Wicked, huh? But that's rock 'n' roll."

"I mean, I *guess*."

"You have to do what you love, Nina. Nothing could keep me off that stage. It's like a drug. I always wanted to be a rock star. Bought my first Stratocaster when I was four-teen. But, that's not a very stable life, you know? I think my dad would have had a heart attack if I'd tried to go for music instead of going to business school. And it worked out OK. I have a good balance."

"I didn't realize you were so *serious* about music." (As se-rious as one could be about a David Bowie cover band, I guess.)

"Oh, I am!" Jaime's head bobbed up and down eagerly. "You know, I was voted 'Most Musical' in high school. Played in a few bands, rocked all the dances. When I went to my reunion last year a lot of people were surprised that I hadn't become a musician. Couldn't believe I was in banking."

"Wait, you went to your high-school reunion last year?"

"Yes. You didn't know that?"

"No. You know mine's this week, right?"

"I know! Aren't you excited? You get to see all of your old friends and laugh at how your enemies turned out. Really, fate does some pretty vindictive things."

"No kidding."

"Oh my gosh, you'd be so surprised. Most of the cheerleaders actually got fat!"

"They probably all had babies but forgot to stop eating for two."

Jaime snorted, and essence of purity and restoration spewed onto her bathrobe.

"*Hyuh, hyuh,*" she laughed, not unlike a hyena in heat. "*Hyuh hyuh.* You're so funny! Oh my gosh. That's the one thing I tell all the girls at work about you. My roommate is so funny! Honestly, I don't understand why you're not the one up onstage at that club every night."

"I dunno," I shrugged.

"So where is your reunion going to be? Probably someplace nice. You grew up in Ashford, right?"

"So?"

"Isn't that kind of an affluent town?"

"I guess. But we weren't, you know, *rich* or anything. There were seven of us."

"Really? All boys except you, I bet."

"Oh, I already told you."

"No, no. I can just tell that you grew up around all boys."

How does everybody *know* that? Do I unconsciously exhibit boyish behaviors, like adjusting my crotch or biting my greasy fingernails to the skin? Oh God, do I have some kind of pattern baldness? I patted my hair cautiously. Nope, still all there. What gives?

"How can you tell? Am I just really sloppy or something? I'm sorry; I try not to swear too much. And I'll stop drinking from the carton. But I figured that since I bought the orange juice and you don't really like it that it was OK—"

"Nina!" Jaime laughed, barely missing another tea-spewing snarf attack. "Nothing like that, silly. You're assertive. And not afraid to make jokes. And very outspoken. I figure you had to fight to be heard as a kid, most likely because you were surrounded by boys."

"Huh. Well, it's not some kind of reactionary feminist thing. I've never shaved my head or anything."

"Well, feminist or not, I admire how strong and independent you are. An inspirational woman."

Me? "Um. Thanks."

Is Jaime trying to make out with me? I inched closer to the edge of the couch, ready to bolt in case she pulled out wineglasses or roses or a dental dam. I also sniffed my teacup for traces of Spanish Fly.

"Want some more tea?" she asked. "I'm going to get some."

"NO—ahem—no. No thanks."

"OK. I'll be right back."

I wish there was a potted plant around so I could stealthily dump out my cup of lesbian healing essence.

"So, anyway." Jaime emerged from the kitchen with a fresh, steaming cup. "Where is the reunion?"

"It's on a harbor cruise."

"Ooooh! Like, one of those huge boats that leaves from the Long Wharf and takes you out to sea for a few hours?"

"Yep."

"That's so fun! Go get the invitation! Do you know what you're going to wear? Who are you taking with you? What kind of food are they serving?"

What's the color scheme? Will there be a DJ? What about ponies? Will there be ponies? I could see this going on forever; large functions *are* Jaime's thing. She's a woman obsessed.

"I didn't pay that much attention. I haven't even decided if I'm going to go."

"What? Why? Don't you want to see how terrible everyone's lives have turned out? That's the best part of those things, Nina! You get to feel better than everyone else because you're not a whale trapped in a miserable marriage working a dead-end job."

"Well, two out of three. Although my fat jeans have been feeling a little snug lately. And besides, Bellyaches is having this thing that—"

"Is that the phone? I'll get it. Go find the reunion invitation and bring it out here! I want to see it again. What kind of paper is it printed on?"

"I don't know; the papery kind. It's somewhere in my room."

"Go get it, silly! Hello? Wade! Hey baby, I was hoping you'd call . . . Oh, it was terrific. Nina and her friend showed up and I didn't get nervous at *all*. How's your tongue feeling? Oh . . . uh-huh . . . uh-huh . . . uh-*huh* . . ."

Ew. I left Jaime and her "uh-huh-ing" in the living room and went to my room to sift through the ten thousand piles of crap that have become a fun little morning obstacle course.

"I don't have much time!" I called. "I've got to be at work soon."

"Hold on, babe. That's OK!" she called back.

I found the offending invitation and booklet on my desk, under a shoe that was covered with grimy floor bits from Bellyaches. Ew. Dutifully I pinched them between my fingers and took it to Jaime in the living room, who was, thankfully, wrapping up her lovey-dovey conversation.

"OK babe . . . uh-huh . . . uh-huh . . . I miss you, to! OK . . . Ok, I'll talk to you later . . . OK, 'bye . . . you didn't hang up! . . . No, you hang up first . . . no *you* hang up! . . . No, YOU . . ."

I reached over and took the phone from Jaime, punching the "talk" button with my middle finger.

"There. Hung up. Here's the invite."

Jaime blinked. "Oh. OK, great. This is so cute!" she exclaimed, thumbing through the booklet with a wistful look on her face. Honestly, am I the only person I know who's not feeling nostalgic about *my* high-school reunion? I wish I could just send Jaime in my place.

Hey, that's not a bad idea.

"But you're not in here! Look, it's just—"

"A gray question mark. I know."

"Well, why?"

"Because I didn't fill out the form they sent me."

"But . . . why?"

"I don't know . . . because I didn't have a pen."

"*Hyuh hyuh!* No, but seriously, Nina, why didn't you send them anything? Don't you want all your old friends to know what you're up to?"

"Why does everyone I show this to ask me that? What am I up to? I dropped out of college, I'm tending bar at a crappy little shit hole in the wall, I'm single, I'm cranky. Honestly, I'm not exactly the kind of success story that Ashford High School wants to advertise in their annual PTA booklet."

"Ah," Jaime said, her "ah" a wise, Yoda kind of noise, "I get it now."

Get what?

"What exactly do you 'get,' Jaime?"

"You're ashamed."

"Excuse me?"

"You think there's no way your life could possibly measure up to the lives of everyone else that you used to know, so you're hiding."

"Well, when you put it that way . . ."

"And I overheard you talking on the phone last week, to somebody named Jacob? Sorry, I was looking for Kitty and you were talking in the kitchen. Who is he? I bet he was your high-school boyfriend."

"How the hell did you—"

"I could tell by the look on your face! And you've never talked about him before, and let's face it, you don't usually talk to anybody you've been out on a date with. Don't look embarrassed! We *all* had high-school boyfriends, Nina. True, some of them existed only in our heads, but the fact is that everyone you've ever met, *ever*, has someone from their past that they're simultaneously dying to see and terrified of seeing."

Jesus. When did the cat lady get smart all of a sudden?

"That makes sense," I said to the hands in my lap, my thumbs duking it out over a snagged thread in the pillow I was holding.

"Trust me, I know how it feels," Jaime continued. "More tea? No? Anyway, when I got *my* high-school reunion invitation I was all nervous and giggly about it. On the one hand, I was confident that the lives of at least half the people in the room wouldn't have turned out as well as mine. But then there was the other half of the room, of course."

"Yeah."

"And, like I said, the whole 'Most Musical,' rock-star thing. I kind of felt like a failure because of it."

"Really? But you *do* play in a band!"

"Yeah, but not the way I always wanted to, you know? I mean, banking pays the bills and all, but there are days when I want to throw it all away, hit the road with the band and really tear it up all over the country."

Didn't David Bowie already take that music on the road, though?

"And there was this guy," Jaime blushed a little, "that I always had a crush on, and we kissed at prom. We actually *kissed* at prom; he was there with someone else, and *I* was there with someone else, but prom—so *magical*, you know?"

"I didn't go."

"Really? That's terrible!"

"Why?"

"I don't know; because it's *prom*."

"Jaime, you're starting to sound like a character from a bad teen-movie parody."

"So you didn't go to your prom, and now you don't want to go to your reunion."

"Not exactly war crimes."

"Oh, so let me finish. So I had this crush on this guy that I kissed at prom, and it was like a fairy tale. But we never spoke again. I don't know why; it just seemed like we got caught up in the magic of the evening, you know?"

"Yes, I can imagine how easy that must be to do in a gymnasium draped with crepe paper. But you saw him at the reunion last year."

"Oh yes. I sure did."

I didn't like the accompanying wicked little grin. Creepy.

"Do I want to know what that means, Jaime?"

"All I'm saying is that if I hadn't gone to that reunion, even though it was ten years later, I would have always wondered. Wondered what he was doing, who he was spending his life with, if he ever thought about me."

"Just because of one kiss?"

"Just because of one kiss."

"Huh. So I guess you can understand why I'm driving myself crazy over nearly two years of dating and then ten years of wondering."

"Two years! Wow, Nina, I didn't know that about you!"

"What, that I've had a boyfriend? A real one?"

"No, that you were capable of such commitment."

"Are you in cahoots with Ben?"

"I'd be *dying* inside! Have you spoken with him at all since high school?"

"Only twice on the phone, and that's in the past month or so."

"Wow. His name is Jacob? Jacob what?"

"Ryan."

Still holding the booklet, Jaime flipped through until she found his page. "Here he is. Oh, wow. He's adorable!"

"Yeah."

"And single!"

"Yeah."

"Ooh, and he's, like, a professional mountain man!"

"Yes, these are all things that I'm well aware of."

"So what's the problem?"

Hmm.

"I don't know."

"Are you still upset about the breakup?"

"What? No, that was, like, ten years ago."

"So what's the problem?"

I knew Jaime was waiting for me to have some giggly revelation that was straight out of a Cosmo article with a title like "Sassy, Single, and Ready to Mingle!" or "Get with Your Ex and Have the Big O!," but it was much more complicated than that. Actually, it had just become clear. Just then.

"The problem is that I'm not what anybody expected me to be."

"So that's it?"

"What the fuck? What do you mean, 'so that's it'? That's a *lot*."

"I mean, it is, but Nina, what do *you* want to be?"

"I don't know."

"Let's start with something easier. What *don't* you want to be?"

"What do you mean?" I asked.

"Well," Jaime mused, "you're upset with your job, right?"

"Not upset. Just not exhilarated."

"But you've been working there for years. Have you looked for another one?"

"No."

"And what exactly is it that everyone has expected you to be?"

"I don't know . . . funny."

"You *are* funny."

"No, I mean, funny, like, onstage."

"What, like a comic?"

"I guess."

"So why don't you?"

"I don't know."

"So, really, you're embarrassed that you haven't been proactive about your own life, and you've never had to think about it until something came along to make you feel threatened. That something, of course, being this reunion."

Damn, Dr. Freud, don't you have a kitty to spoil or a boyfriend to sit on? This is getting waaay too analytical for me.

"Jaime, you sound like a Psych 101 textbook. How did you get in my head like that?"

"Oh." She bowed her head modestly. "I minored in social psychology."

"Really? Hey, listen, if things don't work out with the fire-eater, I've got a terrific match for you. He's a therapist."

Jaime wrinkled her nose. "No thanks. I like my men a little less vanilla and a little more rock 'n' roll."

"His 'plan B' is to tame wild horses on a ranch out West."

That perked her up.

"A cowboy?"

I nodded.

"And he's single?"

"Yep."

"Does he play any instruments?"

"Um . . . his stepfather plays the bagpipes."

"Awesome," she nodded her head slowly. "Wade's hot but he's never around. Give him my number."

"I'll pass it along."

"Awesome," she said again. "OK, let's get back to you. What are you going to do about your deep-seated feelings of underachievement and inadequacy?"

"Can we stop talking about this, please?"

"No."

"I have to go to work."

"Why? You hate it."

"I'm sorry, did you want to cover rent this month?"

"I will if it means you stop moping all over the place."

"You think I mope? I'm a moper?"

"A little, yeah. And you don't give me enough credit, Nina. You've been acting weird since my show on Sunday and I think it's because you're a little jealous."

"You think so, huh?"

"I do."

"Hmm."

"Am I right?"

"No."

"Really?"

"No." Dammit. "Fine, so I'm a little jealous."

"Why?"

"It was so easy for you. To get up there, entertain a group of people, make everyone happy. Or whatever emotion it is that rockers feel. Can they get happy? Anyway, I think I've always wanted to do that too, but I'm too . . ."

"Scared?"

"Yeah."

"But I felt the exact same way the first time I got on a stage, Nina!"

"You did?"

"Yes! You think that Bowie rocked the house the first time he pulled on a wig and some platform shoes?"

"I hadn't given that too much thought."

"Everyone is scared to try anything for the first time. But if you're not afraid to do something, then it's probably pretty boring, right?"

"Didn't Confucius say something similar?"

"*Hyuh hyuh.* See? You're a funny woman. The world needs more funny women. Get up on a damned stage and make people think."

"Think about what?"

"Who cares? About anything. Everyone watches too much TV. Too many heads are filled with sitcom sludge."

"Hmm. Actually, there's this thing at Bellyaches that I was thinking about doing. An amateur contest."

"Yeah? That's terrific!"

"Yeah. Five hundred bucks and a regular gig to the winner."

"Oh my gosh, Nina, you should go for it! Then you could walk into that reunion feeling like you're doing something!"

"They're on the same night."

"What, the contest and the reunion?"

"Yep."

"Oh no!"

"I know."

"So go to both!"

I gently reminded her that, unless I wanted to jump ship and brave the sludge-steeped waters of historic Boston Harbor in a party dress, attending both would be impossible.

"Darn it!" she said. "Well there must be other comedy contests going on around the city, right?"

"I know, but . . . I don't know. I guess if I'm going to start somewhere, it kind of has to be at Bellyaches. It's the only place I'm comfortable enough, you know?"

"I understand. So go to the contest!"

"Yeah, but . . . there's that guy, too."

"Jacob?"

"Yeah. It's not just him, though. I mean, it is, but he kind of . . . I don't know . . . could give me some answers about a few things."

"Ah," Jaime made the Yoda noise again, "sounds like he represents something to you."

"I guess."

"But what?"

"I don't know."

"Success?"

"Success . . . Yeah, I guess he does! Wow, Jaime. You're wasting your time at the bank."

"It makes sense, though. He was the longest relationship you've ever had, right?"

"Pretty much the only one."

"And I've heard you complain that most of your dates are intimidated by you."

"Too much woman for them."

"Or not enough?"

"Not girlie enough."

"Exactly."

"Hmm. So, Jacob liked you for exactly what you were."

"Yep."

"And it would be nice to see him again."

"Yep."

"Maybe find out what you did right?"

"Have you been reading my diary?"

"You keep a diary?"

"No, but maybe I should so you can help me with more shit, Jaime. It's like a pony trick; go ahead, tell me how I feel about my mother."

"You wish you two had more in common."

"How did you *do* that?"

"I heard you on the phone last week." Jaime winked, scooping Kitty up in her arms as she rose from the couch. He gave a lazy mew of discontent, which she coddled with a kiss on the nose. "What can I say? It's a small apartment and sometimes there's nothing on television. Anyway, sounds like you have some thinking to do."

"Yeah."

She left me in a stew of confusion, thoughts doggie-paddling through my head, jagged black letters racing against white empty space.

Crap. Jaime was a little *too* much help. An hour ago I didn't particularly want to go to the reunion *or* the stand-up contest, and now . . . now I wanted to go to both. Terrific. Terrible.

Eleven

T minus two days and counting.

Ben's been uncharacteristically compassionate this week. We spent years choreographing a friendship around slicing each others' egos to bits with sharp banter, and I'm unsure how this newfound sensitivity was conceived. I'll blame it on the Girl Scout cookie. Still, it's been . . . nice.

He took me for breakfast this morning, listened while I whined, and then agreed to accompany me to the Laundromat, his least favorite place in the whole wide world. I can't really blame him; it's hot, it's loud, it smells like dirty clothes and anonymous B.O. Finding an apartment in Boston with a laundry room is like finding a hundred-dollar bill at the bottom of a bowl of clam chowder.

I take my clothes to All Washed Up, the only Laundromat in the city, possibly the state, that's up to hipster standards. Besides a slew of space-agey washers and dryers that vary in size and load capacity, there's a coffee bar, free wireless Internet, and a wall lined with old-school arcade games. There's always a line for Donkey Kong.

The place is great for people-watching. I've honed a lot of comic material just by sipping on a latte and observing. The contents of a laundry basket can be more revealing than a polygraph test.

For example: Princess over there, by the dryers.

The towels piled in front of her were impossibly white, a tower of crisply creased terrycloth that could have tumbled from a catalog. The woman was blonde and petite, undoubtedly in a well-functioning relationship and a huge fan of Ann Taylor, given her tiny pearl earrings, impeccable manicure and powder blue pullover that cuddled her slender body like a cloud. She was folding methodically, pulling things one by one from the dryer and divvying them up like a machine, a homemaker robot: T-shirts in this pile, linens in this, socks over here. I watched as she folded and refolded a thong. A thong! White cotton butt floss that was too small to shape into anything but an oblong crumple. I can't stand those things. I know they're supposed to be sexy, but I spend enough of my day trying to keep my underwear *out* of my ass. The last thing I need is a permanent wedgie and a raging infection, the inevitable aftermath of a night out in a G-string, cotton or silk. That's a secret Victoria keeps to herself. Deceitful, yeasty bitch.

This woman clearly had no over-the-counter hang-ups, with her tiny underwear. Over and over she folded countless tiny bone-white thongs, stacking them in a tiny pile on the green plastic table across from the dryers.

I nudged Ben, busy wadding his indie rock T-shirts into balls and packing the cheapest washing machine as tightly as he could.

"See that?" I whispered. "That right there is a pile of Tuesday-night sex."

"What?"

"Tuesday night. Maybe Wednesday. Missionary. Maybe

in a chair if she's had a chardonnay, but definitely nothing kinky."

Ben wrinkled his nose. "What does that mean?"

"White cotton underwear, so it'd be run of the mill. Vanilla. You know, a little in and out but probably for his sake."

"What if she's a lesbian?"

"Don't be ridiculous. She's wearing Shreve, Crump and Low; she's not a lesbian. Probably married to a Republican."

"She's wearing what?"

"Shreve, Crump and Low. Sounds like a skin rash, but it's fancy jewelry. My Dad buys my mother some earrings once in a blue moon when he's pissed her off. Only WASPs shop there. No lesbians."

"OK. Go on."

"That's all. Just making conversation."

Ben put down the worn, yellow Wilco T-shirt he was shaking free of stray cat hairs. "Gross. This is the last time I lend you any of my clothes, Kurtz. I always get them back covered in Kitty fuzz. Why are you staring at that chick's underwear?"

"It's just a thing I do."

"Really?"

"You can tell a lot about someone by their underwear. When I was in college my brother Paul and I used to do laundry together every Sunday, and it's a habit we got into—checking out people's underwear and trying to guess what their lives were like. After a few months I got to be something of an expert, if I do say so myself."

"How could you tell if you were right about these women?"

"I'd send Paul over to chat it out of them. That kid could

charm the peel off a banana. More often than not I hit it right on the head."

"This is interesting. And very arousing."

"Ew!"

"What's 'ew'? I'm a red-blooded male and we're talking about underpants!"

Giggle. Ben knows I think "underpants" is one of the funniest words in the English language.

"This is an entirely new insight into the female psyche," he continued. "Keep going. Tell me about that woman over there."

"The one eating a bagel?"

"Yeah."

"Single. Long-term single. For one thing, she's eating carbs like it could rid the world of cancer, so that's no big mystery. But if I had to go just by her underwear . . ."

"So what do you think?"

"Hang on, I'm trying to see what's in her basket without looking like a perv. Oh. Yeah, definitely single, and definitely hates herself. She's got boy-cuts that say 'Cutie' in pink script on the front."

"So?"

"It's like below-the-belt affirmation. If she has to remind herself that she's attractive by stamping it on her underpants, she definitely has issues."

"Interesting. What about that one?"

"Cheating on her husband."

"What?!"

"All gray, elastic waistband Hanes, *except* the lace crotchless panties she just threw in with her delicates."

"And you don't think she's just trying to spice up her love life?"

"Sure she is. With easy-access undies and some sous chef named Paolo."

"I'll take your word for it."

"You don't have to. Check out the dude that just walked in. You think that's her husband?"

Sure enough, the front door swung open with a jingle, as a tall, lean, extra-virgin-olive-skinned man came in and made a beeline for the woman I'd been talking about.

"Paolo!" She gurgled with delight, touching a hand to her disheveled curls and slamming the washer door on a load full of her husband's dismay. She looked around nervously. "What are you doing here?"

"I had to see you." His accent was as heavy as a steamy night in Rio. "My life, it is empty without you, Gertrude."

"Oh come on," I whispered to Ben, "her name is fucking Gertrude? She doesn't deserve that hunk of jalapeño."

He clamped a hand over his mouth and swallowed a snicker. "How do you know that's not her husband?"

"Because she just took her wedding ring off. Didn't you see?"

"No! She did?"

"Slipped it in the pocket of a pair of jeans in her basket. Ten bucks she forgets it's there until that puppy's already on spin cycle."

Ben had snagged the last washing machine, so I had to wait for someone's cycle to finish before I could cram a load in. No matter; plenty to see. Additional case studies included a bald guy wearing a calf-length leather trenchcoat and a pair of earplugs, a few grannies chatting in Portuguese, and an intolerably annoying little girl who flip-flopped between racing in circles around the room and screaming for her parents to listen to her while she told a story about a pony that died because a monster wanted more mashed potatoes. Even if I were stoned out of my mind and unwittingly catapulted into an alternate universe where everyone's destiny was to be determined by David Lynch, that story wouldn't have made any goddamned sense. I wanted to pull the parents aside and tell them they sure as hell weren't raising a Pulitzer Prize winner, but from the way they "mmm-hmmed" halfheartedly while the girl demanded a captive audience and endless bottles of orange soda, I think they must have known.

Ben didn't find the surveillance to be nearly as interesting.

"I'm going to play Ms. Pac-Man," he yawned, after about ten minutes of people-watching. "Want to watch?"

"No thanks. That washer just freed up, so I'm going to throw a load in."

"OK."

He ambled over to the arcade and jump-started Ms. Pac-Man with a handful of quarters and a few well-aimed kicks.

My laundry basket was stuffed to the gills; I usually wait until I'm down to my last pair of underwear before making the laundromat trek. I like to see how creative I can get with my wardrobe.

That's a lie. I'm just lazy.

If someone else in this place were playing my analytical laundry game, I shudder to think what picture the contents of my basket would paint of me. Hell, it had been so long since I'd done laundry, I couldn't even remember what was in there, but I imagined it was mostly work clothes and pajamas. Such is my sad, sad life.

Let's see: black pants, black pants, apron, black pants, black shirt, apron, gym shorts (a.k.a. sleeping shorts), underpants, underpants, underpants, stray sock, black pants, underpants, apron, black shirt, *Dukes of Hazzard* T-shirt, stray sock, *Monkey See, Monkey Poo* T-shirt, apron, apron, *DeathWish Rapids Whitewater Rafting* T-shirt . . .

DeathWish Rapids Whitewater Rafting?

Oh my God.

I forgot all about this shirt.

Jacob Ryan was the kind of guy to give seashells for birthdays and handwoven hemp jewelry for Christmas. When we'd graduated from high school he gave me his favorite T-shirt, given to him by his father after they took their first river-rafting trip together in the Colorado Rockies. The shirt had been black once, long since faded to that endearing blue-gray that accompanies countless wearings and spin cycles.

I used to live in this shirt, but I hadn't worn it in years. Christ, I didn't even know I had it anymore. Must have thrown it in there by accident. Or maybe it had been *that* long since I'd done laundry. Shudder.

I held the shirt to my nose and breathed deeply. Unbelievable; it smelled *exactly* like Jacob, that inimitable aroma of pepper vanilla corduroy and freshly cut ryegrass.

It's so strange, how smell or taste can evoke such vivid memories.

Chamomile tea reminds me of the middle-school summers I spent in Maine at my grandparents' cabin, sipping Celestial Seasonings on our cedar porch and tracing the constellations with whittled twigs sticky with remnants of marshmallows.

Cinnamon on my tongue tastes of Mexican Christmas. When I was seven, one of my father's college buddies came to spend the holidays with us after pulling the plug on his second disastrous marriage. Raoul was from Oaxaca, but had been living north of the border ever since freshman year at UMass. He'd been my Dad's favorite sit-in companion, and best man at my parents' wedding. When he showed up at our door that December morning, he had a pocket full of chocolate for the kids, cigars for Dad, and a cardboard bakery box for my mother. Inside were a dozen crusty pastries, shaped like seashells and covered with a delicate ivory glaze.

"*Pan dulce*," Raoul had said simply, before hitting the eggnog with my parents. "Sweet bread."

We'd devoured them with cinnamon hot chocolate, and a Kurtz family tradition was born.

Inhaling that T-shirt was like inhaling summer midnights warmed by tangerine moons.

"Nina, do you have any quart—whoa." Ben, having unwittingly stumbled into a tender, nostalgic, girlie moment, was totally caught unawares. He wrenched his neck into a double take when he noticed I'd sunk to the floor, clutching a T-shirt to my face. "Are you OK?"

"What? Yeah, I'm fine."

"But . . . but you're crying."

"Shut up, I am not."

"OK." Ben sucked in his cheeks and raised his eyebrows. "But your face is leaking."

Son of a bitch.

I've never been one for dramatic exits prompted by unbridled emotions, but hey, no time like the present. I nearly knocked over a tiny Asian goth chick as I sped from the washers to the front door.

Ben caught up with me in the parking lot.

"What's . . . what's going on?" he panted, purple from sprinting and, likely, a lifetime of cheesy arteries.

"I don't know." I half laughed, half sniffled, wiping sentimental brine from my cheeks. "I don't know what just happened. I haven't cried in years."

Ben took me by the elbow and steered me to a wooden bench, shielded from the autumn wind by an obsolete phone booth and a small grove of trees.

"Here. Sit. Talk," he said.

"This feels awkward."

"Why?"

"I don't know. Because you're being nice to me."

"Well that speaks well of our friendship." Ben laughed, fishing in his jeans pockets and producing a crumpled tissue. "Here. I haven't used it," he said when I wrinkled my nose.

"OK. Thanks."

"Better?" he asked after I'd blown my nose. "You can even give it back to me if you want."

"Gross."

"Ha! Good, a smile. So, tell me what's going on. We were having this great conversation about ladies' underpants and then I was leading Ms. Pac-Man by the nuts to an unprecedented high-score tour de force, and all of a sudden I look over and you're smelling an old T-shirt and getting all misty. Somehow, I missed something."

"Do you think I'm a loser, Ben?"

"Do I think you're a loser? What kind of question is that? You're the person I spend all of my work time and most of my free time with; if you were a loser, what would that say about me? That I spend my time with losers. Come on, Kurtz. I think you're a winner. A big, big winner."

"You don't spend most of your free time with me anymore; you're always with your lady. Although, I don't think I mind—Samoyed seems to be having quite an effect on you. You're almost benevolent."

"Her name is Samoa."

"Right. Sorry. Anyway"—I sniffed—"sensitivity isn't

good for a stand-up comic. You should try and hold back on that shit before it colors your act. Snarkiness is really your most endearing onstage quality."

"I thought it was my airtight material?"

"Yeah, but that's not really yours, is it?"

"Touché." He smiled. "Can we get back to the subject at hand?"

"Politics?"

"No."

"Global warming?"

"No."

"Boxers or briefs?"

"Why are you crying, Nina? You might as well tell me."

"How can I tell you when I don't know?"

"You must have some idea. Come on, I hate seeing chicks cry."

"I thought I don't count as a chick?"

"You do for the purpose of this conversation."

I could tell that was supposed to make me smile, but instead, I just started bawling again.

"Shit." Ben looked uncomfortable. "I knew I'd say the wrong thing. Shit. Um . . . want me to do a little dance? That might cheer you up."

"Sure." I sniffled.

"What? No. Fuck. I thought you'd say no."

"Why would I say no to seeing you do a little dance in a parking lot? *That's* comedy."

"No, Kurtz. Me dancing is tragedy. Look how white I am."

"You mean you're going to go back on your dance offer, even though I'm crying?"

"You're kidding, right?"

I sniffled again and squeezed my eyes so tears would run down my face.

"All right," Ben sighed, rising from the bench and glancing around the parking lot to make sure nobody was looking.

"There are, like, five teenage girls over there by the soda machine," he whispered tightly.

Sniffle.

With a roll of his eyes and a sheepish grin, Ben shuffled his feet and gave me some jazz hands, spun a hundred and eighty degrees and wiggled his butt in my face.

My burst of laughter wasn't unaccompanied. The girls had spotted him and promptly began hooting and cat-calling.

"Yeah, cutie!" one of them screamed. "Shake whatcha mama gave ya!"

"Wooo! Look at the booty on that fly white boy!"

"Go on, girl! Slip him a dollar!"

"I *know* that bitch didn't say nothin' bout yo mama!" I laughed as Ben took his seat on the bench next to me, cheeks the color of a ripe autumn apple.

"I can't believe I just did that. Do you see what a good friend I am?"

"I'll admit, that did make up for most of your smarmi-ness."

"Ha! Don't expect a Christmas present this year."

"*That* was my Christmas present?"

"And your birthday present."

"Ouch."

I sniffled for another minute or two, trying to calm my-self by staring at my sneakers, tracing circles and stars and unbridled squiggles in the dirt.

Finally Ben spoke.

"You've got to get over this, Kurtz."

"Get over what? Jacob?"

"No, this whole insecurity thing."

"Humph." I snorted. Like it's that easy.

"I don't even get where it comes from," he continued. "I mean, you're funny, you're smart, you're beautiful. There's no reason for you to be so down on yourself all the time."

"You think I'm funny and smart and beautiful?"

"Yeah," he said, "I think you're all of those things. So does Cuse. So does Hal, and your mom and dad, and probably every one of those idiots you've been set up with."

"So why do I always get the 'friends' speech? Wait, I already know the answer to that. Because I'm intimidating. Because I'm too abrasive, and I make jokes aggressively, and I'm too much like a guy."

"Those things are all true," Ben said, "but that doesn't mean you're *wrong*. You're *you*. You're independent and sassy and obnoxious and tough and quick-witted, and, as I've just figured out, beneath all of that, you're very delicate."

Huh.

"And of *course* that's all intimidating to men," he continued. "We're idiots. We're fragile, self-obsessed monkeys who force ourselves to ignore any emotion that doesn't have to do with food, sex, or sleep, and if anything upsets that balance, we freak out and have to go prove our manhood by rock-climbing or surfing or skydiving or some other crazy shit like that. Men like control. And if a man meets a woman who clearly has the upper hand, he runs. He runs like his balls are on fire."

"Why?"

"Because men are caretakers. Whether that's born or bred, I have no idea. But we like to be the one to take care of everything. And if we don't feel needed, we get all insecure and babyish. It makes us feel weak."

"So you're saying, I should act less like I can take care of myself?"

"No! I'm saying that you have yet to meet a man who is man enough for you. Myself included."

"Are you going to deny saying this tomorrow?"

"Probably."

"OK. Just wanted to make sure."

"As for the comedy thing—"

"Oh, we're not done talking about me?"

"Not yet. As for the comedy thing, sure, it's scary. It's scary to get up on a stage and have a group of strangers outright judge what's coming out of your mouth. It's terrifying. Totally different from making a friend laugh, or your family laugh. You have to work harder. You have to act like you're just being yourself without being yourself at all! You can't limit stand-up comedy to a singular perspective, you know that; you write all my damned jokes! So, as you know, you have to get inside as many heads as possible with as few words as possible. And that's hard to do."

"I know. That's why I'm scared of it."

"But everyone's scared of something, Nina! You know, I count the most commercially successful comics not as the funniest people around, but the ballsiest. Those are the people who've gotten booed offstage and booed offstage and heckled and heckled and heckled, and each time, they've worked a little bit harder to get their material a little bit better. And eventually, they didn't get heckled anymore. That's true about any job. You start off at entry level, kind of sucking, and eventually you work your way up the ladder."

"This is all well and good, Ben, but why the hell did you wait so long to say any of this to me? You've been acting like a jerk! When I intimated that I might want to enter the contest at Bellyaches, you got all pissy about it."

"You said it yourself, Nina: I'm afraid you might win."

"Why?"

"Because you write all my jokes. And you're funnier than I am. 'Job security' and 'stand-up comedy' aren't usually found in the same sentence, and I'm lucky to have that running gig. I'm terrified of losing it. And I'm terrified of losing it to *you*. Because I know that eventually when Hal replaces me, I'm going to hate the person who follows in my footsteps. And I don't want to hate my best friend."

"Wow. Thanks. Thanks a lot, Ben. I needed to hear all of this."

"I should have said it all a long time ago, instead of just whining at you all the time. I'm sorry."

"It's OK."

That night, I brought a flashlight to bed and pulled my covers all the way up over my head like I used to do as a kid.

My bedtime reading was a little more contemplative than it was in my *Teen* magazine days.

That stupid gray question mark, the cause of all this trouble, looked enormous next to all of the smiling snapshots of my former classmates.

I wonder how many of these people are actually going to show their faces? I've seen enough reunion movies to know that most of the "popular" kids will have made mediocre progress with their lives, and will go to the reunion to see each other. The nerds will all be enormously successful and will go to the reunion to see the popular kids. At least one of them will arrive in a limousine, maybe even a helicopter. The cheerleaders will be smiling from a corner of the room, tittering together behind perfectly manicured hands. People will show off engagement rings and wedding bands and pictures of their kids. Someone will still hold a grudge, and since we're now all old enough to be openly drunk, I'm sure a fistfight will ensue, or at least a catfight. Someone will cry. Someone will have died. We'll all have to stand around and talk about how we never really knew them but wish we had.

And I'll have to face my fears. One of them, anyway.

Twelve

"Woooow!" Jaime wolf-whistled from my bedroom door. "You look hot!"

"You scared me!" I cried, missing my eye with a mascara wand and jabbing myself in the cheek, leaving a jagged black streak across the left side of my face. "Shit."

"Sorry." She giggled. "Hang on, I've got eye-makeup remover in the bathroom."

"That stuff never really works. I'll just wash my face."

"No!" she protested. "The rest of your makeup looks great. This stuff works; trust me. I use it after gigs to get the Ziggy Stardust lightning bolt off of my face. Don't move." She spun and bolted, stepping on the cat in the process.

"*Mrrrrrrrrrroooooooooowwww!*"

"Sorry, Kitty, Mama's in a hurry."

I stepped back from my mirror and took a good look at the babe that stared back at me. Besides the mascara stripe, I *did* look pretty fierce, if I do say so myself.

In atypical Nina fashion, I'd spent pretty much the entire day getting ready for the big night.

I folded yesterday, and let my parents take me shopping. This was a big deal; shopping with my parents has never matured beyond what it was in middle school. You know:

Mom and Dad take you to the mall, you're all embarrassed about being *seen* with them in *public*. Like nobody else around you has parents, like these people trailing you while you stomp around the mall in disgust are tumors or leeches, when actually, it is *you* who suck things from *them*, like money and patience.

I tried to be mature about it, but now that I'm not a teenager, I was embarrassed for a completely different reason: I'm twenty-seven years old and my pops was buying me a party dress. It's a little pathetic. And can certainly be misconstrued as creepy.

Dad is hilarious to watch when he shops, though, because Mom and I drag him into all kinds of girlie department stores and he just smiles to himself and wanders, checking prices on Capri pants and three-quarter-sleeve blouses. He usually chats up the staff for a while, works them over, procures himself some kind of discount, especially when someone recognizes his voice from the radio.

Yesterday afternoon he was on *fire*, flirting up a storm with all the salesgirls, who think it's a hoot that a shaggy-haired hippie dad can charge up some tank tops like nobody's business. Three times I walked away from stores empty-handed, while my father clutched bags of discounted goods: neckties, trendy socks, sweaters for my mother. Sale prices winked away in favor of a sizeable manager's discount. A champion flirt, that man.

Mom thought it was hilarious.

"You pathetic old man!" She laughed and poked him in the belly, practically drooling as he pulled from a shopping bag some variation on fancy Mom clothes, like a sparkly, fir-trimmed cardigan. "Trying to wrap all those young girls around your wrinkly finger!"

"Hey, I can march this lamb's-wool blazer right back to the Limited, young lady!"

"You wouldn't dare!"

It was cute. Still embarrassing, though.

The dress we picked out was a rich, emerald green; Mom insisted. She feels so bad that all of her kids turned out red-headed that she's accepted it as her mission to make sure we all dress in a flattering way. She's always been especially vigilant about me, raising a stink if there was a chance of wearing pink for a ballet recital, sewing Halloween costumes specifically for redheaded Disney heroines and cartoon characters, stuffing my chest of drawers with every shade of green and blue in the spectrum.

Normally, I hate trying on clothes in department stores. It's just so uncomfortable, cramming into a mirrored cell, staring at every pucker on your body underneath those horrible, horrible lights. Why do they put unflattering lights in dressing rooms? What are they, fluorescent? It makes no sense. Don't the people who run these places want you to *buy* the clothes, not run screaming from your own reflection like it just broke through the glass and tried to maim you with a hanger? If I ran a clothing store, I would make sure that half of my budget was invested in flattering lighting, so that even the lumpiest of women would see themselves as smooth and sleek when they tried things on. Makes sense, right?

Fearing the worst when I zipped myself into this delicate cocktail dress that my mother had snatched from a rack, I was surprised when I didn't hate what was staring back at me. The dress was strapless, but then had feathery bits of chiffony-stuff that fastened over my shoulders to create the illusion of sleeves. Most strapless dresses billow out like ball gowns, or else are tight enough to evoke the memory of the blonde chick from *Married . . . with Children*, but this one was a compromise, an ecstatically happy medium. The skirt had jagged, flouncy layers that danced around my knees. Against such a perfect contrast, my hair looked hot to the touch.

Mom clasped her hands together and sighed contentedly when I emerged from the dressing room.

"Oh," she breathed. "Oh *Nina*."

"Very attractive!" Dad boomed. "Linda? Maggie? Ladies, can we get my daughter some shoes to go with it? No? You don't sell shoes? How about a necklace or something? That's the ticket; thank you, ladies. They're getting you a necklace, Jellybean."

"Thanks, Dad."

Mom's eyes were shining like I'd just done something brilliant or pride worthy.

"Mom, are you crying? Jesus, Ma, it's only a dress!"

"I know, but . . ." *Sniff* . . . "I don't think we've ever shopped for a fancy dress before."

"We haven't? What about . . . oh, didn't go to prom. Really? We've *never* gone dress shopping before?"

"No." *Sniiiiifffffff*. "You look beautiful. Just stunning."

"Thanks. Thanks, Mom."

"You're welcome."

At home, in front of my own mirror, lighting adjusted to my satisfaction, even *I* had to admit that I looked . . . better than usual.

"Here," Jaime panted, frantically bursting back into my room. "I brought you some cotton balls, too."

"Jaime, calm down! I'm not bleeding from the head or anything; no need to panic."

"What time does the boat leave?"

"Seven o'clock."

"Well, it's quarter past six!"

Shit. There *is* need to panic. If I can just get my hands to stop shaking.

"Hold still," Jaime said, snatching the makeup remover back from me and tipping the bottle onto a cotton ball. "I don't think I've ever seen you nervous before, Nina!"

"My life isn't usually calling for this much excitement."

"It's kind of cute! You're trembling!"

"Ha! Imagine if I'd decided to go to the stand-up contest. You'd have to hold my tongue while I convulsed in nervous seizures all over the apartment."

"I have to admit," she said, dabbing carefully at my face with the cotton ball, "I'm still surprised that you chose the reunion, after the talk we had after my gig."

"Yeah. I'm still not sure I made the right decision."

She finished with my face and perched cautiously on the edge of my bed. "I don't think either decision is right or wrong," she said, "they just serve different purposes."

"Yeah."

"But stop thinking and start heading for the door! If you miss the boat you'll miss out on Jacob."

She's right.

"OK. Thanks so much, Jaime. I'll see you when I get home tonight, OK? 'Bye, Kitty."

"Mmmmrrrceeeooooooowwwwwww."

Aw. For the first time, when the kitty mewed, I didn't want to kick it across the room. Must be my nerves. Or the half bottle of pinot that's swirling in my gut. I tend to chug the vino when I'm nervous.

Jaime followed me to the door, holding Kitty in her arms and making him wave his little paw at me as I left the apartment. It took a minute to hail a cab, but when I was safely in, Jaime gave one final wave and turned, hoisting Kitty over her shoulder so he was facing me as she retreated. The little bastard hissed at me, bobbing up and down as Jaime walked. I knew it was too good to be true; as soon as Mommy's back is turned, that thing turns into Franken-Kitty.

Long Wharf charges into the water with New England courage, directly across the harbor from Logan Airport. It is south of the North End (Boston's Italian neighborhood and home to some of the best cannoli you'll ever taste), east of historic Faneuil Hall, and boasts the only outdoor bar I know of that will serve you a bright blue mystery cocktail in a fishbowl.

It's also located smack in the middle of a notorious construction disaster called the Big Dig. Since the late 1980s, the City of Boston has been bumbling away at "America's most ambitious public works project," or, as most Mass-holes like to call it, "the money pit that's fucked up our roads for two decades." Basically, the goal of the Big Dig is to put all of Boston's major highways underground. In theory, it's an ecologically friendly, architectural innovation. In practice, it's a traffic nightmare, an ever-shifting labyrinth of tunnels and detours.

It almost made me miss the boat.

The cabbie pulled up by Long Wharf at six fifty-seven, giving me three minutes to toss him the fare and race to the cruise ship (over cobblestones! In heels! Damn you, historic urban planning!)

I heard them before I saw them; dozens of voices that I halfway recognized but whose accompanying names I had pushed out of my brain in favor of more relevant factoids. A crowd was milling about at the foot of a rickety-looking ramp, sipping drinks out of plastic cups and picking at a sad-looking hors d'oeuvre table, waiting to be marched two by two onto our moonlit cruise like Noah's animals. I'm sure that at least half of these people will get Biblical by the end of tonight, after a few too many martinis and memories.

Most of the men were in khakis and blazers, a few wearing decent-looking suits, one fat guy in a Hawaiian print shirt. The women were dressier, replete with body glitter and push-up bras. Women my age are just hitting their prime; men are just giving up.

They all looked familiar. Older. But familiar.

I made eye contact with one of them. Then another. And another. Each one strained, squinting their eyes, tilting their heads, as though trying . . .

As though trying to figure out who I am.

Shit.

I nearly broke both ankles speeding back to the curbside. What were the chances my taxi was still there?

None, of course. This wasn't Hollywood. Still, it *is* a city, and one was bound to come along any minute now . . . come on. Come *on*.

Finally I spotted a cab and waved my arms like a frantic airport controller.

"Hi," I spat breathlessly.

"Where to, miss?"

"Bellyaches Comedy Club. It's near—"

"Bellyaches Comedy Club," the pungent cabbie cut me off, rolling the words around in his mouth like marbles. "Bellyaches . . . oh yes. I have been there before. Not a place for a lady. Are you sure that's where you want to go?"

"I'm sure, I'm sure. Do you know how to go?"

"Of course I know how to go." The cabbie was indignant. "But it will take some time because of the construction."

Boy, he wasn't kidding.

"Turn left here. No, left! Aaah, that was the exit. Don't you want to go toward Government Center?"

"I can't go this way for Government Center, miss. Why don't you relax and let me drive, OK?"

"What do you mean, you can't go that way for Government Center? I just went that way two days ago!"

"That was two days ago. The detour has changed since then."

"Aaaarg. OK, what about taking the next—son of a BITCH, that exit is closed, too!"

"It's the Dig," the driver said matter-of-factly. "It has really fucked up everything in this part of town. Oh, pardon my language."

"What? Oh no, that's OK."

"I forgot myself. I don't usually swear in front of a lady."

"Don't worry about it, OK? Fuck. See? See, it's fine. Swear all you want. Just get me there."

It took almost forty-five minutes to make the two-mile drive. It seemed like every few yards we'd miss a closed-off exit, or be redirected to a street that wound back up and around the harbor, bringing us three steps forward and two steps back every single time.

"Fuck!" the cabbie and I would scream in unison. "Shit! Shit! Fuck!"

"Oh, I can't *believe* this!" I fumed.

"This is not my fault, miss."

"I know. I know it's not your fault. It's the Dig's fault."

"I have to say," the cabbie chuckled, "you curse more than any lady I have ever met. It's very amusing."

"Well," I said, "I'm a special kind of lady, my friend. Oh, stop. Stop right here, this is perfect. Thank you so much.

What time is it? Almost eight? Crap. OK. Here, keep the change. Thanks!"

It's weird to approach Bellyaches after dark. The place almost looked welcoming tonight; the windows glowed with neon that seemed to pulse in time with the pizzicato laughter that escaped through the cracks in the concrete wall. I could tell from outside that the place was packed; I felt like a street urchin with my nose pressed against the glass, watching as the amateur comic onstage owned the room.

"Hoping for a handout?" came a voice from behind me.

I nearly jumped out of my dress.

"Jesus, Henry, you scared the pants off of me!"

"That doesn't look like pants, Kurtz."

"What, this old thing?"

Ben was leaning in the doorway, arms crossed, eyes smiling.

"Why aren't you on a boat right now?" he asked.

"I missed it."

"Really?"

"No. Not really."

The smile spread to his mouth.

"Come on in, then. You're up in about twenty minutes."

"I'm . . . what?"

"You're *up*, Kurtz. As in you have to go onstage. Stage, you know, that elevated platform thing at the front of the room?"

"But, how did you—"

"I had a feeling. So did your roommate; she's in the front row. Next to your mom and dad. And Cuse is sitting in the back. He said something about five-alarm fries and not wanting to be too close to a microphone. We all know you better than you think."

Ben grinned when I didnt respond, clearly too shocked to speak. "Now, are you coming in or not?" he said.

"I don't have any material."

"Come on."

"I'm serious!"

"I'm not going to hold this door open forever. My arms will get tired, and the boss will come out and bitch about the draft."

"Ben?"

"Yeah?"

"Thanks."

We stared at each other for a moment, me wearing my emerald green dress, Ben wearing a smile. He moved a step closer. Then another. Then—

"Oh my GOD, you're not going to kiss me, are you?" I sputtered.

"What? Oh my God, Nina, I was going to offer you my arm and, like, escort you in or something!"

"What?"

"Well, you're wearing a dress! I felt like I should try to be a gentleman or something."

"Oh. OK. Good. Good. Ew."

"Oh my God. You thought I was going to kiss you?"

"Well . . . hey! Don't look so grossed out!"

"Well I'm sorry, but kissing you . . . don't take this the wrong way . . ."

"Was like getting CPR from a jellyfish?"

"What?"

"A jellyfish. That's what it was like to kiss *you*, Ben. Like being resuscitated by a jellyfish."

"Actually, I was going to say that kissing you was like licking a bowl of oatmeal, but I can see how you might have mistaken my lips for something with tentacles."

"*Oatmeal?*"

"Cold oatmeal."

"Eeeew!"

"Tell me about it, Kurtz." Ben threw back his head and laughed. He smushed his lips together, and stepped forward to offer me his arm, which I took.

"Ready?" he asked out of the corner of his tightly clamped mouth, leading me through.

I took a deep breath. "Ready," I answered. "Here I go."

Want More?

Turn the page to enter
Avon's Little Black Book —

the dish, the scoop and the
cherry on top from

SARA FAITH ALTERMAN

GET UP, STAND UP

Ever since I was a prepubescent choir geek, I've been attracted to artsy types—most especially, guys who can work a crowd. Actors. Guitarists. Singers who can croon about their wanton sensitivity and still project an image that is fiercely heterosexual. After over a decade of swooning over such alluring artisans, I, to this day, harbor crushes on men who can hop up on a stage and, for an hour and a half, shed their very identities and dedicate every fiber of their being to a desperate, animal sort of dress-up game, sweating unabashedly under the scrutiny of white-hot lights and the eyes of hundreds of spectators.

Once I learned to appreciate the allure of ambivalently shaggy hair, of free-trade coffee and freelance lackaday, it was as though I'd tasted enigma, like my lips were privy to an exotic romantic delicacy. To me, a man with a message smolders with passion and mystery, reeks of earthy sex and whispered promises. My appetite for entertainers is relentless, insatiable. Watching a man hypnotize an audience with a single breath, an E-minor strum, an hour-long bat of midnight eyelash fringe, is like candy-coated, chocolate-covered, peanut-butter bliss. I'll take a man who can earn applause over a man who earns a reasonable salary any day of any week.

Ladies, I beg you, I *beg* you: don't fall into this same trap, this ruse, this abysmal vortex that draws each drop of love and life directly from the unsuspecting veins that pulse with such optimism, such giggly girlish hope.

And for God's sake; don't you *dare* date a stand-up comic.

For while musicians and actors will break your heart and channel their wistful pain into an achingly poetic emotional tourniquet, a stand-up comic will crumple what was once a tender relationship into a crude, foul, unapologetic narration of self-deprecation that details your every flaw and most profound apprehensions to a crowded room filled with tattooed swine gorged with cheap Chinese food and watery beer.

Comics are like sponges. Miserable, tortured sponges. They absorb every experience and wring themselves onstage, dribbling delicate details of their personal lives with unabashed glee. To enter into a relationship with one is like getting your dignity drunk on tequila and allowing it to pass out on train tracks. The spectrum of misery runs the gamut from suffering a splitting headache to being completely and irrevocably pulverized by an anvil the size of Montana.

Poor dignity.

My own dignity got a good kick in the ass the first time I watched my then-boyfriend, He Who Shall Not Be Named But Who Knows Deep Down in His Soul That He's a Heartless Moron, perform a five-minute, two-drink-minimum gig at some seedy watering hole in New York City. I was young; I didn't know any better. Had someone warned me that every move I made during the course of that relationship would be fodder for material, I would have made sure to go down in history as the blandest girlfriend that ever lived.

The night went a little something like this:

"So my girlfriend and I have reached the point in our relationship where we're all talking about the future and shit. I know, I know. A guy's worst nightmare, right? So besides all the usual bullshit like marriage and kids and where to settle down, there's the big issue of religion. I'm as Catholic as they come, like, you walk into my mother's house and immediately all you can hear is the hushed murmur of monks chanting *'Domine ad adjuvandum me festina. Agnus dei qui tolis peccata mundi.'* Creepy. And my girlfriend . . . brace yourselves . . . is agnostic. Which is a four-letter word at my house. She was raised by a Jew and a Christian, and they basically told her that she could believe whatever she wants. Which is *also* a four-letter word at my house. So she wants to raise her kids the same way, and I want to raise the kids Catholic. Not that we have kids. We might. Someday. So we're arguing over a possibility, over the ghost of a chance that someday, somehow, we *may* legalize our union and she *may* allow me to impregnate her. This has been the cause of several huge, huge fights. I haven't been too worried, since God's on my side, but I think I may have a compromise all worked out. By show of hands, how many of you dudes out there have tried to get your lady to let you throw it in the back? You know what I'm talking about, guys. Take a Sunday drive up the Hershey Highway? Yeeeeah, you have! So here's my proposition. I let her raise the kids however she wants, and she lets me do her in the butt. Thoughts? Good idea, right? Yeah! Listen to all that applause, honey! Everyone *else* thinks it makes sense! She's right over there, folks. Stand up, babe! Show 'em your ass. That's what I'm *talking* about!"

Suffice to say, *that* was one of the most mortifying nights of my entire life.

And it didn't stop there. It seemed everything about our relationship was fair game. Our fights, our sex life, my quirks and fears and PMS. Night after night I watched as he picked me apart in front of a live audience, spewing cheap one-liners and agonizingly detailed anecdotes about the time I drank too many whiskey sours and tried to pee in the closet, or the snowy Tuesday night we spent running around the West Village trying to find an open store so I could buy tampons, chocolate milk, sausage pizza rolls and chewable orange-flavored fiber tablets. (Don't judge.)

I tried everything to get him to stop; I cried, I begged, I threatened. But in his opinion, material that's generated from real life experiences is easier for audiences to identify with, so it gets better laughs. And that's what he wanted; better laughs. Not dignity of his own, not a happy girlfriend. He wanted people to think he was funny, at whatever the cost.

It cost him my love and affection, that's for damned sure. It also cost him all the stuff he left at my apartment (two DVDs, a baseball cap, four books and an iPod. Score!).

At least I salvaged my dignity. And I can keep my back-door an exit only. Phew.

This Diary Belongs To: Nina Kurtz

(Some excerpts from Nina's high-school diary...)

August 29, 1994

Dear Diary,

I hate that: "Dear Diary." I sound like one of the vapid cheerleader morons. I wonder if those jerks even understand that the Smells Like Teen Spirit video is, like, totally making fun of them. I wish I was easily amused too.

I doooon't want to go back to school next week. Mom took me and the twins clothes shopping today and it was utter hell. She's so unfair! Paul and Jeremy have been going to the mall by themselves since they were thirteen. Why can't I? I'm ALMOST SIXTEEN. It's such total crap. I had to stand there like a loser while Adam and Cory picked out UNDERWEAR. So gross. Then Mom was like, hey Nina! While we're getting underwear, why don't you run over to the girls' section and get a bra!

OH MY GOD.

I couldn't believe she said that. It was in front of, like, four hundred people. But she MADE me get a bra. She said that I have to start wearing one because I'm starting to embarrass myself! I hate her SO MUCH.

September 6, 1994

Dear Diary,

My classes are sooo sucky. I at least have Sheck for history, so that's good, but besides that I have stupid math, stupid classical literature, stupid Spanish, stupid, stupid biology, and stupid, stupid STUPID gym class. It's totally unfair. They don't even make us do anything hard in gym. I guess I would understand if we did something like running or step aerobics or lifting weights, but volleyball? It's not even with a real volleyball, it's with one of those foamy things so the fat kids don't lose an eye. Jeremy said that they don't make you take gym in college. I can't wait.

Lizzie's only in one of my classes, but it's bio, so at least she can be my lab partner. AND that bratty, bitchy, pain in the butt Gretchen Strong is in bio AND Spanish with me. I hate her so much. How can she expect me to forgive her for tripping me in the cafeteria last year? Does she think I forgot? I only had my face planted in my macaroni and cheese in front of six thousand people. Some asshole called me Mac Attack in the hall today. I wish everyone would forget about that. Who came up with that nickname anyway?

Only seven more months until I can take my driver's test! I can't wait until I can drive. Mom said she might let me get an after-school job if my grades are OK, which would be totally awesome because then I could buy a car. So rad. I think I want a VW bug. Or a van. Something vintage like that.

September 16, 1994

Dear Diary,

I'm trying to decide if I want to go to the fall dance. The Fall Fling. I bet Gretchen Strong came up with that name.

It's kind of early to be deciding, I guess, since it's not till October, but I don't want to be stuck without a date again. I haven't been to any dances, not even when I was a freshman. Personally, I don't really give a crap if I go to a dance without a date, but Lizzie said that's lame and everyone will probably think I'm a lesbian if I just go to a dance without a boy.

September 17, 1994

Dear Diary,

I asked Mom what a lesbian is, and she said that it's something that I'd better not come home as, or God will send me to hell.

September 18, 1994

Dear Diary,

Paul and Jeremy just told me that the only thing cooler than a lesbian is two lesbians. I'm now totally confused.

October 1, 1994

Dear Diary,

I'm definitely NOT going to the stupid dance. Everyone else got asked, even GRETCHEN got asked by Ian Levy and he's a SENIOR. He's got zits on his neck and he smells like roast beef and B.O., but he's got a car and Gretchen was bragging about how she might let him go to third base with her if he brings her flowers.

Gross.

I had like a seventh-sense feeling that Sam Craig was going to ask me, but not only did I hear him say that kissing me would be like kissing his friggin' sister, but when I told Lizzie that, she said she heard Ross Adams telling Chris

Culler that Sam told him that I didn't even count as a girl.
Why not? I have bigger boobs than Gretchen, and half the
hockey team can attest to the fact that she's a girl.

October 4, 1994

Dear Diary,

OK, so I might not have known what a lesbian was (I do now.
Thanks, MTV), but I definitely know what a two-faced pricky
little bitch is. That would be Lizzie Lee, the girl who was
SUPPOSED to be my best friend, but who forgot to mention
the teeny little detail that she was going to the dance with
SAM CRAIG. She swore up and down at lunch that he asked
her before she knew that I wanted to go with him, but it's
such B.S. She's known since last year that I liked him. And
anyway, if he had already asked her, then why didn't she tell
me?

I almost kicked her ass but there was a lunch monitor there
and I didn't want to get in trouble. So instead, tomorrow I'm
going to pour the oil from a tuna-fish can in the bottom of her
locker. Should never have given me that combination when
you broke your leg last year, Lizzie. That was your first mistake.

October 10, 1994

Dear Diary,

Oh my God. Oh my GOD.

I think I fell in love in Spanish class today.

There's a new guy who just moved here from Connecticut.
His name is Jacob and he is so so so cute. He's like six feet
tall and he has the softest eyes, and he dresses like Axl Rose,
without the long hair and heroin chic.

It went down like this:

Señor Zahowski asked me some stupid question about the homework, which I didn't even do, and then the classroom door flew open and in walks this guy, and he answered the question for me. Then he sat at the desk next to me, and I was trying to make him laugh without making any noise and I totally smacked him in the face. In the FACE.

I have never been so embarrassed in my whole entire life.

And it's worse. Zahowski is making us be partners for our midterm Spanish project, which means I'm going to have to go over to this guy's HOUSE sometime to do extra work.

Either I'm going to die, or something big is going to happen. Not like sex big, but like maybe-I'll-finally-have-a-boyfriend big. I haven't decided which one. Maybe I can get him to be my boyfriend before he figures out that I don't count as a girl, like everyone else thinks.

I hope he likes me.

SARA FAITH ALTERMAN

SARA FAITH ALTERMAN is an author, a comedy writer, a film journalist, and a workaholic. She currently lives in Massachusetts, where she tickles funny bones as the head writer at ImprovBoston and barely makes her deadlines for *NewEnglandFilm.com*. *Tears of a Class Clown* is her second novel. Please visit her website, *www.sarafaith.com*.